William H. Mallock

In an Enchanted Island

A winter's retreat in Cyprus. Third Edition

William H. Mallock

In an Enchanted Island
A winter's retreat in Cyprus. Third Edition

ISBN/EAN: 9783337255879

Printed in Europe, USA, Canada, Australia, Japan

Cover: Foto ©Andreas Hilbeck / pixelio.de

More available books at **www.hansebooks.com**

A WINTER'S RETREAT

IN CYPRUS

AMONG THE RUINS OF FAMAGUSTA

Frontispiece.

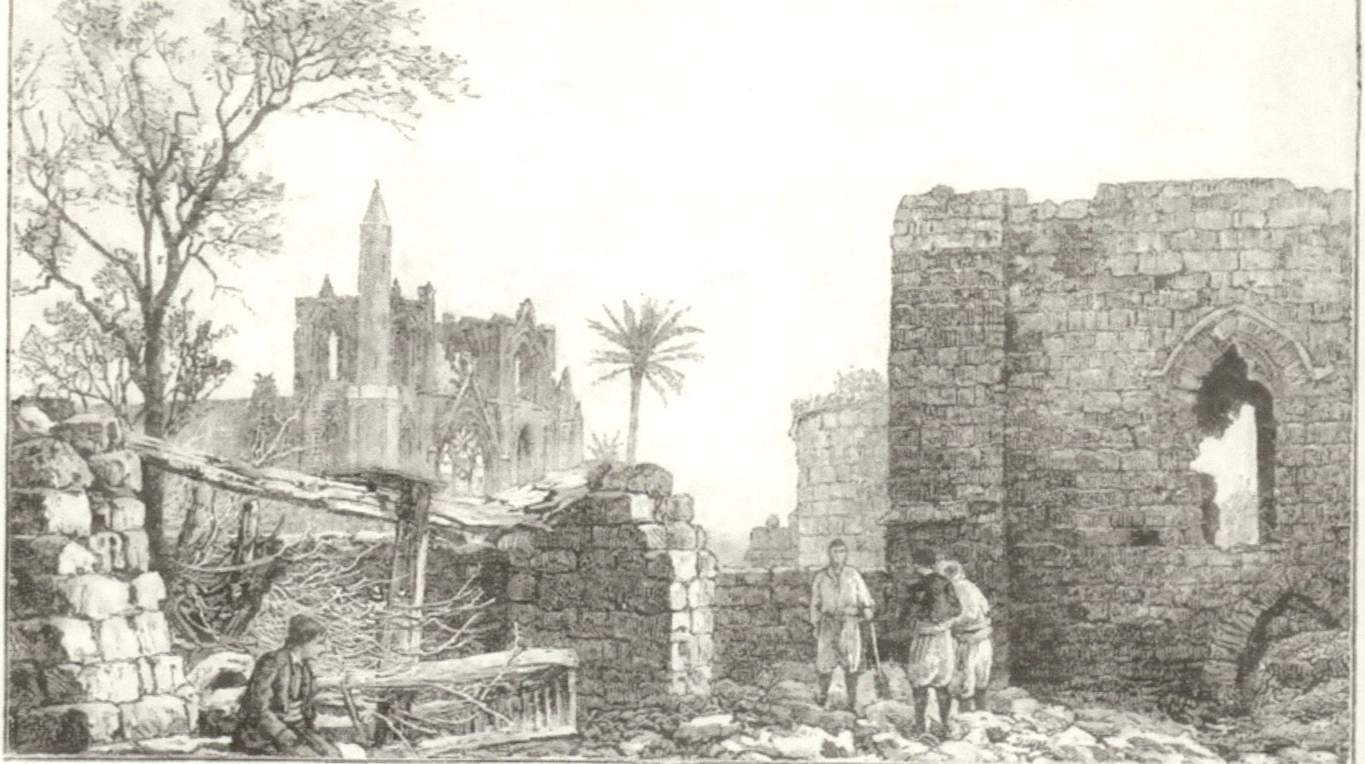

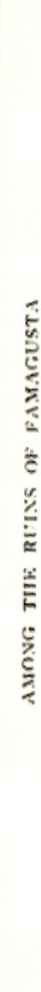

IN AN ENCHANTED ISLAND

OR

A Winter's Retreat in Cyprus

BY

W. H. MALLOCK

AUTHOR OF 'IS LIFE WORTH LIVING?' 'SOCIAL EQUALITY'
'THE OLD ORDER CHANGES' ETC.

' For always me the fervid languid glories
Allured, of heavier suns in mightier skies '

THIRD EDITION

LONDON

RICHARD BENTLEY & SON, NEW BURLINGTON ST.

Publishers in Ordinary to Her Majesty the Queen

1892

NOTE

On the day of publication of this book the Publishers and the Author received an intimation of a fact before unknown to them, that Mr. Wyke Bayliss had previously published a book with a title which, though not identical, was unfortunately similar. It is hardly necessary to say that, had this been known earlier, the title of the present volume would have been altered, and that both the Publishers and the Author regret the accidental coincidence.

It is hoped, however, that, as the subject of the two books is wholly different, and as that of Mr. Mallock's is unmistakably indicated by the second portion of its title, no confusion in the public mind is likely to arise from the circumstance.

November 1889.

CONTENTS

IN AN ENCHANTED ISLAND

CHAPTER I

THE TRUE TRAVELLER

I SUPPOSE that this book, if classified in the usual way, would be called a book—a very slight book —of travels ; but I would rather call it myself a record of a fragment of life which was, by the magic of its unfamiliar surroundings, detached like a dream from the things of the modern world—from steam, from progress, from the glorious march of democracy—and suddenly came between them with the lulling and luxurious charm of an interlude from an opera heard between the acts of a farce.

I tell the reader this by way of a timely

I

warning, so that he may know at starting how
much or how little to expect of me.   The scenes
I shall have to dwell upon lie in a classical
country which is full of interest for students,
for politicians, and for speculators—indeed for
earnest or practical people generally—but whether
the reader will be interested in what I may say of
them, will depend very much on what are the
tastes or temper with which, if occasion offered,
he would visit these scenes himself.   Would he
visit them eager to unearth prehistoric pots for
·museums? to throw a new light on the relations
of Phœnician art to Hellenic? or else to collect
facts with which to discredit the Colonial Office?
or to see what money might be made out of the
place or people?   Would he be a man with a
special object, or still worse, a man with a special
subject?   If he would, let him throw this book
in the fire.   It is not written for him—it would
certainly not appeal to him.

If it appeals to any one, it will appeal to a
class of men who take to travel in a different
spirit altogether, and who frankly admit that

what they seek under other skies is neither profitable, nor useful, nor edifying information of any
kind, but merely this—the stimulant of a new
mental experience. No doubt their taste in this
respect is for nothing but a more refined form of
dram-drinking ; and that perhaps may be thought
sufficiently immoral and frivolous. And yet such
men after all are the only true travellers, for it is
they alone who really love change for the sake of
change, taking it into their system as a smoker
inhales smoke, and finding it exhilarate them like
a kind of spiritual haschish. All other travellers
are travellers merely by accident. They go to
distant places for some definite object, which it so
happens is to be had at a distance only—a
picture gallery, a gaming-table, or a good climate
in January—but they would like it as well or
better if they could find it nearer home, whilst as
for the excursionist, who in the course of a single
holiday is " personally conducted " through India,
Japan, and America, it can hardly be said that he
has ever left home at all. He has virtually sat
still and looked at a moving peep-show. The

globe has gone round before him, he has not gone round the globe.

But the true traveller seeks precisely what the excursionist dreads, and what those who travel with a definite object are indifferent to. It is a sense of escape from all that is homely and habitual—from an earth and a heaven grown sordid with the dust of vain associations. It is the refreshment like that felt by a fevered cheek when a pillow is turned and the touch of the linen is cool again, produced in the mind by new colours on the mountains, new scents in the atmosphere, forests with unknown borders, roads that lead into mystery, castles that rise from the mists of an enchanted past, and men whose aims and characters one cannot despise, not knowing them. Amongst influences such as these there steals upon the true traveller a delightful sense of being born again to youth. Once more, for the time, he is buoyant with bright illusions ; the world is once more fresh to him as it was to the eyes of twenty ; life is once more a bubble iridescent with all the colours of hope.

Is the reader a person who can understand this? Do his own sympathies in any way make it intelligible to him? If so, it may prove that he is the very reader I wish for; but, before he decides as to how far he really agrees with me, there is an important part of my meaning which it still remains for me to explain to him. It perhaps may have struck him that what I have said about the charm of newness is capable of being applied to the newness of a new country—to a clearing with its log houses in some colonial forest, or to the white stores and the printing office of an infant Higgsville or Briggsville, appearing like pustules on the face of an expressionless prairie. I must therefore tell him that in my mind it has no such application whatever; that the newness which I speak of is a very limited thing; that it is essentially connected with the past, and essentially opposed to the present; in fact, that for me the only new world is the old. Nor is this limitation arbitrary. There is a very excellent reason for it. The present, with all its mortal coil of weariness—that is to say, our natural and habitual

surroundings—is the very thing which a traveller,
as I have tried to describe him, travels on purpose
to shuffle off.   Now the present, for us in England,
what is it ?   It is a modern order of things,
gradually effacing and defacing a traditional :
still the traditional order is not yet quite obliterated.   But in a new country there is no
traditional order at all ; and life there for the
traveller, instead of being any escape from the
present, would be simply the present itself in a
balder and more unmitigated form.   The only
real change for him, the only travelling which is
travelling for his spirit as well as for his body,
he must find in countries which have an historical
past behind them—amongst valleys and mountains
which retain the echoes of chivalry, in cities where
the painted ceilings have looked down on powder
and periwigs, in scenes where the past fills the air
with a sense of it, like the smell of pine forests ;
or where it actually survives, as it does in the
tents of the immemorial East.

Here, however, I confess that if we try to be
seriously logical, we find ourselves in a certain

difficulty. The charm, the fascination, of the past
—of the plunge into the deep waters! How well
some of us know it! But not only is it impossible to describe it to others : it cannot logically
be even justified to ourselves. Let us fix our
sentimental preference on whatever period we
will, letting the imagination escape to it as a
happy refuge ; and we cannot avoid thinking, if
only we think too closely, that all the littleness,
all the vulgarity, all the rawness of life, had we
really lived then, would have been plain to us
then as now. The Pyramids, as they rose under
the hands of the Egyptian bricklayers, smelt from
top to bottom of chewed garlic and onions. The
Athens of Pericles was as modern as South Ken-
sington. The farther a man, with an imposing
pedigree, dives into what he fancies to have been
the statelier times of his ancestors, the nearer he
gets to the time when those ancestors were
parvenus.

Fortunately, however, we have an answer to
these reflections ; and the answer is, that logically
they are quite unanswerable, but that our nature,

with a delightful obstinacy, refuses to be in any
degree influenced by them.   It behaves, in fact,
just as it does in another case, which is analogous,
and is familiar to all of us.   Let us stand on a
stony   hill-side—colourless,   herbless,   waterless ;
let us realise how forbidding and bare it is, and
then let us look at the distant mountains.   We
may know as a fact that they are quite bare also,
and that their slopes, if we stood on them, would
be even more forbidding.   But in spite of that
knowledge, to our eyes they have all the colours
of heaven on them.   We cannot tell why nor
wherefore, they trouble the soul like music ; they
lift our longings above the life that fetters us,
and they carry them beyond the regions of care.

And with distance in time it is the same as it
is with distance in place.   The imagination has
its atmosphere and its sunlight as well as the
earth has ; only its mists are even more gorgeous
and delicate, its aërial perspectives are even more
wide and profound.   It also transfigures and
beautifies things in far more various ways.   For
the imagination is all senses in one ; it is sight,

it is smell, it is hearing ; it is memory, regret, and passion. Everything goes to nourish it, from first love to literature—literature, which, for cultivated people, is the imagination's gastric juice.

And this reminds me that I may as well explain the allusion, which I made at starting, and which may perhaps have sounded contemptuous, to ancient art, and the temper of the professional student. I meant by it nothing disrespectful to literature generally ; indeed, how could the traveller whose pleasure is in contemplating the past be indifferent to that through which the past is mainly apprehended ? Such a traveller values literature quite as much as the student does. I only mean that he values it in a different way. The professional student, no matter how distinguished, is, after all, merely a maker of roads for the minds of others to travel on as far and as luxuriously as possible : but the student himself, with his spectacles, cannot realise this or see that his work means nothing but the convenience of post-chaises ; and the difference between him and the traveller may be bluntly

expressed as follows: that he cares only for
making the roads, and the traveller cares only for
using them. The traveller is sensible of the
importance of exact history; the traveller is
sensitive to all the magic of poetry: but facts
and dates, as he moves from one historical place
to another, are for him merely so many sticks on
which to train the tendrils of his imagination;
and poetry appeals to him only in so far as it
melts into the moonlight, as it peoples again old
cities and gardens, and fills the air with echoes of
lutes that have long been silent.

He values literature for these reasons only;
but could any reasons be stronger? Where,
without it, would be the charm that lurks in the
iron *grilles* of mediæval Italian palaces, in the
twisted ciphers and coronets forlornly rusting on
their gates, in the shadows of the grimy archway,
or the discoloured marble fountain? Except for
literature it probably would be almost imperceptible; and the more literature the traveller has
been able to apply to quickening and expanding
his own emotions and prejudices, the more potent

and enthralling does this charm become for him. It is thus that, as he wanders amongst scenes of the kind I have alluded to, he moves in a world of sights and sounds and associations undreamed of by the tourists who flourish at *tables d'hôte*, and eye with interest each other's luggage and labels, and unvalued by the student—that odd intellectual Methodist—who has his life in his books, instead of having books in his life.

Such is the sort of person whom I call the true traveller. Such is the sort of person I should now desire for a reader. What the *frou-frou* of petticoats and the odour of *poudre de riz* is for the devotee of the modern *Vie Parisienne*, that for him is the odour of antique life which still clings to so many existing walls, and the murmur of which in certain places is still alive in the air. For him the present is masculine, and he deals with it as he would deal with a man; but the past is feminine, and he loves it as he would love a woman, of whom he never could weary, because he could never entirely win her. Or to treat the matter to a simile which is perhaps more respectable, and certainly equally true, we may say that the past is to him what an opera or an oratorio is to others. The present may strike his ears as a medley of objectionable discords ; but as it drifts away from him, and becomes part of the past, its sound changes to the sound of a distant orchestra or of the sea, by turns august and plaintive with the burden of human destiny ; and each ruined marble temple, each desolate baronial banquet-hall, is a shell which murmurs with a fragment of the illimitable music.

And now I think I must bring myself to make a certain confession. I have said that the pleasure in the past is not logically defensible. I doubt, however, if such is wholly the case. I suspect that most of those who feel it have one logical reason for it ; only it is a reason which the modern thinker would consider far worse than none. I arrive at this conclusion by reflecting that for myself individually the past in England begins before the first Reform Bill, and on the Continent before the French Revolution. I am also certain that if we discovered a new Pompeii,

of which all the inhabitants had been radicals, no
matter how perfect the remains might be—even
if they comprised a complete file of a Latin *Pall
Mall Gazette*—the principal satisfaction the discovery would afford myself would consist in the
feeling that all these people were dead. If then
I may imagine myself speaking to those excellent
leaders of men, and guides of popular aspiration,
who make serious faces about a race which,
according to their philosophy, began in a gas
and will soon end in a glacier, who spell the
People with a capital P, and think that we one
day shall have a better religion than the Catholic
—I would ask them to run over all the things
that they are proudest of in the modern world ;
and I will venture to say that a part of our
pleasure in the past is due to the fact that in the
past every one of these things was wanting.

In other words, to make a long matter short,
the true traveller is mentally the *émigré* of contemporary Revolution ; and he exiles himself
from his country in order that he may escape at
intervals, if not from himself, at all events from

his generation. In one way, however, he differs from those other *émigrés*, his prototypes. He is a far more practical man; and for all practical purposes no one is better able to recognise and accept the inevitable. His many enemies will of course call him a sentimentalist; but his sentiment is generally kept sweet by the brine of some cynical humour; and though it renders him contemptuous of modern life in general, it leaves him none the less equal to dealing with, and making the best of, it. The optimists will probably ask him, Why, if that best is bad, he does not give his fine sentiment to the future instead of to the past, and so throw himself hopefully into the ranks of progressive Humanity. The pessimists will ask him, Why give any sentiment to either? The past died yesterday; the future will be dead to-morrow. But such remonstrances will have very little effect on him. The hopes of the optimists he will leave to the brutal refutation of events; whilst as for the pessimists, he will content himself with saying this to them: that if the present is really nothing but a path between two cemeteries, he finds more to interest him in the full graves than in the empty ones.

And now, if the reader is a traveller in my sense of the word, or if he has anything of such a traveller's interests, or sympathies, or temperament, he may perhaps be amused and pleased in acquainting himself with the following experiences of my own : and though the best descriptions of the writer "are but shadows," yet they may perhaps, if the reader's "imagination mend them," bring to him a breath from a land of remote mountains, rarely looked upon, except officially, by European eyes—a breath that has touched the weeds on Phœnician tombs, the marble columns of shattered Grecian temples, and Gothic towers on which once the flags of crusaders fluttered, which has borne on its breast the hoarse notes of the muezzin, and the wings of the crows that wheel round rustling palm-fronds and round minarets, which has whiffs in it of Byzantine incense, the freshness of summer seas, and the soul of the plain and of the mountain-side in a perfume of thyme and wild flowers.

And in case such a reader, with the pudicity of common sense, should, in spite of a lurking sympathy with me, fear that I may lead him too far into the regions of the sentimental, he will perhaps be reassured when he hears, as he shall hear directly, how eminently unsentimental and sordid were the motives which prompted me to visit a country where I certainly soon forgot them.

CHAPTER II

A HINT OF THE EAST

IN the August of 1887 I happened to be staying in Devonshire, with a friend and neighbour who had returned recently from the East. He was a man of as many wanderings and as many exploits as Ulysses; and his house from top to bottom was a museum of barbaric treasures. Enormous heads with horns, from the most secret places of Africa, peered down on the glass and flowers of the dinner-table; the distended jaws of a crocodile yawned over the grand piano; one went upstairs to bed past rows of poisoned arrows and the blazing ruby discs of enamelled Eastern shields. Indeed, hardly an object caught the eye anywhere which did not literally, to quote a sentence of Macaulay's, carry the mind "over boundless seas

2

and deserts, to dusky nations living under strange stars."

One morning, as I was sitting with my host in the smoking-room, he produced from the cupboards of a Japanese cabinet a number of gems, and began telling me their histories. This, I confess, I did not find specially entertaining ; and I was not sorry when, pausing, he pulled open a drawer, and proceeded to rummage in it for some new subject of conversation.

"Here," he said at last, "is another curious specimen." And he produced and handed me a small triangular something, heavy, rough in surface, and in colour a dusky green. "That," he went on, "is a fragment of Verd Antique, the famous marble which was so much prized by the ancients, and the quarries of which have for so long been unknown to the modern world."

I asked him where he found it. "I found it," he said, "in Cyprus, in a remote part of the island ; and all about the spot the same priceless stone was to right and left of me in enormous detached masses. More than that, too," he added ;

"close beside them are other masses of a beautiful clouded yellow. There they lie! Nobody knows of them; nobody but a peasant comes near them. I myself found them only by accident."

I asked him if it might not be practicable to work those quarries profitably. He replied, though without much enthusiasm, that it very possibly might be, provided a man with sufficient knowledge and enterprise should be found willing to undertake the experiment. His tone was not encouraging, and the matter accordingly dropped; but there was a mixture of romance and speculation in the train of ideas it had suggested to me, which kept constantly bringing back at odd intervals to my mind the far-off Eastern island, the unvisited silent spot in it, the veined and grained masses of luxurious green and yellow.

Some weeks later I was at a country house in Yorkshire, where portraits, books, everything— even the screens and chintzes and bell-pulls— were redolent of the last century. It was Sunday; it was the sleepy hour that succeeds a Sunday luncheon; and my hostess, by way of imparting

a little life to a guest, asked one of her daughters
to show me a certain book—a picture-book, so I
gathered, but I was unable to catch its name.
Presently a folio, bound in faded russia, was
deposited on a table and its thick leaves were
being turned over for my benefit.   I now realised
that it was a French book of travels, dealing
principally with the eastern shores of the Adriatic,
dedicated to the First Consul, and illustrated with
fine engravings.   Many of these were of unexpected interest—for instance, several of Pola,
and of Diocletian's palace at Spalatro; but
there was one above all that at once arrested and
fascinated me.   It represented a castle, lying somewhere south-east of Trieste, of the most singular
aspect, and in the most singular situation imaginable.   It was perched on the spur of a mountain,
with a river and woods below; and close behind
it, gashed in a frowning precipice, was a monstrous
cavern, out of which the river issued—a cavern
whose mouth, full of unfathomable shadow, was
large enough to have swallowed the entire castle
at a gulp.

This scene took such hold of my imagination that I began seriously to contemplate altering my winter plans so as to visit it ; and the more I dwelt on the scheme the more attractive and practicable it appeared to me. Another castle between Trieste and Venice, which I had long thought of as a place of possible pilgrimage, came back to my mind ; I reflected that I might take it on my way : and my original prospect of a winter and a spring on the Riviera began to undergo a change, like a transformation scene at a pantomime. Presently, all of a sudden, another idea struck me, which at once joined itself to the others, giving them an illuminated background. This was the idea of Cyprus, with its quarries of virgin marble. I had a general impression that one could go by steamer from Trieste to it ; and at Trieste I should be already half-way on my journey. I resolved, therefore, that I would add Cyprus to my programme ; and that its possible treasures, which had for weeks been amusing my fancy, should in sober earnest be examined, and perhaps exploited, by myself.

I immediately wrote two letters—one to a friend who had lived for years at Venice, and could tell me much about the neighbouring regions east of it ; the other to the distinguished traveller who had shown me the green specimen, asking him for a description of the exact spot where he had found it, and also for his advice as to the business side of my project. It was from him that I heard first. A fat envelope came from him with the specimen itself inside ; and crumpled round the specimen was a letter to the following purport :—

Along the northern Coast of Cyprus runs a chain of lofty mountains, one of which rises into a peculiar peak, in shape rudely resembling the distended hand of a man, and called by the Greeks Pentedactylon, or The Five Fingers. Near this peak is a grotto, within which is a fountain. It is well known to the peasants, and should not be hard to find. Close beside it stands an immense solitary cypress tree ; facing it, on the far side of a gorge, is a sheer wall of rocks, to be recognised by their colouring of brilliant red and orange ; and above it, at a height of some hundred feet, are to be traced the ruins of an old Byzantine church. Here, in front of the grotto, is lying the green marble.

A few words followed of plain practical advice.

I was to get the specimen polished, and submit it to a London expert. If in his opinion the stone would be worth working, I should make an application to the Cyprian Government with regard to it ; the initial expenses would not be great, and it was quite possible that the venture might be really profitable.

I did as I was told. I sent the specimen to a polisher. I then took it to a marble merchant, and at the same time wrote to the Governor of Cyprus and explained myself. The marble merchant gave me an answer exceedingly like that which natural science, if it were only honest, would give in connection with the Progressist's schemes for man. The stone, he said, was not Verd Antique, though at first sight, no doubt, it very strongly resembled it. Still, he admitted that it was of considerable beauty, and would, were it procurable in sufficiently large blocks, be also of considerable value. The size and soundness of the blocks were the things on which the value would depend ; and his own opinion was, though he did not profess to feel certain of it, that the blocks would be small, or, if not small, ruined by flaws.

Disappointments, as we know, never arrive singly ; and on top of this verdict I received a letter from Venice to warn me against my project of visiting the two castles. If I went at all, said my friend, I should go in the latter spring : such an excursion in the winter months would be miserable. Here was a second blow to the fabric of my delightful plans ; and I began to fear that possibly, after all, I should have to subside on those I had so lightly thrown over in their favour. But I found that, in spite of discouragement, it was hard to submit to this. The castles might wait till a more convenient season ; but the idea of Cyprus I could not let slip so easily. For six weeks, beyond horizons of Highland heather, and through mists scented with leaves of November woods in England, I had been seeing visions of tall clustering date palms, ruined temples, and faces turning towards Mecca. My hopes had tasted the unusual as a tiger tastes blood ; and I felt that I should not be satisfied until I had had a draught of it. Besides, it was still possible that the marble quarries might prove to be valuable ; the belief that they were so, having been the parent of my wish to visit them, was now in its broken condition kept alive by its child ; and it endowed, in my eyes, an impatience to be off somewhere with a semblance of sense and meaning which might else have been wanting. Add to this that, in the course of a few weeks, I received two letters from the two chief officials in Cyprus, offering me help and welcome with a cordiality so charming, that, though springing as I knew it did from their own natural kindness, I modestly set down some degrees of its warmth to the well-known pleasure of expecting a new face.

Cyprus, therefore, now remained in my mind for a month or so, much as heaven does in the minds of respectable people, as a place I should shortly go to, though I made no preparations for getting there. I went on with my visits, I wrote one or two papers on Socialism, and here and there I spoke at a political meeting. In fact I ate and drank like the people before the Flood, until one day I surprised myself much as Noah surprised his contemporaries ; I entered into the Ark—that is to say, the offices of the Peninsular and Oriental Company—and took my ticket by the overland route for Alexandria.   I had already made enquiries as to how Cyprus was to be reached, and, unless I wished to waste time on the road, Alexandria—this seemed certain—was the first point to make for.   But how from Alexandria, to get across to Cyprus—by what line of steamers, or on what days the steamers sailed—no one in London was able to tell me confidently.   I was obliged, therefore, to rest content in the faith that I should learn particulars on board the boat at Brindisi, and in the hope that I should not—as I learnt was perfectly possible—have to wait at Alexandria for the best part of a week.

I had taken my ticket a fortnight only in advance, just in time to secure the last berth in the sleeping - car which runs to Brindisi every Friday from Calais ; and during that fortnight I found it hard to believe in the reality of the future which I had now definitely prepared for myself. In fact, as so often happens when once a decisive step has been taken, I began to regret what I had done and listlessly to avoid thinking of it. The date of my departure was to be the last Friday in December. I spent Christmas and the preceding days in Devonshire ; and the season of goodwill was appropriately enlivened in my neighbourhood by the rival meetings of two Parliamentary patriots, both of whom I knew, and one of whom I assisted. On both sides we wielded the usual phrases ; we breathed polite and yet profound distrust of each other, and profound trust in all the rest of the nation. We drew cheers by resounding and reverential allusions to the Integrity of the Empire, to Truth, to Consistency, and to Justice—indeed, to almost everything not a vice that could be spelt with a capital letter. The whole proceedings were fertile in that unintended humour which is the redeeming feature of modern popular government. By Christmas Eve, however, they had perforce come to an end ; and I felt that I owed to them one of the keenest pleasures of life—the pleasure they caused me by their cessation. The day after Christmas day I came up to London to collect some necessaries I had already ordered for my journey. If it had not been that I found myself thus occupied, I should hardly even yet have realised that I was on the point of starting. I dined out twice, I went to the theatre once. Everything happened in such a natural and habitual way that it seemed as if it would go on happening so indefinitely ; and I felt as if I were dreaming, rather than as if I were awake, when, on the fourth evening, somewhere about eight o'clock, I found myself muffled on the platform at Charing Cross, with the curves of the huge roof glimmering dimly in the gaslight, and a wind, which seemed like a message from foreign seas, sweeping in through the open arch at the end, along the chimneys of the dark Continental train.

Five minutes later I was drifting out into the night, and my thoughts dwelt regretfully on a room not yet two miles away from me, where a pear half eaten was still perhaps lying on a dessert plate, with a glass half full, as if waiting for me to return to them ; and on another room, where a bed which I should not sleep in was still tumbled with the last disorders of packing.

CHAPTER III

A VOYAGE TO DREAMLAND

LONDON that Christmas had had brighter sunshine than usual, and never before had I seen from Hyde Park Corner the evening skies flush redder over the bare westward trees. My surprise, therefore, was great when, some ten minutes after starting, I saw from the window the first suburban fields gleaming in faint moonlight as if dusted with white sugar. I instantly recollected that that day at a club I had caught in the conversation of some one the words "snow at Chislehurst." I had not at the time paid them any attention, but I now appreciated their meaning, and realised that this whiteness was snow. "A local fall," I said to myself as I turned away to my paper; but half an hour

later, when I again looked out, and the suburbs
had given place to the stretch of the open
country, the whiteness was not only present,
but was wider and more unbroken, and the
hedges and trees were lying on it as if they
were scrawled in ink. The farther we went the
deeper the snow seemed ; and when I emerged
from the carriage on Dover Pier, the peculiar
smell of it at once came to my nostrils.

There was no wind, however ; the air, though
keen, was pleasant ; and the tall funnel hardly
swayed or trembled as the packet moved with its
lanterns out into the cadaverous waters.   Still
half dreaming, and seeming to be wandering
in my sleep, I stood on the deck and looked
at the coasts of England.   There they lay, an
odd glittering vision, which with fantastic per-
verseness reminded me of a birthday cake, and
also completed the strange feeling in my mind
that suddenly out of autumn we were plunged
into mid-winter.   Perhaps, so I thought, things
would be better at Calais.   But at Calais I saw,
as we slowly steamed into the harbour, snow

shining on all sides, in the wheeling rays of
the lighthouse ; and the moment I landed I felt
the ground like iron.

There was, however, no time for shivering.
Directly facing me, amongst the customary trucks
and carriages, was an object on wheels, dark
and of unusual length.   This I found to be the
Pullman sleeping-car for Brindisi, and I was at
once hurried off to it with my bundle of rugs
and dressing-bag.   The door was already very
much like the mouth of a wasp's nest, beset by a
swarm of obscure-looking men in ulsters.   They
were going in, and then again they were issuing,
with all the apparent aimlessness that annoys
us in winged insects ; they were asking the conductor the same question three times over, and
their lamp-lit faces seemed set with a vague
anxiety.   With some difficulty I at last effected
an entrance.   The car was a passage with berths
upon each side, and my own berth having been
shown me, I entrenched myself in it, and watched
my fellow-travellers.   One by one they were at
last settled in their places ; there was an opening

of bags, with revelations of socks and handkerchiefs; white collars were being unbuttoned from
flannel shirts, and long overcoats dangled from
every hook. Presently the conductor brought
me some coffee, which I had asked for on
entering; whilst I was drinking it there was a
low rumbling and a tremor. The train was in
motion: we were off for the South and Italy.

Waking next morning, I turned round to the
window, in hopes that we possibly might have
left the snow behind us. The glass was opaque
and gray; I brushed it, but made no clearing;
and then I saw that it was coated with thick
ice. I took a pen-knife and scraped a small
aperture. I looked out on a scene that would
have done honour to Siberia. That whole long
day we drifted through frozen France, the ice on
the windows freezing as fast as one flaked it off.
All my hopes had now been sent on to Italy;
and south of the Alps, at any rate, I dreamed
that blue skies would await us. Evening fell;
and my spirits began to rise as my pen-knife
laid bare for me a pageant of Swiss mountains,

a gloomy lake, the glow of a red sunset, and crags and peaks piled high in the air like thunder clouds. Early in the night we passed the Mont Cenis tunnel; and, before going to bed, I wrapped myself up closely and went out at the end of the car on to the balcony, hoping to feel on my cheeks the touch of a suaver air. Never had its bite been sharper, although not a wind was stirring, except that caused by our own motion. But the spectacle before me was almost staggering in its beauty. The naked moonlight falling on peak and precipice dazzled the eyes with an unearthly illumination. Passes and gorges towered to right and left of me; the snow, like birds' nests, hung in the climbing pine woods; and the stars, clear as diamonds, rested sparkling on the mountain-tops. And through it all, with its swing and its fierce clanking, feeling its way, the black train was sweeping. Below me were frozen rivers, expanses of silent ice, which now and again flashed with a glare like fire; and down the middle, a ribbon of curving darkness, hurrying water flowed with

a noise that was heard fitfully. I waited and
watched, expecting every moment to see the
prospect open, revealing the plains of Italy. But
I waited in vain, till my ears stung with cold.
We passed out of one gorge only to find ourselves in another; and still in the distance was
range after range of whiteness, and walls of
dazzling snow that seemed to rise up to heaven.
My feet presently began to grow cold also. I
made my retreat into the drowsy, lamp-lit car,
and was soon falling asleep in a world of curtains
and dressing-bags.

By nine next morning we were already far
into Italy, and I soon was conscious of a distinct
and surprising change. I call it surprising because it was the very opposite of the change I
had expected. The sky last night had been
clear. I counted on its being blue this morning. But instead of being blue it was livid
with leaden gray; the winter seemed far more
savage than that we had left behind us, and
we entered Bologna through snow-drifts ten feet
high.

We hurried on southward; but no change came, except that the white desolation seemed to grow more desolate. The green shutters of villas built for sunshine, the gaudy paintings on the walls — Madonnas on blue clouds, or vistas of impossible gardens — looked haggard and piteous in this unnatural weather, like rouged cheeks at five o'clock in the morning. We skirted the Adriatic; its colour was a cold menacing purple; and Ancona stood out in it, squalid like unwashed linen. We seemed to be passing through an extinct or forsaken world. That evening we stopped at a wayside station, and dined in a cold restaurant, under a ceiling daubed with flowers, having had previously all our meals in the train. We were to reach Brindisi by an hour or two past midnight; so we turned to our berths early, and slept without undressing. At length we were roused by the intimation, half welcome, half odious, that we should, as the conductor put it, "be there in half an hour." In a minute or two the car was alive with the folding and the strapping of

rugs, a search amongst blankets for novels and
pocket-handkerchiefs, and a great cramming and
dragging about of bags. My own preparations
made, I escaped outside to the balcony. I was
presently conscious that our speed began to
slacken ; some houses gleamed ahead of us ; we
slid by some walls and watch towers ; a moment
more and we were out on a frosty platform,
surrounded by porters and a babble of quick
Italian. After a little confusion, and many
illustrations of the belief that English is a universal language if only spoken loudly enough,
passengers, porters, all in a straggling crowd,
were hurrying over a ringing pavement down
to the moon-lit pier. There, lying close to it,
was a tall shadowy mass with masts and towering funnels—our steamer for Alexandria. We
ascended its side. Its port-holes were eyes of
lamp-light, which showed the monster wakeful,
although it appeared asleep.

I was soon pacing the deck, my luggage
collected and disposed of, and was thinking
over the journey which had just come to an

end—a journey which, though taken weekly by
some fifteen or twenty Englishmen, has rarely
been taken through a Europe so swathed in one
bitter winding-sheet, and which still dwelt in my
mind as something spectral and bewildering.

On the steamer, however, there was nothing
spectral at all; though certain reminiscences, not'
entirely commonplace, even now mix in my
memory with that smell of the night's keen air.
After the three days' rumbling of the train, the
sounds which I heard now—detached voices,
and the dragging and pushing of boxes—touched
the nerves like a pause of solemn expectant
silence; whilst the gleam of the harbour lights,
the sway of the still waters, the huddled, mysterious houses of the unfamiliar town, all brought
home to me, with a sudden and pleasant sharpness, the thought that I was now on the verge
of the Western world, and was soon to be
floating off from it into the hollow darkness
beyond. The imagination, with one of its many
passing flatteries, was breathing a sense into
me of personal loneliness and adventure when,

passing a group of men, I heard my own name
called out to me ; and I presently recognised
in the speaker a certain well - known Life-
Guardsman, whom I had last seen with a
gardenia, at supper in a London ball-room.
I then began to put names to his companions
—all of them men of much the same stamp,
whose talk seemed, when I joined them, to
have been of cigars and rifles. This meeting
at first I found rather prosaic and disappointing ; but when we began to compare notes as
to where we each were going, and found that
one was bound for the Soudan, one for Australia,
one for Burmah, and two for the deserts beyond
Damascus, a common thought slowly stole over
all of us. Here were four or five lives—four
or five out of millions—so often and so closely
touching each other in England, united now by
chance under the stars in the south of Italy,
and soon again to be separated for the remotest
ends of the earth. My friends' faces, in spite
of gossip and laughter, looked wan in the shadow,
and seemed to be touched with seriousness ; and

as I moved away from them a sense of illimitable distances, stars and sea winds, and the
riddle of human destiny, wove itself into the
consciousness of the moment, and made all life
seem larger.

I descended to the saloon in quest of some
sort of supper; and the first sound that greeted
me was a female voice from America—that of a
young lady sandwiched between two male ad-
mirers—declaring in ringing accents that " she
couldn't stand Jerusalem." The last thing I
heard before I retired to rest—which we all did
before we had left the harbour—was the same
young lady informing the same gentlemen—she
called one " Bill," the other she called " Darling "
—that she had learnt in Paris a new song for the
banjo, " lovely, but so wicked that Máma forbade
her singing it."

The following days were for the most part
sufficiently weary and monotonous. The Ionian
Islands lifted their snowy summits up to the
clouds as if modelled from Turner's pictures ; my
eye lingered on the jagged outlines of Crete—that

country seen by so many, explored or visited by so few. In front of these classical scenes the admired of Bill and Darling paced the deck in a sky-blue " Tam-o'-Shanter," with Bill on one side of her, and sedulous Darling on the other, each provoking her wit, and assailing her with devoted glances ; but nothing else impressed itself much on my memory, except this : that I could not get from any one any news whatever about any steamers to Cyprus, that the cold still followed us, that the waves of the Mediterranean were slate-coloured, and that finally, late in the gloom of the third evening, we entered the harbour of Alexandria under a deluge of soaking rain.

All the passengers, with the exception of two or three, were going to proceed at once by train either to Suez or Cairo. The few others, amongst whom I was included, were allowed by the captain to remain for the night on board—a kindness on his part to which he added another, that of instant inquiries for me as to my future journey. His success, however, was not equal to his wishes. He first came to me with news that there would

be a steamer in three days. Then he came again
to tell me he had been misinformed, and that I
should have to wait for six days or a week. My
delight, therefore, was great when, in the course of
another hour, everything was cleared up by an
agent of Messrs. Cook, who announced that a
steamer was going to start next morning, and
arranged that some one, by the time I had done
breakfast, should come to take me off to it without
further trouble.

The steamer was an Austrian Lloyd, which
would touch at the ports of Syria, and only reach
Cyprus after four days of coasting. This was
tiresome; but in one way I was repaid for it, for
I found that two of the friends whom I had lit on
so unexpectedly at Brindisi would be coming with
me as far as Beyrout.

At the hour appointed we were all three in
readiness; and a brown man like a wizard, in
flowing Eastern raiment, with the word "Cook"
written large on a linen ephod, was faithfully
awaiting us, who convoyed us across the harbour
to a vessel of moderate size about half a mile

away. We were somewhat apprehensive as to the sort of accommodation that might be in store for us ; but our apprehension only heightened our pleasure at what we found. The saloon and cabins were not merely clean, they were luxurious ; a *déjeuner* which we ordered revealed the hand of a *chef* who would, without any exaggeration, have been a prize to a London dinner-giver ; and, best of all, we three were the only first-class passengers.

And now, for the first time since I started, I felt that I was really travelling. During the earlier part of my journey I had been in a sort of trance. On the boat from Brindisi I had been perfectly wide awake ; only camp stools, novels, canvas boots, and opera glasses had given the deck an aspect of Margate jetty ; and men haunted the bar, their moustaches wet with cocktails, who suggested a garrison town and breathed Angostura bitters. But here suddenly all had become different. Instead of majors and doctors and young ladies going out to be married, there were strange steerage passengers in turbans and floating draperies. I was very soon conscious of a new

nasty smell, which I have learned since is peculiar
to Arab pilgrims, and which made the very air
feel foreign ; and at last amongst the crowd, that
was slowly growing by boat-loads, I detected
some outspread prayer carpets, with their owners
squatting in devotion on them. The only thing
that disappointed us was the persistence of
English weather. It was not raining, but the sky
was dim and cloudy, the wide harbour was swept
with a long lumbering swell, and a chilly wind
seemed to breathe a blight over everything.

So the day wore on, finding us still stationary.
Our own part of the ship was not invaded by
anybody, except one solitary figure. He was a
man in European dress, with wistful eyes and a
fine Hellenic face. He spoke English well, and,
advancing to us with dignity, he asked us if we
would buy what he called " special photographs."
" Be off," said one of my friends. " Take the
beastly things away with you." " Not beastly,"
he said gently, " academic." Then opening a
leather case which he carried, he produced from
its depths some polished cubes of olive-wood, and

with no change of manner except an increased
gravity. "Perhaps," he went on, "you would like
a piece of the true Cross."

In the course of the afternoon the wind began
to freshen. We had not started yet. It was
evening before we did so. By that time a stiff
breeze was blowing; a drop of rain occasionally
spluttered in our faces, and we went out over the
bar into the gathering twilight, plunging through
crests of foam.

By the following morning we were at Port
Said, where we passed a long, wearisome day.
There was rain there also, and the sandy roads
were in puddles. The sense of the East was by
this time distinct in all of us; but it was an East
blighted and draggled, a forlorn mockery of its
fame. The day after, however, things at last took
a different turn. I found, on waking early, my
cabin aglow with sunrise. I looked from the
window: sparkles were leaping on the waters. I
went on deck, and there—how shall I describe
the spectacle?—rose-coloured fleeces wandered on
wastes of transparent purple: the naked dome of

the sky was soaring and arching over me ; and
the dark waves heaved, waiting to be lightened into
azure.   It was some moments before I realised
something else : then it burst on me—we were
hardly two miles from land.   Opposite to us
Jaffa was gleaming ; and stretching to north and
south of it were the brown coasts and the tufted
palms of Palestine ; and inland, the violet outlines
of the hills about Jerusalem.

And now began the process of a new birth, for
which all that had gone before had been a preparation—the birth, so long delayed, out of the
Western winter, and the homely associations
which thus far, like winter birds, had been following us — the birth out of these into a world
increasingly different.   At Beyrout, where I spent
a day on shore, and where in the evening I said
good-bye to my companions, the air was already
mild and balmy, the mud walls looked as if they
were baking in the sunlight, the hotel garden was
grateful with green shadow ; and as I sat there,
confronted by seventeen Persian cats who were
smiling and purring on seventeen empty biscuit

tins, a babbling fountain and a tree with scarlet flowers seemed to say to me that I was entering unknown seasons.

By and by I returned to the ship alone. The pale twilight fell, and enfolded us with unutterable tenderness, just revealing the glimmering snows of Lebanon, and leaving the glass of the sea just distinguishable from the air. Lights glistened from the town; a sound like a fairy bell—I suppose it came from a boat, though in the dimness I could not see one—made at intervals a mysterious tinkling on the water. In due time a term was put to the quiet. There was a dragging of ropes and chains, and a splash of the revolving screw. The funnel buzzed, our bows turned round to seaward, we began to move rapidly, and the sea and the night received us.

Some eight hours later, after a windless passage, I woke up in my cabin, and in sight were the coasts of Cyprus.

CHAPTER IV

THE THRESHOLD OF A NEW LIFE

I STOOD on the deck.   I found myself solitary in
the opening morning.   Bars of crimson and
purple were brightening over unseen Palestine ;
our white wake was a road reaching straight away
towards them, with the black smoke from our
funnel travelling back over it ; the waves splashed
and tossed in a chorus of fresh whispers.   My dress
was of the scantiest, a thin overcoat and *pyjamas* ;
and the air, breathing through all the fluttering
folds, seemed to enter the skin as it enters a bird's
pinions, and gave me a feeling as though I were
akin to the wind and foam.

And there Cyprus lay, stretching far along the
horizon, a bank of hoary blue with curious pallid
gleams on it, and dark purple markings that

hinted of cliffs and headlands. At this distance, however, it had no definite meaning. I could only wonder what it would mean to me one day, and allow the sensations and fancies of the moment to play with me.

In some ways they played delightfully, as if full of the spirit of the early, adventurous hour. But along with this elation I was conscious of a rising anxiety as to what was going to happen to me before the day was over. I was, on arriving, to be the guest of the Chief Secretary, who lived in Nicosia, the immemorial seat of government ; and so far as kindness went I was sure of a kind welcome : but as I neared the island I began to realise keenly how very little I, after all, knew about it, and to ask myself if in coming to it I had not been a fool for my pains.

As an island of the imagination in the world of fable and history I could have recited a roll of magnificent names connected with it — antique Egypt and Hellas, luxurious Rome, Byzantium, and crusading Europe ; or, again, Adonis, who was wooed on its sloping hillsides ; Balaam and

Ezekiel, who sang of its power and riches ; Solomon
and Alexander the Great, St. Paul and St. George
the dragon-slayer, Catharine Cornaro of Venice,
and the conquering Sultan Selim.   The mere
catalogue would have come to the ear like a
passage out of *Paradise Lost.*   But as for the
dates and details which underlay all these
associations, my knowledge, I now found, was
forlornly less than fragmentary.   And what sort
of present remained after all this past ?   My
knowledge of this was more inappreciable still.
Six weeks ago I was not even aware of the
existence of the city in which I should sleep that
night—this obscure capital, Nicosia, hidden away
far inland, and full, as I had learnt already, of
strange relics of antiquity.   It was   still the
merest dream to me except as regards one point,
that I should have, as soon as I landed, to drive
some thirty miles to it.

The situation, as I gradually thought it over,
caused me, I confess, a certain sinking of the heart ;
and presently, feeling chilly, I sought relief in my
cabin, where, pulling a rug over me, I dropped off

into a doze. When I awoke and emerged again things had quite a different aspect. The air was mild, the sky was a full-blown blue, and the coasts of Cyprus, hardly three miles away from us, met the eye like the canvas of a moving diorama. So far as I could see, they were utterly bare and treeless, and they glittered from every facet with a pale dazzling brilliance, in some places colourless, in others suffused with pink, so that now and again one might have fancied them half transparent, as if with all their crags they had been formed out of solid amethyst. I looked long in vain for any sign of a human occupation, and was wondering for how many hours the process of coasting would continue, when, taking a turn forwards, I saw that right ahead of us, shining like snow, and apparently standing in the water, was a row of houses, with a cupola, a campanile, and a minaret, and at one side of it a dot of intensest green—the green of a grove of palm trees. This I knew must be Larnaca, the port of landing. We were now nearing it rapidly. Detail after detail began to grow more distinct. Hollow arches and quaint balconies were discernible ; the light of the morning began to flash in the windows, and soon we detected boats putting out to meet us.

Larnaca has no harbour ; there is only an open roadstead ; and we dropped our anchor about half a mile from shore.   I was busy in the saloon over some coffee, when voices and shouts outside proclaimed that the islanders were already beginning to board us ; and when I passed presently into my cabin, which was, like the saloon, on deck, there was a red fez cap at the window, and a brown bearded face, courting my attention with a plaintive, enquiring smile.   I lowered the glass, and a voice in delightful English (by which I mean that it was just bad enough to be pathetic) asked if I was the gentleman who was going to land at Larnaca.   I said that I was.   " Right, sir," the voice replied.   " You show me your things.   I have good boat here ; I put you ashore directly—take you to custom-house ; if you want it, get you a carriage.   Yes, sir, I manage—yes, sir."   The man's manner had

something very taking in it, and so had his whole
appearance when I saw him at full length outside. His dress, except for his Oriental head-gear,
might very well have belonged to a British sailor
—a loose pea-jacket and trousers of blue serge—
but his face, handsome in feature and dark in
colour, had the curious expression only to be
found in the East, an expression of appeal and
devotion like that of a faithful dog. He was as
good as his word. He very soon had me in
a boat, manned by a negro and two brigand-like
Greeks. As I sat by him in the stern he told me
he was an Arab from Syria, but that he knew
Cyprus thoroughly from end to end. I told him
I wished to go to the house of the Chief Secretary, and was charmed when he answered
promptly, " Right, sir ; I know the gentleman."

After heavily mounting and falling for some
time on the swell we arrived at last at a short
wooden jetty, with a small steam crane pertly
peering over its side, and a square building facing
it like a new village school in England. The
British flag flying over this last told me that it

was the custom-house. Experience presently
told me the same thing, for all my luggage was
instantly carried off to it and deposited in a
verandah, before a door which proved to be
locked. The officials, it seemed, were all of them
away at breakfast, and my Arab protector suggested that I should follow their example. " If
you like," he said, " I take you to the hotel.
While you eat I go order the carriage—good
carriage, sir ; three horses—and I arrange with
these fellows for the price of him. Come, sir,
come this way."

I assented and went with him. In something
like thirty seconds I had passed out of sight of
the steam crane and the custom-house into a
world whose suggestions were utterly strange and
different. I was moving rapidly along an ill-
paved species of esplanade between the sea and
a succession of houses, perforated with pointed
arches. Some of these seemed to my hasty
glance in passing to give access to nothing but
caves of darkness ; others revealed glimpses of
primitive shops, like fragments of mediæval Italy ;

and above, protruded on quaint supports over the road, were sleepy Oriental windows, blinded with wooden lattice-work.

Presently my guide plunged into one of the arched interiors, which seemed a sort of cross between a grocer's shop and a drinking-bar; and having spoken a word or two to a woman hidden in the background, he led me out into a wide, echoing passage and up a flight of bare stone stairs at the end of it. These brought us to a stone-paved, capacious landing, in the middle of which stood a table, with a white cloth and some plates on it. Here my guide begged me to sit down and wait, and engaged, as he hurried off, that some breakfast should at once be sent to me. It came duly, brought by a sallow Greek; and whilst I was finishing it my guide again showed himself; and coming up to me with an air of engaging apology, put into my hand a packet of dirty letters. After a moment's puzzled inspection I realised what these were. They were testimonials to his character, from stewards of yachts and from men-of-war's officers, for whom, I gathered, he had often acted as interpreter. He also told me a fact which gave me more interest in him—that he had, at one time of his life, been servant to Colonel Valentine Baker. I asked him his name. He answered in a word of two syllables, which I mentally spelt S, k, ô, t, i, with a circumflex accent written large over the ô. I was, therefore, amused when a moment later he said, "Once, sir, I been at Glasgow. That why they call me Scotty. Abdullah Scotty, that my name, sir. This coat, these trousers, I get him both in Glasgow. I think, sir," he added, "if we go now, they ready by this time at the custom-house."

This proved to be true. A dapper Maltese, in a check shooting-coat, did what was necessary in the way of inspecting my luggage; and whilst waiting for the carriage, which Scotty told me he had ordered, I wandered about in an open space close by and tried to realise my first impressions of the island. I found them delightful to a degree which I could hardly account for, and which must have been mainly due, at this time, to the sunshine and the enchanting air. I, who a week ago had been shivering in the gloom of Europe, was here moving under a sky of the softest turquoise. The sunlight was penetrating soul and body at once; and my nostrils were touched by the smells of aromatic leafage. On three sides of me were low Government buildings, as raw and new as mortar and red tiles could make them; but they were half hidden by a whispering fringe of pepper trees; and on the other side was the town I had just left, with its white flat-roofed houses, the plumes of its feathery date-palms, and, blue above these, the crags of some distant inland mountains.

Presently, turning round at the end of my beat, I could hardly restrain a laugh at an object I saw before me. It was the carriage—"the good carriage"—standing at the custom-house door, with my luggage, under Scotty's direction, already being placed upon it. This singular vehicle was a battered English wagonette, which had once been black, but was now a permanent dust-colour. It had been adapted to its present climate by the

addition of an iron framework, roofed and enclosed by curtains of pink and white diaper,
which exactly resembled a patchwork of house-
maid's dusters. There was a lean negro on the
box, with a pair of ropes for reins, and standing
in front of him were three gaunt horses abreast,
whose harness, I must say, showed traces of real
care, for in every part it was mended—indeed,
kept together—by string.

"Perhaps, sir," said Scotty as I approached,
"you like me come with you to Nicosia. This
fellow, he not know the house." I had been in-
tending to make the same proposal myself to him,
and was glad to find him already prepared to act
on it. I climbed to my seat in the transparent
shade of the dusters; and was beginning to
wonder why we did not start, when my ear was
caught by some words which, though strangely
familiar to me, I had never before heard or expected to hear in conversation. " Ὀκτώ," said
Scotty's voice to some one I could not see. Then
followed a murmuring, and then his voice said,
" Δέκα." Then came " "Ενδεκα," and in a minute

more, "Δώδεκα." It was like a page of the
Eton grammar suddenly come to life. My ear
for the first time was catching the accents of
modern Greek. I at once perceived what it
meant. It was Scotty bargaining in shillings for
the price of the carriage. The bargain was
struck at thirteen—thirteen shillings for something like thirty miles. Certainly, I thought,
whatever else it may be, Cyprus at any rate is
not an expensive place.

The next moment there was a noise from the
negro's mouth, a whip cracked, the vehicle gave a
jerk, my dressing-bag opposite me fell forward on
my knees, and at a very decent pace we were
moving away from Larnaca. We passed some
gardens surrounded by tumble-down mud walls,
above which appeared the dark leaves of orange
trees; we passed a Catholic convent, whose
church had a pale pink dome on it; and then,
when these disappeared behind some sandy
acclivities, we entered a country as bare as a
Scotch deer forest. Slopes strewn with boulders
descended towards the road or away from it;

rocky surfaces glittered as if they were wet with
water ; and far and wide was growing some harsh
brown vegetation, that seemed, as I passed it,
like stunted and withered gorse.   The patchwork
of dusters was drawn so closely round me, that I
had no view except through the opening above
the door.   I leaned out occasionally to see if on
either side of me any prospect of a different kind
was visible ; but I looked in vain.   Everywhere
the horizon was formed by low undulating ridges,
whose summits broke occasionally into fortresses
of natural crag, and which here and there, where
they receded, enclosed morass-like levels.   In a
northern climate it would all have formed a
picture of dreariness ; but I found, to my surprise,
that it did not do so here.   The sunlight and the
air lay on it, like a love philter endowing it with
fascination.   Everything — shrub and boulder,
brown soil, and naked rocky ridge — was softly
luminous, as if it were seen through water ; and
every breath which I drew into my lungs excited
me as if it had been drugged with some strange
stimulant.

The landscape itself, however, I soon felt, was
monotonous ; so I gave up staring at it, and be-
taking myself to a map and to a guide-book, I
tried to identify the road on which I was
travelling, and I re-read a meagre description of
Nicosia. The description told me of gardens,
palaces, and minarets, Venetian fortifications, and
mediæval Christian churches, of the palaces of
crusading kings, and the tombs of Turkish
warriors. The whole was comprised in a few
mechanical paragraphs, and when I read it before
it had conveyed very little to me ; but now the
words seemed to become alive, and their very
inability to satisfy my curiosity made them all
the more powerful in exciting it. Occasionally
my attention was called again to the road, by our
passing some travelling group, or else some solitary figure. So far as I could see, they were
shepherds or peasants mostly, with scarlet caps
and long shaggy capotes ; and once or twice
came a rude cart drawn by bullocks. The men,
as we went by them, all glanced back at the
carriage, showing bronzed wild faces and dark

eyes and moustaches, and were presently lost to sight, like images seen in a dream.

After two hours or so of this kind of progress I gathered from the map that we were approaching a place named Dali—the site of the old Idalium, where a hundred altars once were fragrant to Idalian Aphrodite. Presently the carriage stopped, and Scotty's voice through the curtains explained to me that the horses would rest here for twenty minutes. I descended and looked about me. We were on the summit of a low ridge of hills. Close at hand was a cluster of flat-roofed mud cottages, and on the opposite side of the road some corresponding outhouses. A few cocks and hens were strutting amongst fragments of broken crockery; a mule's head protruded through a dark crack in a wall, and from the door of the principal cottage a man came with cups of coffee. Scotty informed me that we were now half-way to Nicosia. "It over there, sir," he said. "We get there in two hours." I looked, but no town was visible. It was hidden behind intervening ridges.

The country now before us had the character
of an open plain, littered with low brown hills
and bounded by purple mountains. The outline of these last was singularly bold and fantastic, cutting the sky with summits like spires
or isolated citadels; and I presently realised
that amongst them was one eminence, curiously
splitting itself into five several peaks, which I
at once knew must be Pentedactylon—the Mountain of the Five Fingers. The recognition, in
its reality, of what was already familiar to me
in words—this seeing of the object which I
had heard of in homely Devonshire actually
towering in its far-off native air—sent an odd
thrill through me; it was like seeing a dream
come true.

In a few minutes more it was time to be
off again, and the curtains of the carriage again
narrowed my view. I saw, however, that we
were getting into a district which was somewhat more fertile. The road soon began to
show a border of asphodel, and on wide tracts
I had glimpses of goats and sheep wandering.

So the time wore on—an hour and then two
hours—but, though I looked out anxiously, there
was still no Nicosia. The only new feature
was a number of isolated hills, perfectly flat at
the top and looking like artificial fortifications.
At last, against the side of a bare yellowish
cliff, I detected a mud village squalidly simmering in the sunshine. "Good heavens!" I thought,
"and is this the city of the Crusaders?" But
the carriage passed on. My alarm was, happily,
groundless. Presently by the roadside was a
stream and a grove of palm trees. A mile
farther on was a group of men who were road-
mending. I cannot say that I thought their
expression agreeable; nor is this to be won-
dered at, as I learnt afterwards they were con-
victs. Then after another mile or so was a
group of another character—three young men in
tweeds, with the air of Government clerks, who
looked after me with a smile of suburban curiosity, and exhibited British freckles and British
briar-wood pipes. Then came Scotty's voice
saying something or other through the curtains,

which I took to mean that we were nearing
the end of our journey. I stretched my head
out to see if the environs of any town were
about us, but I still saw nothing but rocks and
open country. I was wondering at this and
beginning to be a little impatient, when suddenly
a shadow for a moment fell over everything. On
each side appeared masses of ancient masonry.
We had passed through some thick walls; we
were next in an open space, surrounded by
a vision of vague mud-coloured buildings: a
moment more, and with a hollow echoing rumble
we were rapidly moving along a narrow shadowy
street, and at last abruptly the carriage came to a
standstill.

On descending I found myself before a large
arched doorway, with heavy folding doors in a
blind whitewashed wall, and above it a mass of
overhanging roofs and windows. But I had no
time to distinctly realise anything before, in response to Scotty's efforts and the bell-pull, the
doors were opened, and revealed a smart-looking
Greek servant in a dark braided jacket and dark

voluminous trousers. I was a little apprehensive that we might have come to the wrong house, but the man, who spoke English, instantly reassured me. Crossing the threshold, I found myself in a wide passage, opening into cloisters supported on pointed arches. These last ran round two sides of a garden, green with orange and lemon trees and the tall fronds of bananas. There was a murmur of water somewhere softly splashing into a basin, and the air was full of a faint but delightful smell of violets. I was conducted along the cloisters to a flight of stairs that led from them, and was just preparing to mount when my hostess came down to meet me. By way of a thin disguise I will speak of her as Mrs. Falkland. Her greeting was of the kindest, and, with a thoughtfulness which I fully appreciated, she told me that in the dining-room she had ordered some luncheon to be awaiting me. We went there. It was a room on the ground-floor opening on the cloisters. It was lofty, if somewhat narrow. It was spanned by a pointed arch, which helped to sustain the bare beams of the ceiling. The walls, covered with a smooth pinkish plaster, gave the scene an aspect of non - European simplicity, whilst a sparkle of plate on the side-board and on the table at once betrayed the presence of European comfort and luxury. It was a pleasant, piquant mixture, and produced a strange sense in me of conditions untried hitherto and altogether mysterious.

My repast over I was taken to the rooms above. The stairs led to a sort of lofty hall, shaped like the letter **L**, directly over the cloisters. Its stone floor was strewn with Oriental rugs ; its bare plastered walls were hung with Oriental embroideries, and here and there were some small tables and ottomans. Out of this opened the drawing-room and various bedrooms—my own amongst the number. My portmanteaus, I found, were by this time duly in their places ; and my hostess left me to arrange myself after my dusty journey. I resolved, whilst annoying myself over the troubles of unpacking, to engage Scotty for my servant during my stay in the island—a

contingency which, I believe, he foresaw from the
first himself.   By the time I had shaved and
dressed it was already five o'clock, and the dim
blue twilight without was falling rapidly over
everything.   As I emerged and approached the
drawing-room, I was surprised by a babble of
voices, and on entering I found Mrs. Falkland
entertaining a large tea-party.   The high room,
roofed with dark open rafters, was full of shadow,
despite some glimmering lamps ; and the forms
and faces of the company were all mysterious and
uncertain.   I was never able to identify a single
member of it afterwards, but they all must have
belonged to the English colony of officials, to
whom Mrs. Falkland was at home on periodical
occasions.

I listened in silence to the conversation round
me, and never had I listened to any with a more
singular flavour.   The dozen or so of visitors, it
seemed, were of all ages—girls, old ladies, and
youngish and middle-aged men.   Some of them
talked of practising hymns for the church, others
of hunting, of races, of last year's picnics, and the

glories of a possible ball.   In many respects, no
doubt, it was just what might be heard any day
in the outskirts of any provincial town in England ; but the names of the places mentioned and
certain pieces of slang, as if in a mad dream,
were all of them metamorphosed into Greek.   It
was like a dialogue from Homer entangled with
a dialogue from Miss Austen's novels.   There
was something inexpressibly grotesque in the
idea of a curate who had lost his copy of "Hymns
Ancient and Modern" at Paphos, and in hearing
a young lady date some delightful memory as
"the time when Mr. Button was so ridiculous
on Olympus."

Amused as I was, I confess I was somehow
mortified at the thought of Mr. Button profaning
these august localities.   I felt that his presence
would act on the ghosts of the gorgeous past,
as a cross-handled sword is supposed to act on
the devil.   But as soon as his friends were gone
he slipped away from my memory ; and a sense
of surrounding strangeness once more took possession of me.   Now that the room was quiet

I was introduced to my hostess's daughter, and before long her father, Colonel Falkland, entered. I learned presently that I was not the only guest, but that a young professor from Cambridge, with his wife from Girton, were also staying in the house, being in Cyprus to superintend some excavations. They had just come in, having been out at their work all day, and I did not see them till dinner time. We assembled at eight o'clock, and our conventional evening coats showed curiously amongst our semi-barbarous surroundings. Our way to the dining-room lay through the open cloisters; and faint odours of the East touched our nostrils as we passed.

The dinner was the work of an excellent Scotch cook; but it derived a charming and unmistakable local flavour from the early vegetables and the woodcock, from the strong Cyprian wine, from the fine preserved apricots, and from the pale Oriental sweetmeats. The conversation, though very different from that of the afternoon tea-drinkers, was saturated, like theirs, with a local flavour also. Mr. Adam, as I will

call the young professor, discussed, in a tone of
placid academic refinement, which came to my
ears like an echo of an Oxford common-room,
the various spots where it might be desirable
to excavate, and the various objects which had
been unearthed already. Strange names of unknown places and people—men called Demetrius
and Georgos, and places called Paraskévi and
Morphou—buzzed in my ears like a sort of un-
intelligible spell. During dessert a basket was
brought in full of prehistoric pottery, with a
bronze spear-head in addition—the fruits, as I
gathered, of that afternoon's work. Mrs. Adam,
though, like Don Juan's mother, "her favourite
science was the mathematical," betrayed in dis-
cussing these objects the fact that she was a Greek
scholar. Colonel Falkland, who had lived much
in the East, interwove with his talk about archæ-
ology many interesting observations as to the
unsuspected power, the politics, and the future of
Islam. He explained to us problems of which
in the Western world the very existence is hardly
so much as dreamed. As he spoke, mysterious

regions with sounding legendary names, which had always seemed to me to belong to the land of fable—Armenia, Karamania, and even Thibet and Persia—began for the first time to assume a sort of spectral reality ; and when at half-past ten we all of us separated for the night, I felt that my mind, like my body, was moving against a new background. Strange mountains seemed to be towering up around me whose snowy passes shut out the Western world, and I seemed to discern, half-transparent in the air, the gigantic shadowy shapes of new powers and presences.

CHAPTER V

IN A FORGOTTEN CAPITAL

I HAD reached my present quarters in the most charming way possible, having been brought to them practically blindfold ; and I awoke next morning with the sense that I was lying in the middle of mystery. Of what the town was like, of what the people were like, or of what sort of sentiment I should find abroad in the air, I hardly knew more than I did when I left London. I lazily looked up at the sloping ceiling above me, which was formed of some fine matting, stretched upon beams of olive wood. My eyes wandered to the unpainted door, on which fanciful iron hinges branched into lean crescents. I glanced at the stone floor, with a thick Persian mat on it. The chest

of drawers and the looking-glass I recognised as
European.

Presently through the perfect stillness came a
long-drawn lilting sound, something like a crow
imitating a town-crier. I turned towards the
window, which was close beside my bed, and
drew back from it the semi-transparent curtains.
The sight of the blue sky at once made me
wakeful and vigorous. I rose and I looked out.
Before me were the tops of dark and glossy
orange trees, with their golden fruitage glittering
on them. Then came a gleam of walls, and
again more trees beyond them—oranges also,
with here and there a cypress—and ending the
vista rose a tall feathery palm tree, and close
beside it the spike of a slender minaret. The
minaret showed me the nature of the sound I
had been listening to. It was the voice of the
muezzin, still calling from the gallery. Every
detail was vividly unfamiliar. A closely-latticed
window or two peeped in the distance through
the leafage, doubtless looking down upon hidden
and inaccessible gardens. Near the minaret was

a glimpse of a low white dome, and far away was
the peak of a faint silvery mountain.

After breakfast that morning I was left to my
own devices. The garden of the house, with its
sense of seclusion and secrecy, was so attractive
that I felt no impatience to leave it, and I was
pleased at dallying a little longer with my uncertainty as to things outside. I therefore spent
the time before luncheon in unpacking a photographic apparatus, and erecting a portable developing room in a quiet corner of the cloisters—
an occupation which I lightened occasionally, by
pausing to watch the ways of the native servants.
In especial, my attention was caught by a curious
Greek girl, who rushed to and fro on her business
like a good-natured wild animal, and eyed me
and my appliances with a laugh of undisguised
curiosity. My attention had also been caught
by some brilliant flashes of colour, coming and
going through the leaves at the far end of the
garden ; and I at last discovered that these were
part of a brown groom called Mustapha, with a
white turban and crimson and yellow stockings,

who was as tall as a lamp-post, and whose legs were like those of a Chippendale table.

Mrs. Falkland proposed to take me into the town after luncheon, but something happened to occupy her, and I was warned not to go by myself as I should certainly lose my way, and, not speaking Greek or Turkish, might find myself unable to ask it. About five o'clock, however, Colonel Falkland returned from his office, and suggested that we should go for a stroll outside the walls to visit something—I did not quite realise what. We went through the garden, and out of a side gate near the stables; and passing along an exceedingly narrow lane, in less than a minute we found ourselves on the ramparts. The slight gray parapets, loop-holed for old-world musketry, were broken and ragged, with tufts of weed growing on them. Beyond was an open plain, which stretched away to the bases of far-off mountains. Here and there were a few children playing; a Greek girl passed with a pitcher poised on her head; below a voice called —it came from a shepherd with a crook—an occasional hen ran by, and some wrangling dogs barked.

We went to the edge of the walls, and though the parapets were broken, the sloping surfaces below were in most places as perfect as when— so Colonel Falkland told me—they were built by the Republic of Venice four hundred years ago. Here and there, however, the stone-work had been torn away, and left a practicable descent over the earth and rubble underneath. Down one of these places Colonel Falkland and I scrambled, and he began to lead me out over a bare tract of plough-land. Presently we paused and looked back at the town. What I saw was a girdle of walls fast growing dim in the evening —walls which at intervals bulged into rounded bastions. Above them peered the eaves of some flat-roofed houses, with some palm trees and one minaret, dark in the clear air. At that short distance nothing more was visible.

Pursuing our walk we arrived in a quarter of an hour at a barren space of ground, littered with fallen building stones, columns and capitals and fragments of carved arches. A cross which caught my attention showed me that the relics were Christian, and a second glance showed me that the building they belonged to had been Gothic. "Here," said Colonel Falkland, "is the site of a palace of the Lusignan kings. In mediæval times this spot was inside the city. Its walls then had three times their present circuit ; but the Venetians destroyed them at the time of the Turkish invasion as being too extensive to defend, and instead of them built the present ones. Do you see," he continued, "what this place is now? It is a burying-ground—the Armenian burying-ground." As he spoke he pointed first to a prostrate door jamb, then to a moulded plinth, then to the mullion of some vanished window, set upright in the earth : and rude crosses cut in them, and inscriptions in the Armenian character, which traversed their original ornamentations, showed me that they were used as grave-stones, and that the dead were resting under them—the ended trouble of life hiding under its ended pride.

Had a poet like Gray been there, he might have written a new elegy, but the scene at this hour seemed to be an elegy in itself. Far away in the west the fading sunset gleamed over a darkening sea-like plain, flanked on either side by lines of converging mountains. A faint breeze came sighing out of the solitude, and passed on to rustle the palm-fronds of the mysterious city. A feeling of sadness rose up out of the earth, with hints of remote races, and the splendours of forgotten history ; and as we walked back over the twilight fields, and through the alleys now black with evening, and found ourselves in the lamplight of Mrs. Falkland's drawing-room, the spirit of the place kept sounding in my mind's ear, faint and plaintive like the voice of an Æolian harp.

After tea Scotty made his appearance, and I agreed to take him into my service. Our dinner that evening was as pleasant as on the night preceding ; and my sense of the contrast of things was more keen than ever when a dull tramping was heard in the street outside, and the sound of camel bells came tinkling through the taste of our Scotch broth.

That night I retired to rest with a strange feeling possessing me—who would not be grateful for it were it only his privilege to experience it? —a feeling of escape from the Furies of modern life, disillusion, doubt, and democracy. People often talk of their heart being brought into their mouth. Life in these days brings the hearts of many of us into the devil's mouth, and he gnaws them as Dante's devil gnawed Judas and Brutus, whilst the eyes and lips of their owners seem to smile with enjoyment. But here was a sudden rest, and peace breathed upon my pillow. Nor was this merely a night's passing illusion. Happy was the light that came to my eyes next morning. Joy came with it, freshness, and expectation. Nothing interfered with my mood except the rapid discovery that Scotty was not very clever at folding or brushing trousers; and Colonel Falkland's garden, when I came down to breakfast, smelt like the gardens I had known in the morning of boyhood.

Mrs. and Miss Falkland said that at twelve
o'clock they would come out with me and give
me a glimpse of the unknown world I was living
in. When the time came we all of us sallied
forth into the street through which I had driven
two days previous. It was perfectly silent, but
there were a few figures moving in it. The walls
of the houses to a height of twelve or fifteen feet
were, with rare exceptions, perfectly blind and
blank except for doors occurring at wide intervals.
Above were irregular windows, many of which
projected ; and the roofs, which projected still
farther, in places nearly touched those opposite to
them. Out of this street we passed into another
—a narrower one—then into another, and so on
into more. Some of them were merely alleys
running between high mud-walls, above which
peered the leafage of palms or fruit-trees. I felt
that it was lucky for me I had not come out by
myself. The place seemed as intricate as the
Cretan labyrinth, so that very soon I had completely lost my bearings ; and everywhere it was
pervaded by a sense of hush and secrecy. The

6

narrower alleys were generally quite deserted, only now and again a grave, bearded figure, in a turban and long robes, went by stealthily; or suddenly round a corner came a white-veiled girl gliding.

As my eyes grew gradually accustomed to the look of things I began to realise a number of strange details. I noticed that though the upper parts of the walls were of mud or of sun-dried brick, the lower parts were mostly of finely-cut ancient stone-work, and that most of the doors were early Gothic arches which might, with their mouldings and their ornaments, have belonged to an English abbey. Here and there, too, in an odd angle was a conduit or fountain that suggested mediæval Europe, and in one place, embedded in a shadowy blank wall, was the chancel end of an exquisite Gothic church. The window, with its mass of florid carving, was perfect; indeed, so to all appearance must the whole structure have been. It was now the barn or the stable of some Turkish mansion, and a black Nubian in a white tunic was leaning against it.

He eyed us as we passed, as if he were some en-chanted figure. Wherever we went there was the same hush. The ripple of a conduit was often the only voice in the street, and yet all around was a sense of unknown ambushed life.

My own feelings in making this singular ramble recalled to my mind a passage in a certain sensational novel, hardly known even by name to ninety-nine out of a hundred novel-readers. It is a Latin novel of the ancient Roman Empire. It takes us into the heart of a Roman province, into Thessaly, and it shows us the daily life of forgotten luxurious cities—of the hearth, the theatre, and the banquet-room ; it shows us country cottages, secluded mills, picnics in shady valleys, and even the by-lanes of those far sub merged centuries, with the petals of the dog-roses fluttering on the wayside brambles. Those who have read the book, or have even glanced at it, will know that I mean *The Golden Ass* of Apuleius. The hero is the heir of a noble African family, and his one ambition is to be initiated into the mysteries of magic. His

mother was a Thessalian, and affairs take him
to Thessaly.   Now Thessaly at that period was
renowned as the special home of witches.   The
entire country was a kind of gigantic Brocken,
and by the time the young man has arrived at
his destination—the house of an old miser in the
rich city of Hypata—magic and not business is
the thing that fills his brains.   "The morning
after my arrival," he says, "when the night had
been shaken from nature, and a new sun re-
created the day, I started from sleep and from
bed at the same instant, and, full of the thought
that I was now in the very heart of Thessaly,
which the whole world celebrates as the native
land of enchantment, burning with eagerness and
curiosity, I went out and examined everything.
And there was nothing in all that city which I
could believe to be really what it seemed to be,
but I fancied that everything was enchanted and
changed into another shape by sorcery, that the
stones I tripped against were human   beings
petrified, that the trees, in the same way, were
human beings with leaves on them, and that the

pouring waters of the fountains were human lives wasting. Every moment I expected that the statues and the frescoes would begin walking, that the walls would speak, that the oxen and cows would prophesy, and that from the very heaven itself and the dazzling circle of the sun there would issue some sudden oracle."

I cannot say of Nicosia that I expected to hear oracles in it, but it filled me with precisely the same sense of unreality as that with which Hypata filled the hero of Apuleius. Everything seemed to be something more than it appeared to be on the surface. The air seemed charged with some latent romantic life. Any moment I could have expected to hear the notes of some Oriental love-song or the guitar strings of some wandering troubadour, and my imagination would have been satisfied rather than surprised had there issued from any door some gorgeous crusading knight, grown effeminate in the East, some veiled Circassian beauty, or a disguised caliph with his vizier.

Mrs. Falkland was not an archæologist, and

could not tell me much of the history of the
Nicosian houses ; but there was one house she
knew of, of very considerable size, belonging to a
certain Melek Jahn, an Armenian, which had been
in his family for three hundred years, and of
which—in case I wished it—she said she could
show me the interior.   To this house we accordingly bent our steps.   Though Mrs. Faikland had
known Nicosia for years, so intricate are its
tangled streets that we twice lost our way.   At
last, however, we came to the junction of three
lanes, where a small mosque and a minaret formed
an unmistakable land-mark.   Here we turned
sharply round by the tomb of a Turkish warrior,
adorned with droppings of candle grease and the
ends of votive candles, and went up a narrow
passage under the shadow of a Franciscan convent.
Presently over the opposite walls rose the open
arches of a campanile, which Mrs. Falkland told
me belonged to the Armenian church, and passing
in through a pair of broken gates we were brought
by a weedy path to a mouldering stone doorway.
The nail-studded doors we pushed open without

ceremony, and within we found ourselves in a lofty dilapidated arcade, beyond which glowed the green of a neglected garden. The arcade under which we stood rose the whole height of the house. Its roof was of timber, supported by slim circular columns, and on it looked a succession of dark windows, framed and latticed with wood-work of delicate carving ; the doors, which had horse-shoe arches, were masses of carving also ; and everywhere there were traces of bygone taste and splendour. We strayed on into the garden, an acre and a half in extent. Part of it was nothing but a bare space, squalid with rubbish ; but part was still covered with orange trees, palms, and mulberry trees, various shrubs, and a mat of neglected violets. There was nowhere a sign of life, except from some ragged children who had come in after us, and stared at us from a distance, and from the struggles of an extra-ordinary hen, which we found tethered to a black-currant bush. As we turned to go, in the middle of an open space I saw lying the broken shaft of a white marble column, evidently the relic of some

old Grecian temple ; and the next moment, under
the green shade of a bush, I discovered also a
white Corinthian capital.

My mind, when we reached home, was full of
delightfully confused impressions, which I felt I
could add to and disentangle at my leisure—
minarets, convents, palazzos, and Grecian temples ;
and they all seemed to be woven like patterns
into a sense that the world was out for a holiday,
and that life had lost its burden. The strange
men and women that we had passed in the street
—more or less consciously I said to myself of
each of them that the words *democracy* and *progress*,
if uttered to them, would seem as meaningless as
they are in reality. And yet, on the thought of
these, other thoughts obtruded themselves, which,
as we sat down to luncheon, suggested to me this
question : Of the two kinds of vision which does
the most for man—to see things, or to see through
them ?

CHAPTER VI

A PURPLE EVENING

PERHAPS that morning I had been too happy, for one of the low troubles of life presently did its best to irritate me. Colonel Falkland proposed at luncheon that we should take a four-mile walk to the place where Mr. Adam was digging for Phœnician crockery. For my own part I hate Phœnicia. It is far too old, like a wine that has lost its flavour, and none of its social abuses are distinct enough to excite sympathy. I therefore assented to the plan with an unexpressed reluctance, and reluctance was changed into very distinct annoyance when I found that we were to start as soon as we had done eating. There was, however, no help for it. Miss Falkland and Mr. Adam were coming, unconscious of any inconvenience, and accordingly four of us were presently setting forth. We had soon quitted the town by some break in the wall, and I had no time to look for any fresh curiosities. We took a road that led over the bare plain, and when we had passed the first rise in the ground, walls, houses, and minarets were completely hidden from our view. Meanwhile the sky, which had been cloudless all the morning, had grown dim, as it does in an ill-tempered May in England, and in half an hour or so, on a bleak open moor, rain spat in our faces, and thickened into a driving shower. This naturally did not increase my complaisance. All the same, however, I could not help being conscious of the wild purple colours that were settling down over everything, and the mobile way in which level and rocky ridge all about me took the complexion of storm. At last the prospect was relieved by a definite feature, a grove of trees near the road, with some cottages crouching under them. I asked what the place was, and I was told it was the settlement of the lepers. I felt that at all events there

was some consolation in that; a foreign feeling
at once stole into the rain. A little beyond this
we turned off the road, and followed a faint foot-
path over a series of stony ridges. This brought
us to a sloping mud-built village, with a huge
public rubbish heap, and a little Greek church
beside it. The walls of the cottages and their
precincts were oddly like those in Devonshire,
only a glimpse into a farm-yard showed arched
colonnades and orange trees. By and by we
descended over a dip in the hill on a luxuriant
palm garden, surrounding and hiding a house, in
which lived a mysterious Turkish lady; and
farther on, beyond a stretch of level ground, we
saw before us one of those isolated eminences
which had caught and surprised my eye as I
drove from Larnaca—in plan a rude circle, and at
the top absolutely flat. This was the scene of
the excavations. By a zigzag path we scrambled
up its sloping sides, and an object came in view,
which was better than anything I had bargained
for. It was the ruin of a solitary square tower,
the masonry of which, as we approached it, was

seen to be of a most singular character. Externally it was rusticated as if by the workmen of Palladio. Inside, the stones were entirely smooth, and the jointing was so fine as to be very nearly invisible. My own fortuitous guess would have set it down as Italian, but I was told that there were certain signs about it which proved its extreme antiquity—that it was certainly pre-classical, and probably early Phœnician.

I was anxious to believe, but I confess I was a little incredulous : and looking at the stones, fresh as if cut yesterday, I profanely asked myself if the Phœnicians had ever been in the neighbourhood. I presently saw that my companions had wandered to a little distance, and had joined an Englishman, whom I divined to be Mr. St. John—a young and accomplished scholar, a colleague of Mr. Adam. They were all standing in a group, plainly doing something particular, but I could not tell what till I came close up to them, and I then saw that they were peering into a narrow, open trench. I caught in their voices a certain note of excitement ; and looking into the

trench myself I discovered a man at the bottom
of it, kneeling down, and scratching at the earth
with a knife. Some one said to me, " Look, he
is coming to something!" And, following the
movements of the glimmering steel blade, I saw
appear amongst the clay another glimmering
surface. It was brown, it was rounded, it had
some rude patterns on it ; and presently a small
bowl was handed up to the archæologists. The
scratching was resumed, and in a minute or two
was a like result ; then another and another ;
and before long, in a basket, there was a numerous and growing family of jugs, lamps, and
vessels with a spout like tea-pots, most of them
oddly diminutive. I asked Mr. Adam what these
things were. He knew their character perfectly.
They were, without doubt, Phœnician ; and as
for their size, he said, that told its own story.
The trench that had just been opened was the
grave of a Phœnician child. My doubts of a
moment ago were to some extent wrong anyhow.
I had never been present at an occasion like this
before, and it changed at once the whole character

of the afternoon for me. I did not, as I have said, care sixpence about Phœnicia ; but there was something that touched the feelings like a knife or a note of music in seeing, after all these centuries, the earth giving up her dead, and the toys of a child thrown back to the light which had shone on them last before the dawn of history.

I presently left the group, and walked along the brink of the hill, like a dog with a bone, taking this thought away with me. The rain, meanwhile, had ceased, and the air was soft and fragrant ; but the sky was still charged with masses of purple cloud ; and a purple, dark as the bloom of the darkest grape, had settled down over the whole of the distant landscape. I almost fancied, as I looked, that I was in the heart of Inverness-shire or of Ross-shire ; and a feel of the Scotch Highlands came back to me with a gust of memories. I saw once more the silvery mists of morning, asleep over their own reflections in the glass of gray Loch Shiel : I saw the shining birches of Kinloch-Moidart. I felt the wet and

heathery wind of evening, sweeping over the hills
from Dalwhinnie to Loch Laggan. I half expected to see on the wide expanse before me the
Highland train go by, with its load of autumnal
cockneys. Then through these fancies the real
landscape asserted itself. Its colour was deeper
than any on the hills in Scotland ; and, tried by a
Scotch standard, there was somewhere something
uncanny about it. The clouds lifted over the
mountains ; and their leagues of spires and
summits rose jagged against a clear streak of
saffron ; resting on Pentedactylon was the base of
an immense rainbow, of which so little was visible
that it looked like a luminous leaning column ;
and where, a moment ago, I had imagined a
whistling train, I saw slowly moving a small
caravan of camels.

The approach of evening was perceptible when
we began our return home. As we descended to
the plain, faintly from every quarter came to our
ears a tinkling of sheep-bells and of goat-bells.
As the earth grew darker, a wild orange glare
answered in the east to the fading embers of the

sunset ; and against this we saw nameless shaggy
figures, home-going men and women, in unfamiliar
clothing, journeying, like phantoms, we none of
us knew whither.   Who were they—what were
they—these nomads of the twilight ?   To us they
seemed like figures out of a poem or Eastern
story book ; and they suddenly deepened in our
minds the sense that we were in a strange land.

Of experiences such as this one thinks less at
the time than afterwards.   Their meaning unfolds
itself as one looks quietly back on them.   Then
one sees sometimes how foreign places have dyed
the mind for ever with foreign colours—how
Eastern sunsets and the blue of Mediterranean
bays have entered into the blood, and become
part of one's life ; and I knew, as I walked home,
that thoughts of that purple evening would come
back to me hereafter, with many others that go
tinkling like sheep-bells across the waste places
of memory.

CHAPTER VII

A CITY OF THE CRUSADERS

AT night I took to bed with me a number of books about Cyprus, and tried, till my candles burnt down into their sockets, to put together some coherent history of Nicosia. To begin, I gathered that it was a town of immense antiquity; that it was certainly wealthy and populous before the days of Constantine ; that it was then adorned with palaces and beautiful Greek temples; and that gradually side by side with the white Corinthian porticoes rose a splendid crowd of Christian churches and monasteries. When the English crusaders came in their gray armour and seized it, it looked like a vision to their rude European eyes. This happened about 1190. A few years later, under circumstances which I afterwards studied more attentively, and which read exactly like a chapter out of the Waverley Novels, it, and Cyprus with it, were handed over to Guy de Lusignan, ex-king of Jerusalem.

This Guy, who when he began life was nothing more than a penniless well-born adventurer, having gained and lost one kingdom, here established another, which took root and flourished for 300 years. Of all dynasties known to European history, the career and the position of this is incomparably the most romantic. It represented more than a mere vanishing conquest. In it the chivalry of the West was rapidly acclimatised to the East, and took, like some transplanted flower, new and unknown colours from it. Its counts and its barons, of French and of English ancestry, settled down over the length and breadth of the island, and kept their feudal state amongst spice-gardens and silken luxury. The peasantry never were displaced, nor was the Greek religion interfered with ; but side by side with the plain Greek basilicas rose Gothic churches with windows of elaborate tracery. Marvellous abbeys like Foun-

tains, Bolton, or Kirkstall, in distant nooks hid
themselves amongst oleanders; and castles like
Alnwick or like Bamborough reared their clustering towers on the mountain-tops. But civilisation
there was not merely at home in fortresses. The
nobles, like those of Italy, inhabited the towns
also; and Nicosia in particular became a city
of palaces. Coats of arms familiar to Western
heraldry surmounted the street doors, and covered
the monuments in the cathedral. The streets in
the fourteenth century were alive with gorgeous
retinues—with ladies on horses, whose housings
glanced with jewels, and knights in velvet bonnets,
and mantles clasped with gold. In some of the
households were as many as two hundred re-
tainers. In the markets were the finest wines,
and the rarest and most delicate provisions. Ice
in the heats of summer was on sale always; and
the monopoly of it yielded a handsome revenue
to the State. In the jewellers' shops were treasures unrivalled throughout the world, and the
rich bazaars exhaled the perfumes of the farthest
East. Outside the gates, where the wide plains

extended, gay and gallant parties would daily ride out hawking. Farther off, near the woods where Adonis died, and where the wild boars still roamed, hounds were kept by the nobles, with huntsmen in brilliant liveries ; and the notes of the horn were daily sounding amongst the valleys. And surrounding and penetrating this pageant of Western mediæval life was the local colour and flavour, not only of an alien Christianity, but, stranger still, of old classical paganism. In the recesses of the forests were still to be seen gleaming the milk-white columns of many a deserted temple, where the old deities were still believed to linger, metamorphosed into saints or demons. The air was haunted with traditions of Venus. Holy hermits praying high in mountain grottos found that the hills were hollow, and that within was the Goddess of the Horsel.

This is what I gathered about the island before I went to sleep ; and my mind was full of it next morning, when, giving my camera to Scotty, I went out to see what I could photograph. I did not believe that all my historical impressions were accurate. I thought that nothing accurate would be nearly so pleasing to the imagination. Still I felt that they gave the place the same kind of interest that might have been given to it by an historical novel. What was my delight, then, when passing along some of the alleys, which here and there I recognised as part of the sights of yesterday, my eye was caught first by a scutcheon let into a wall, and presently by another surmounting a crumbling doorway! Then I detected others, broken or half-obliterated. They started from their obscurity, and showed themselves in quick succession. What I fancied had been romance was reality after all. I was actually walking through the remains of the mediæval palaces I had been reading about; and the existing houses were built upon their foundations.

But the wonder of the morning was yet to come. The special object of my walk was a mosque, which had once been the cathedral—the only important structure of which I had as yet heard anything definite. Nothing that I had

heard, however, had at all prepared me for the
reality.   After many turns and windings I
arrived, under Scotty's guidance, at an open
square, with old stone buildings surrounding it
and a Gothic fountain in the middle ; and close
to one of the sides, with pinnacles and flying
buttresses, was a mass of windowed masonry
which impressed me like York Minster.   As it
suddenly burst on one its entire aspect was
English.   It was not till a little later that the
eye took note of the differences.   I went slowly
round it.   For one half of the circuit a road,
practicable for vehicles, passed actually through
the buttresses, whose arches flung a succession
of shadows over it.   Every shy corner showed
some detail of architectural beauty.   No cathedral
in England could show more.   What struck me
most, however, was the great western front, across
the whole of which ran a lofty and magnificent
portico.   The groined roof of this rested on a
series of fluted columns, in which were empty
niches once filled with statues, and three tall doors
of equal size opened from it into the aisles within.

Here I set up my camera ; and I had, whilst selecting the best point of view, a good opportunity of watching a stream of worshippers who at short intervals were passing in to their devotions. The dress of some of them was semi-European, but they had for the most part turbans and loose robes. What could their business be, my English mind asked—the business of these strange figures within these familiar-looking doors? My eye instinctively looked for a gowned verger extracting a half-crown from some pleased sight-seeing clergyman, and for demure young ladies mincing in with their prayer-books and parcels of slippers hidden under their arms for the curate. But before the doors barbarous curtains hung, marked not with crosses, but huge cabalistic symbols ; and when these were pushed aside, and a faint sound came from within, it was not the roll of an organ or the flute-like response of choristers, but some long-drawn, hoarse modulation, ending with the name of Allah.

When I had done with my photography I strolled to a distance and again surveyed the pile.

I now saw that, in addition to its other ornament-
ation, it, like the old street walls, was covered
with coats of arms, one of which caught my eye
for a very curious reason: it was identical with
that of an extinct Devonshire family—the Pynes
of Axmouth—which in the fifteenth century was
connected by marriage with my own, and which,
along with my own, has not a few of its members
lying side by side under the flag-stones of Axmouth Church. The same device, the same three
pine-cones—there looks down upon homely village
faces, old-fashioned square pews, and the flowers
of Sunday bonnets, which here, amongst alien
races, has all its shadows sharpened, by the sky
that bends over Paphos, and is cut by the shafts
of minarets.

I had plenty of time that afternoon to rumin-
ate over these impressions, and I also received
others of a quite different character. Mrs. Falkland took me about four o'clock to call on one
of the judges who lived beyond the walls. We
went by a broad road bordered with eucalyptus,
which presently took us past the British Govern-

ment's offices, and showed us, a mile or so off, the tiled residence of the Governor on a small eminence, with more eucalyptus sheltering it. Since I had left the pier at Larnaca these were absolutely the first signs I had met by which Western civilisation made the fact of its presence public. In numerous ways, no doubt, England has done much for Cyprus ; but, with rare exceptions, such as these which I now speak of, it has regulated and improved the conditions of native life without producing the least alteration in their character, and a man might wander for days upon days in Nicosia before he encountered a single English face. It is true that on the road we were now traversing clerks and officials—the whole of them few in number—were at stated times to be seen going to or from their work ; but, except at such times, whatever life might be stirring, as I found this afternoon, was even here entirely Oriental.

The judge's house, however, which stood at some distance from the road, was amongst the objects tainted with Western progress. It was

a stone villa in fact, which had only been built
yesterday, with English grates and a porch like
an English parsonage.   It seemed to profane
the landscape, and I was sorry I had set eyes
on it till, after a minute or two spent indoors,
we were taken out into the garden, and back
we were plunged again into all the strangeness
of Cyprus, which here showed itself in a fresh
and delightful form.   The garden was as new
as the house, and as yet little labour had been
spent upon it ; but already it was enclosed by
hedges of trellised creepers, and tall luxuriant
shrubs made it green and private.   Its beds were
rich with a mixture of flowers and kitchen vegetables.   Violets, hyacinths, and anemones made
borders along the paths, and the soil enclosed by
them, though it was yet in the depth of winter,
showed beans and potatoes sprouting into exube-
rant life, huge cauliflowers, spikes of matured
asparagus, and rows upon rows of peas, whose
pods had been full at Christmas.

By and by we came to the secret of all this
fertility—to a well half-hidden by foliage, with

a date-palm standing over it, whose deep waters
were raised by a rude Persian wheel. This
primitive contrivance in every detail of its structure is probably the same to-day as it was three
thousand years ago. The principal wheel is
horizontal, turned by an ox or mule, which com-
municates its motion by another to an endless
chain of pitchers—red clay pitchers, fastened
by bands of straw to ropes, apparently twisted
out of lithe brown twigs, and each of these child-
like vessels as it comes to a particular place spills
its tribute into a broad wooden shoot. Had the
house been out of the question, the garden and
well together would have formed a scene in which
Ulysses might have found Laertes. Indeed, I
felt that the spot was full of the possibilities
of classical idyls.

There was something idyllic too—at least
I was pleased to think there was—in the golden
butter and the cream which were presently offered
to us at tea, and which our host and hostess
produced from their own farm. At tea, too, I
met one of the principal English officials—an

accomplished classical scholar and a student of mediæval history, especially of such history as touched the romance of Cyprus—in whom at once I discerned a kindred spirit. For him, as for myself, I found that the place was haunted, that mediæval hawking parties went with him as he rode over the plains ; that classical forests were green for him on the bare valleys and mountains, and that in their recesses Adonis still went hunting. He told me more in twenty minutes of the things I cared to know than I had learnt hitherto from all other sources of information. I asked him if any castles existed still in the country, and if there were any recognisable fragments of the Latin abbeys I had dreamed about. To both of these questions he answered, yes. He gave me the names of six or seven castles instantly, three of which were perched on the tops of mountains, where their halls and towers now had few visitors but the clouds. My imagination, it seemed, could have asked for nothing better, whilst as for abbeys, in one instance at least, there were more than fragments remaining; there was a building almost perfect.

My new friend, whom I will speak of as Mr. Matthews, walked home with us, and added to the interest he had excited in me by telling me that he lived in a house which originally was the Latin archbishop's palace. I mentioned the coats of arms to him which I had been noticing that morning. This was a subject with which he was quite familiar; and he promised to lend me a book which contained the genealogies of most of the Western families settled here during the Middle Ages. I parted from him with a promise that I would call on him, in his palace, in a day or two; and a sense, derived from many of the things he told me, that my historical dreamings had not been dreamt in vain.

The practical reader will possibly call to mind my boast that I came to Cyprus with a reasonable and practical purpose, and will think that, if this were so, I was not very business-like in setting about it. I had, however, already made inquiries as to how the locality of my supposed marble was to be reached; and in case I could wait for a day or two, Mr. Adam had promised to accompany me. The expedition had accordingly been fixed for the following morning. Our mode of conveyance was to be mules; and when we came in that evening Scotty was waiting for us, with a lean, tanned muleteer, in order to settle about our saddles and the hour of starting.

CHAPTER VIII

WE were down and at breakfast shortly after seven o'clock, for the journey to Pentedactylon would take us at least four hours, and as it seemed that the paths amongst the mountains were not easy to find, we wished to be half-way home again before the daylight faded. Between sips of coffee and mouthfuls of fried bacon, my companion and I alternately studied a map. For the first nine miles or so our route was simple enough. It lay over the plain to a large village called Kythrea. We evidently must go through this village, which was just at the foot of the mountains, but after that point the map could tell us little. In a straight line Pentedactylon was not more than five miles distant from it. The pro-

blem was how to reach it through a labyrinth of
intervening ridges. Accordingly before us were
two elements of uncertainty ; first, should we ever
get to the peak in question ? and secondly, if we
got there, should we discover the precious marble ?
It is not perhaps a business-like view of the
matter, but I confess I was charmed by all this
uncertainty. It seasoned the day's prospects
with a sense of mimic adventure.

The dining-room door was presently slightly
opened, the red cap and the brown nose of Scotty
showed themselves, and we listened to this an-
nouncement : " The mules and the mule-man he
here, sir ; he say that we best start, for he not
sure of the road." There had before now been
a good deal of talk about saddles, from which I
gathered nothing except that I should find them
peculiar. I was certainly not disappointed. Of
the four animals which we found awaiting us in
the street, two—those meant for the muleteer
and Scotty—had nothing on their backs but
squares of gaudy-coloured camel's-hair cloth, kept
in place by two curved frames of wood, which

were covered with crimson leather, and shaped
like the merry-thought of a chicken. Across
these were slung a couple of saddle-bags, and
rude stirrups attached to a loose rope. Anything
more uncomfortable it is hardly possible to
imagine; but for myself and my companion,
because of the hardness of our hearts, or perhaps
because of the softness of something equally
sensitive, the native fashion was modified in the
following way: over the saddle was thrown a
thick species of feather-bed, which, though halved
in size as well as doubled in thickness by being
folded, left little of the animal visible, excepting
its head and tail. Mr. Adam assured me I should
find this arrangement charming; but he had
hardly made the statement when I had occasion
to doubt it. As he was about to mount, his
mule gave a harmless frisk, and feather-bed and
stirrups together came floundering off into the
dust. They were soon, however, again in their
places, with Mr. Adam on top of them, and I too
a moment later was in a similar proud position.
We had not been long in motion before I made

S

two curious discoveries. One of them was that
the use of a Cyprian mule's reins is simply to stop
it, and that the whole business of guiding is
accomplished by hitting it on one cheek or the
other. My other discovery was that if I wished
to quicken its paces, it was, owing to the extraordinary covering which I sat upon, as invul-
nerable to blows as the ghost of Hamlet's father ;
or if—as I have reason to believe, for I could not
turn round to see—my stick did occasionally
reach some undefended quarter, the only result
was not a trot but a kick. However, with the
aid of the muleteer, we were soon progressing
satisfactorily, and our sixteen hoofs were pattering
along the silent streets of Nicosia. We passed
the walls of long mysterious gardens with door-
ways at rare intervals ; we turned round endless
corners. Sometimes a bough of oranges or a
spray of milk-white blossoms cut the sky overhead,
with dew on them glittering in the sunlight. We
emerged from these narrow ways into a broader
road that ran at the foot of the circling grass-
grown ramparts. Here we came on a few moving

figures — a shepherd driving to market some straggling sheep, whose fleeces were gray in the early invigorating air, and some Turks with the morning bright on their linen garments. At last we came to one of the city gates—a shadowy stone tunnel, about eighty feet in length, which bulged in the middle into a circular domed chamber, lit, like the Pantheon, by a circular opening in the roof; and at the end of it hung the same iron-clad doors which had been placed there by Venice four hundred years ago. Through this tunnel we plunged. For a few seconds the echoes hovered about us, and then we found ourselves launched on the open country.

Never shall I forget the sensations of that moment. We seemed to be issuing out upon the earlier ages of the world. Long luminous hazes were afloat on the plain before us ; and here and there in the distance rose a tall patriarchal date-palm. At first we found ourselves in a road, but we almost instantly left it, and took a rude path between unfenced fields and vineyards. Along similar paths, from one direction or another, were groups of peasants whose clothes were patches of blue and crimson, going forth to their work and to their labour. From scattered primitive cottages came a faint barking of dogs. The clods of the earth were still yellow with sunrise, and a far-off silvery column, that came from some burning weeds, was going up like the smoke of the first sacrifice.

When we had ridden in this way for a mile or two, I turned to look back at Nicosia; and I now for the first time had a clear general view of it. Its long, gray walls lay like a gleaming girdle clasped round a sleeping forest of minarets, palms, and cypresses, with some low domes amongst them, white as wood-anemones, and, looming over all, the bulk of the great cathedral. This was not a time for thinking about architectural details; and the sight produced on me one impression only—that Nicosia was exactly like a picture of Damascus—Damascus, the city old in the days of Abraham, and therefore no anachronism on these patriarchal plains.

As I rode on, under the influence of the scene

and hour, paralysed capacities for pleasure tingled
and came to life again. Hopes, associations, and
illusions which had long littered my mind, dead
and motionless as fallen leaves in November,
began to stir and rustle like the bones in Ezekiel's
valley ; and I laughed as I caught myself actually
muttering to the air, " Breathe, oh breathe upon
these slain, that they may live ! "

The air, which I thus apostrophised, though it
lost none of its freshness, was meanwhile growing
warmer, and the distances more clear ; and our
eyes fixed themselves on the wall of mountains to
which, in a slant direction, we were now gradually
approaching. Detail after detail of pinnacle, crag,
and precipice swam into sight, as if fashioned out
of oxidised silver, whilst here and there a cloud-
shadow made a blue moving stain on them, or a
flock of milk-white clouds settled on some aërial
peak. One such peak specially caught my attention from its great height, from the savage abrupt-
ness of its sides, and the curling vapours about it,
which were making it smoke like Sinai. As these
rolled away from it, I saw that its extreme

summit was marked by a number of pale faltering lines. I pointed this out to my companion. "Ah," he said, "by the way, that is one of the castles of which your friend Matthews was telling you. It is called Baffavento, which means *the defier of storms*, and on one of the towers, which from here is hardly visible, Richard Cœur-de-Lion once planted his standard."

At this, Scotty, who prided himself on his local knowledge, not to be outdone by Mr. Adam, broke into the conversation. "See, sir," he said, "that over there, Kythrea. I came through him last year with a gentleman who want shoot woodcock." I looked in the direction he indicated, and beginning on a spur of the mountains, and extending thence like a long headland into the plain, I saw at a few miles' distance a blot of the deepest green, above which appeared the tops of a belfry and a minaret, and through which gleamed the white corners of a house or two. As we neared this, we struck into a rough carriage road leading to it, and we presently saw what all the greenness was. On either side there began to be groves of

olive trees. Then our ears were caught by the
splash and babble of water. We looked, and we
saw it glancing on a wall, which proved to be an
aqueduct. Then came olive trees planted in
more regular order, and under them—not, as is
usual, the bare ground strewn with berries, but
grass greener and richer than any growing in
Jersey, with lazy cattle standing knee-deep in it.

The first glimpse of the village itself surprised
me. The road took us into a small triangular
place surrounded by a farm-yard, and by two or
three quaint houses, which were several stories in
height, and looked Spanish rather than Oriental.
Thus far our way had been perfectly unambiguous,
but now began a succession of minor troubles.
Passing out of the *place* by an alley between low
buildings, we found ourselves brought up sharp by
a stone wall five feet high. We tried another
turn, and a lane bordered with brambles brought
us to a conduit running between two gardens.
Our third attempt carried us somewhat farther ;
but our course was at last checked, and that by a
garden also, where an old woman was washing

some petticoats in a drain.   Kythrea, in fact, though the largest village in Cyprus—it cannot be much under three miles in length—seemed nothing but a tangle of private paths and water-courses, and it struck us that its houses, which were most of them hidden in foliage, could have no connection with each other, except by a succession of trespasses.

We were well repaid, however, for our slow progress through it, by the series of charming pictures its gardens and groves revealed to us.   At the doors of the embowered houses we saw, through the green shade, family groups sitting and talking in the sunshine.   Here in the grass lay a basket half filled with wild flowers ; there a bevy of children was playing round the silvery olive trunks.   A feeling gradually stole over my mind that during the last ten minutes we had passed into another epoch—from the days of the patriarchs to the days of Hellenic Sicily—from Genesis to the idyls of Theocritus.

This change, as day after day taught me, was one of the things most characteristic of Cyprus.

Like the fruit of the durian, which has flavours of all foods, Cyprus has flavours of all epochs and literatures, and has every mood in its sky, its air, and its scenery. We at last reached a path by the brink of a small canal, which both went curving together between walls of towering reeds, the very same reeds that whispered, " Midas has no ears ; " and this brought us to the upper part of the village, which climbed from the plain over a low spur of the mountains.

Everything now underwent another change. We left the green behind, and great brown hills came sloping down on us with the bare sky on their ridges. Our road was no longer doubtful— if, indeed, it could be called a road, for what lay before us was simply a track of mud running along one of the hill-sides, and sloping like the roof of a house. Such, however, was here the main thoroughfare of Kythrea, and along it, at irregular elevations and intervals, were mud-houses, each with a small loggia, whose pointed arches showed sharp against their own internal shadows.

Presently we heard a buzzing noise in the air,

and just below us we saw the roof of a corn mill.
A little further on, by a zigzag stone causeway
we descended into a miniature gorge, with a brook
and a bridge, and another mill at the bottom of
it.   In the shadow of a dark arch we saw the
flicker of the swiftly revolving millstone, and from
an opening in the wall the water came tumbling
out like wool.   Out of this dip we ascended by a
climbing street, with paved steps like those of the
mountain towns of Italy.   We passed a vine-
trellised café, which revealed a floor within covered
with a regiment of chibouks, all in readiness for
the afternoon smokers.   Higher up we reached
a cluster of sycamores, under which was another
café, with benches on a rude balcony, and the
host with fierce moustache sipping some red wine.
Round the corner of this we turned sharp into a
lane which ascended the hill, steep as a garret
staircase.   Everywhere it seemed that the slope
was traversed by aqueducts, leading away towards
the village, or spilling themselves into white-walled
cisterns, and somewhere far down was the murmur
of more millstones.   When we issued from the

lane, which was walled upon each side, there was only in front of us one lonely cottage, and after that we found ourselves in the heart of the mountains.

For some forty minutes we wound among brown stony acclivities, quite bare of vegetation, and beautified by nothing but the sunlight. Then we issued on a high irregular table-land, with rich-looking red soil, dotted with dark-green caroub trees, tufted with myrtle, and sparkling with lime-stone fragments. Beyond this rose a range of limestone ridges, broken, as we presently found, into a multitude of crooked gorges, and through these we began slowly to take our intricate way. Rock-strewn streams ran by us, and on every side from fissure or silvery ledge young pines were sprouting, and here and there was a cypress. The small noise of the waters came sharp and clear to our ears, and brought home to us the deep silence of the wilderness, which once or twice was made even more profound by a far-off tinkle from the bell of some clambering goat.

All this while we were working our way up-

wards, and the air each moment grew rarer and
more exciting. Little puffs of wind came cool
and fresh on our cheeks, and scents like thyme
and myrtle were breathing on every side of us.
In due time the summit of this range was arrived
at. Before us was a shallow descent, beyond it
a rising slope, and above this, like a castle, the
summit of Pentedactylon. It was a singular
object. Its sides seemed to be absolutely precipitous, and its five peaks, on a nearer view of
them, still retained their likeness to five distended
fingers. Here we halted and scrutinised the
slopes to right and left of it. We sought
everywhere for the signs which my friend had
mentioned—the ruined church, the great solitary
cypress-tree, the dark mouth of the cave, and the
orange-coloured wall of rocks. But not one of
these things could we see anywhere. I had imagined
that when once we were in their neighbourhood we
should instantly recognise all of them. We appealed to the muleteer. He said he had been
there before, but he had never heard of any church
or any cave, or of any cypress. I asked him,

through Scotty, if he had ever heard of a spring.
His face brightened a little. Of a spring he
thought he had heard, and he thought it was
somewhere a mile or so to the left. A distinct
path led in that direction, lying like a thread
amongst boulders and green bushes, and dis-
appearing over the sky line. This we accordingly
took, watching the peak as we went, and hoping
that a cave or a cypress would show itself round
some corner. I was thus employed when something distracted my attention, and looking before
me, my eyes were met by a spectacle which sent
caves, marbles, and cypresses for the time being
to the winds. Facing me, through a pass with
walls of gray limestone, blue like a wild hyacinth,
was the misty, sparkling sea, and beyond it, peak
upon peak of glittering snows and shadows, hung
in the air the mountains of Asia Minor. I am
not much given to quoting Greek in company ;
but as my companion was a scholar, the impulse
may perhaps be excused me which made me in
surprise and delight shout aloud to him, Θάλαττα !
Θάλαττα !

As often as I think now of that glorious vision,
the thrill it produced in me still repeats itself.
Part of it was due to the mere sensuous qualities
of what I looked at—to the colour, the crisp outlines, the bold gigantic distances—but as much or
more was due to a multitude of vague associations,
which suddenly rose in my mind like a swarm of
disturbed bees.   Asia Minor—the very name was
a spell.   The whole lyre of classical poetry
trembled at it through all its strings.   Beyond
those distant peaks, Apollo, Pan, and Marsyas
made their music amongst the Phrygian highlands ; and " bound about with trees," as Catullus
sings, there too, under Dindymus, were the
" shadowy places" of Cybele ; whilst far to the
north-west, the white wild swans of Ovid fluted
their dying songs to the reeds and shallows of
Mæander.   Snatches of hexameters and penta-
meters, mixed with English melodies—sometimes
many together, sometimes singly — like notes
loosened by the different stops of an organ, filled
my mind with a tumult of noiseless music, as I
breathed the breath of the wild thyme and the

myrtle. Literature, I have always thought, is in most places and companies a singularly dull and uninteresting thing to talk about, but one may, as a rule, hate literary conversation, and yet at the right moment, with all its powers of feeling, the mind in silence may feel what it owes to literature. To the poets, whose verses at that moment came to me, no acknowledgment, I felt and I feel, could have been excessive. Let me pay my tribute to all of them—in especial, I think, to Catullus, to Shelley, and Matthew Arnold. It is only at moments like these that one feels all they have done for one. Then, looking around the mind's temple, one sees that on every column they have hung an unwithering chaplet.

It takes some time to describe all this, but it took less to experience it, for, as Hobbes says, "thought is quick." I had stopped my brute of a mule, in order to enjoy my feelings; and I now suggested to Mr. Adam that this would be a good place for our luncheon. He assented. We seated ourselves on some tufts of aromatic herbage, and a gray stone was our table. Our

food—for even eating at times has a poetry in it
which touches the imagination—seemed to be full
of the taste of the world's youth.   There were
meat, bread, figs, and primitive cream cheese,
wrapped carefully in cool, fresh plantain leaves.
It was a repast that might have been eaten without surprise by Abraham—all but some slices of
excellent cold plum-pudding, which he, no doubt,
would have kept, in order that he might show
them to Sarah.

Across the leaves, between the silvery boulders,
between tufts of broom, and the bells of fine wild
anemones, my eyes, as I reposed myself, kept
turning towards the sea ; and it invaded my mind
with a new train of reflections.   As I looked and
looked, there seemed to be a heavy voluptuous
bloom on it, which held some passionate secret.
One sail, far off, lay like a petal of apple-blossom
on it ; or it might have been the shell on which
Aphrodite stood when the winds drifted her over
these very waters.   Why natural objects suggest
human emotion is a difficult question, probably
with a complicated answer.   But any one who

had cared to look long at that blue surface, drowsy under the touch of a breeze, which caressed it lightly at intervals, would have seen in it some suggestion of that hunger or aspiration, of which for man the " Eternal Feminine " is at once the cause and the symbol. The coast was far below us, and I could not see it ; but I felt that along it there ought to be snowy temples, with columns between whose marble the living waters sparkled, and with capitals where the shadows clung sharp to the carved acanthus leaves.

The mundane taste of a cigarette conjured me back from dreamland ; but the Asian coast, when I came to reflect longer about it, recalled to me what I believe are facts, almost as strange as dreams. For the country behind, and under those great snow mountains that were opposite to me, is literally to this day a country of un-exhausted mysteries. Wonderful cities of the superbest days of Rome still exist there, in the hearts of untrodden forests, of which some have been visited only by single travellers, some never visited at all, but only seen from a distance,

whilst some are known of only by rumour and local
legend.   Even on routes which, comparatively
speaking, are familiar, the unexpected is always
lying in wait for one.   Obscure Turkish villages
stand upon broken palaces ; and passing guests
in rude reed-thatched hovels have discovered that
the roofs rested on columns of verd antique.   On
lonely mountain roads detached masses of rock
are found cut into towers, with sepulchral
chambers on the summit ; and by the road-side
in one gorge is a great Roman sarcophagus, with
a winged lion in marble, keeping guard over the
lid.   As to details and places, I confess I was
somewhat hazy ; but I knew enough to excite
my antiquarian sympathies ; and I felt a longing
to charter a Greek caïque, to cross the intervening
sea, and plunge into the regions of the marvellous.

But a glance at my watch warned me that
time was pressing ; and, instead of thinking of
verd antique in Asia, I remembered that at the
moment my object was to find it in Cyprus.
Mr. Adam and I, therefore, now began to

scramble in various directions over the uneven
ground, making from one point and another a
number of geological surveys. But we could see
nowhere any of the signs we were in search of,
and the muleteer was completely at fault as to
the spring. At last, however, as I was straying
along a steep track, I saw at my feet a small
green fragment, of the very same kind as that
which my friend had given me. I went on, and
presently found another. Then the track turned
sharp round an angle of rock, and once more the
extraordinary charm of the view quite distracted
my mind from the frivolities of practical business.
Above me the mountains rose for a hundred or
a hundred and fifty feet, and below me for three
thousand they plunged, at one descent, down to
their base in a torrent of rocks and firs and
myrtles. Their base was formed by a level belt
of country, wooded and cultivated, about a mile
in breadth. Against its indented edge the white
ripples were breaking, and some miles to the
westward, glittering on a miniature promontory,
was a little seaport, the name of which I knew

to be Kyrenia, flanked by a large square fortress, which I remembered to have heard of as mediæval.

In spite of the view, however, I soon recovered my energies; and being duly armed with a geologist's hammer, I struggled along the side of the slope, through bushes and over boulders, hitting and chipping in all directions. But nowhere did my blows lay bare anything green below. I did not even find any more of the green fragments. I was not unnaturally to a certain extent disappointed; but one half of my mind was again playing truant, and amusing itself with fancies which had little connection with reality. What set these fancies going was a cluster of oleanders, which, together with some myrtles close to them, looked as if they belonged to a garden, and suggested some solitary fragment of luxurious European life. With the eye of fancy I saw above the myrtles the corner of a pale balustrade, and a marble vase with an aloe in it; below me, catching the sunlight on some winding path, I saw the glimmer of some

dainty feminine figure, and the charming movement of a bright Parisian parasol ; and presently,
still to the same eye of fancy, the statues and
terraces of a Palladian villa revealed themselves.
For any man rich enough to overcome the practical inconveniences of remoteness, what a winter
paradise might be created in these solitudes !
Civilisation is never so charming as when it is
an island in the middle of simplicity, or of a
civilisation of an alien kind. A villa here might
be filled, by raids on the opposite coast, with
pillars, statues, and pavements from those old
forgotten cities ; and slabs might feel again the
touch of a woman's shoe, which have for two
thousand years known only the movement of the
snake or of the lizard. East and West, old and
new, might meet here under porticoes and painted
ceilings. And the life without ! On the slopes
and mountains near, never a tourist, or a tourist's
hotel, or an advertisement, or the sound or the
knowledge of such a thing as a political meeting ;
but only sunburnt figures, in bright unfamiliar
garments, with a strange language, living on

strange beliefs, and making one feel as if the whole background of life were a child's holiday, or a back scene in an opera. Perhaps this too was a fancy; but it certainly seemed to me that one's own life lived under such conditions would yield clearer music than it can do in modern Europe ; that all its chords would sound—at least whilst the conditions were new—as if there had been drawn across them the bow of a violon-cello.

However, to descend again to practical matters, I found on coming back to the spot where our mules were left, that the muleteer had been in conversation with a goat-herd, and had learnt from him that some two miles farther on there was without doubt a ruined church and a spring, though nothing was said about either a cave or a cypress tree. We accordingly mounted, and went at a brisk trot along a path, which for some distance traversed the side of the mountain, directly above the one from which I had just returned. At last, with many zigzags, it led us into a winding valley, formed by a deep irregular

cleft amongst the mountain-tops, and thickly
wooded with pines and luxuriant undergrowth.
In the heart of this valley we came on a grove
of sycamores. At their roots was a small ruinous
cistern, into which trickled a feeble stream of
water; and a few yards up the slope was the
apse of a broken chancel. Here we dismounted,
and I and Mr. Adam, each armed with a hammer,
again began our explorations—but with no better
result. We accordingly agreed that, so far as
the marble was concerned, we had come to the
wrong place, and that the day's work was a
failure; and we proceeded—I must say not at
my own suggestion—to attempt a short cut home
by the contemptible light of reason.

Slowly ascending the closed end of the valley,
we found ourselves finally on the highest ridge
of the mountains; and far below us, beyond a
multitude of lesser ranges, extended the great
plains we had ridden across that morning, with
Nicosia, like a faint mark, in the middle of them.
The descent was long. We went four miles out
of our way, and had it been dark we should have

gone straight over a precipice. By the time we
found ourselves again in the difficult thoroughfares
of Kythrea the light was waning. By the time
we emerged from them it was dusk. The plains
were purple ; the by-ways had ceased to be distinguishable, so we urged our animals home by the
dusty and stony carriage road. As we were nearing Nicosia, I glanced to one side of me, and was
astonished at the sharpness of the shadows which
I and my mule were casting. I looked up, and
I saw that in the clear liquid sky the moon was
now mistress, and was shining in all her brilliance.
The bastions of the town gleamed as we passed
under them. The passage of the gate was like
midnight. Within the streets were silent. Scotty
rode ahead of us, as he alone knew the way. We
trotted after him through a series of black alleys,
lit only by a lantern at rare intervals. Once or
twice we detected, as we passed close to them,
long-robed Oriental figures gliding silently by the
walls. A kneeling camel waved its shadowy
neck at us. Dogs barked, and the buildings
faintly echoed. At last came a welcome sight.

Scotty checked his mule, and I realised with delight that we were at Colonel Falkland's door. I was stiff and tired ; my expedition had failed in its object, and yet the day had been one—I will not say full of happiness—but full of the best of the illusions which make the absence of happiness forgotten.

CHAPTER IX

A CHARMED LIFE

I NOW realised, with regard to the precious marble, that to find a nameless spot on a range of unfrequented mountains was not so easy a task as I had first fondly imagined it. I resolved, therefore, that, before making any more expeditions myself, I would send Scotty, with some villager of Kythrea, to reconnoitre, and find, if he could, the group of objects that had been described to me—the ruined church, the cave, the spring, and the cypress tree. It was some days, however, before I put my plan into execution. The strangeness of the life around me, I confess, I found far more interesting than thoughts of the most lucrative business; and I gave myself up for a time to the pleasures of exploring Nicosia,

and to quiet cloistral mornings in Colonel Falkland's garden.

Day by day, hour by hour, the charm of the
place sank deeper and deeper into me, like
warmth into cold limbs, or the approaches of
sleep into tired limbs; and further and further
it quietly put away from me all the cares belonging to what is commonly called reality. Who
does not know the delight of sleep that is conscious of itself? There is the same sort of
delight in strange surroundings, as they gradually
become familiar, and yet leave us conscious of
their strangeness. There is the same sort of
delight, and another delight added to it. Sleep
is only an anodyne; but these strange surroundings are at once an anodyne and a stimulant. Perhaps after a time one's own life, by
being lived amongst them, would rub away the
bloom of their freshness, and cover them gradually with some precipitate of its own weariness.
But there is a long interval before this happens,
during which familiarity with the strangeness
only makes it stranger, and completes, cell by

cell, a new environment for our life.   Then, as
we look round us, our ordinary lot is inverted.
We have slipped, for the time being, from the
husk of our past experiences; and the world
shows us our dreams and illusions reflected, instead of showing us our dreams and illusions
destroyed.   This, as I have said already, is the
true end of travelling—this unnatural transmi-
gration of the soul into a new body of circumstance; this flight from the life to which birth
happens to have married one, to the arms, the
lips, the eyes, of a life and land with which
legitimately one has nothing at all to do.

The severe scientific moralist, armed with
terrible phrases about the social organism, and
Humanity, and our natural sympathy with our
kind, will call this pleasure immoral and anti-
social.   I have no wish to maintain that in his
eyes it can be otherwise; for an essential part
of it is the complete escape it offers us from
him, and from all the conditions that have produced him and made him intelligible.   The
moralist of the type of Mr. Herbert Spencer,

the scientific moralist, whose dogmatism about
man in the abstract is based for the most part
on a guileless and scholarly ignorance of the
ways and passions of men and women in the
concrete, amuses himself with the idea that
pleasures become more pleasurable in proportion
as we know them to be shared by a number
of other people. I can assure him that the
pleasures of the true traveller are great in proportion as he has them all to himself, or at all
events in proportion as the general public is
debarred from them. Another element in these
pleasures is even more scandalous, and that
element is absence of social duties. The true
traveller has never reached the goal of his
travels till he reaches a land in which all such
duties vanish — even the suggestion of them.
Then the spell begins to be woven round him.
The men and women he sees are no longer
fellow-citizens, but figures moving in a magician's
crystal. The streets and gardens he passes
through all belong to fairyland, and take the
colour of his own longings and fancies, just like

the woman seen by Faust on the Brocken, who
to each man looking at her had the likeness of
the woman he loved.　We are, in fact, under
happy circumstances such as these redeemed for
a little from what life has done to us, and we
walk amongst images of what we once hoped it
would do.

Most of us must for moments have known
what this feeling is; for it is not always necessary to go into distant countries to experience it.
It will come to us for moments in more familiar
haunts—in gay Mediterranean watering-places,
on light - hearted azure mornings, when bands
play, when coloured awnings glitter, and life
seems made up of the sway of palm trees, and
the movement of music in the air.　Again for
moments it will come to us in the palm gardens
of fantastic villas, when the roses are awake in
the warm winter moonlight, when the fountains
trickle, when the frogs croak, and the flowers, the
air, and the leaves seem bursting with some lost
secret.　Who that has known such scenes, under
favourable circumstances, and in favourable com-

pany, has not been conscious of some such impression? Who has not felt a sensation as if something were about to happen—a passionate something—a something which the nerves call for, but the imagination cannot give shape to? Do we wish that some woman should be born out of the palms and the roses, with the breath of the rose on her lips, and the languor of the moonlight in her eyes? The strings of the heart are strained. What is wanting to strike the music out of them? The voice of the nightingale seems to repeat the question; but not even love quite answers it.

Still, in spite of their incompleteness, perhaps even because of it, moments like these are charming, and colour life for years with memories of their short abandonment. But in familiar scenes the abandonment is short only. In scenes that are strange and remote, it is prolonged from month to month; and as it is less violent, one is able, without any conscious folly, to let it penetrate and change, for the time, one's whole character. Thus at Nicosia a quiet, sustained excitement tingled through my entire days, and gave me nights of childhood. I made no effort to put practical thoughts away from me. On the contrary, during a certain part of the mornings I used to read some treatises on Political Economy ; but my practical thoughts—thoughts about rent, and value, wages, profits, and poverty—all these moved against an unpractical background. Life, in fact, lay upon dreams like rose-leaves ; and I daily wandered for hours about the enchanted town, and gathered the materials out of which the dreams were made.

And of what did these materials consist ? What were the sights and experiences which my daily wanderings yielded me ? There were only a few of them that would bear detailed description, or make any figure in a tourist's guide-book. One of them—the cathedral—I have described already. Next to that in importance beyond all doubt, was the bazaar. To this I was introduced by Mrs. Falkland the day after my return from Pentedactylon. I had constantly heard her mention it ; but, for some reason or other, I had conceived the idea that it would be modern and

uninteresting ; that the young Government clerks,
in tweed suits, who were wholly invisible elsewhere, would be seen sauntering there ; that
Singer's sewing machines and Chocolate Menier
would be advertised ; and that Huntley and
Palmer's biscuits and cheap English stationery
would annoy the eye in shops that aped the glass
windows of Europe. I was never more mistaken.
If anything in Nicosia was like the old world and
a story-book, I found that amongst these things
the bazaar was to be reckoned foremost ; and
amongst these things it was in one way wholly
singular. The rest of the town, with its mouldering ramparts, its cathedral, its mosques, and its
secret tortuous streets, had shown me the past,
embalmed or asleep or ruinous. In the bazaar
I found it full of animation and movement.

Having threaded with Mrs. Falkland a labyrinth of silent alleys, we emerged suddenly,
through an aperture between an old house and a
minaret, into a wide street, lined with low-vaulted
warehouses, their arched doors being all of them
wide open, and showing within a row of shadowy

caverns. In the middle of the roadway donkeys were pattering to and fro; and we almost ran against a bare-legged itinerant tinker, who was about to set up his shop at the foot of a blank wall. On either side in front of the warehouse doors the ground was littered with primitive bales of goods; and amongst these, being laden or unladen, groups of camels stood patiently in the sunlight, with red caps and turbans moving and glancing round them. At the end of this street, which seemed like a *cul-de-sac*, was a large fig tree having a Turkish tomb under its branches; but passing round this we were faced by a covered passage, flickering with lights and shadows, which ran away into a wilderness of old stone buildings, and into and out of which, like ants at the entrance of their nest, men and women, with a sort of busy dilatoriness, were constantly coming and going. This was the entrance of the bazaar proper; or rather one of the entrances, for the passage now before us was only one out of many. The bazaar was a spider's web of them.

Externally the view was of no architectural

interest; but the moment one entered one was
in a world of the curious and picturesque. This
particular passage or street happened to be that
of the silversmiths. As I looked round me and
began to realise the scene, I felt that we were
back again at the beginnings of civilisation. The
little shops were a succession of open rooms or
cells, black with shadow through which the rude
walls glimmered, and on the walls a shelf or two
and some implements hanging by nails: and at
the mouth of each cell, on a wooden stool, sat the
proprietor industriously working at his craft, with
a charcoal forge making a dim glow at his elbow.
Some were fashioning candlesticks, some buckles;
and one was finishing the crook of a bishop's crosier.

At the end of this street was the meeting-
place of several others. They were all covered
in one way or another, some with tattered
awnings of canvas or coarse matting, which
made stripes above one of blackness and blinding sky, some with stone vaulting, and some with
a trellis-work of vines. One was the street of
drapers, and this we entered first. It seemed, as

one looked down it, to flutter from end to end
with gay-coloured triumphal flags, which were
really stuffs for sale — veils, gorgeous handkerchiefs, and beautiful native silks. The shops
themselves were for the most part vaulted, and
looked like a series of chapels with one wall
wanting. The dark interiors of some were piled
high with goods; others revealed in operation
the processes of primitive manufacture. Here
would be three men stitching the shaggy capotes
of the shepherds; here another, shaping red fez
caps over gleaming copper moulds; and here on
a low platform, jutting a little into the roadway,
a Nubian boy lying almost flat on his stomach,
and quilting a coverlet of brilliant white and
purple. And at the entrance of every shop was
— I was going to say the shopkeeper, but the
name sounds far too modern—it is better to say the
merchant. Here was an almond-eyed Greek
twitching with grimaces and vivacity; there an
old Turk squatting superbly calm, like a wax
figure moving to slow clockwork, alternately
sucking at the amber mouthpiece of his chibouk

and stretching a hand with a huge turquoise ring on it over a chafing-dish of live charcoal, looking as if, for him, customers had no existence.

One mentions all this quickly, and then one passes on. But the eye lingered as words cannot linger, as if it would feed on everything and never could have enough — on the masses of quaint detail shining and glimmering in the foreground, on the dimmer objects swimming slowly into sight out of the shadow, on the clear shadows melting into impenetrable darkness, and on all the luminous colours in movement or hanging stationary. Had I only been an artist, I should have longed to be painting everything, and thus to seize it and make its beauty my own.

Passing from this street into another, the longing grew even keener. I felt as if I were in a gallery of living Rembrandts or Van Ostades. What we had entered was the street of the grocers. Here the subdued light flickered on bunches of yellow candles, destined for burning at Christian or Moslem shrines, on huge oil-jars in which the Forty Thieves might have hidden, and on piles

of globular cheeses with madder-coloured rinds.
They all caught the eye, painted on deep shadow.
Then from this street we passed into that of the
fruiterers and the sweetmeat-sellers. The change
was like that of passing to the works of some
other Dutchman. Here in shadow that was
browner and more translucent was the fresh
greenness of vegetables. There were the wrinkled
leaves of cabbages and the faces of creamy cauliflowers, and here and there the whole place was
illuminated by piles of pale gold lemons, of fiery-
red tomatoes, and rose-coloured stacks of radishes.
Farther on one came upon trays of comfits, on
gelatinous strips of *nougat*, and great masses of a
peculiar pallid sweetmeat, of the colour and the
texture of putty, with the large knives sticking in
it, that were ready to cut it into slices.

In another street we came upon the shops of
the barbers, bare to the public eye as the interior
of a doll's house; and not far off were rows upon
rows of cafés—deep vaulted rooms, entirely open
to the roadway, and showing within, dark in the
swarthy twilight. long groups carousing at wooden

tables. Not far from these was the more squalid quarter of the shoemakers, where all down an inky alley busy hands were glancing, and boots brown and black, and slippers crimson and yellow, dangled in front of what were less like shops than sheds. Somewhere too in the same neighbourhood a sharp turn brought one amongst the smiths and the iron-workers, where black puffs of vapour floated faintly amongst the awnings, and far away in the gloom forges spat and sparkled.

And through these shadowy ways, from early morning to dusk, the most motley throng kept moving. Greeks and Armenians, in dark, tight-fitting clothing, jostled their way amongst turbans and flowing robes, amongst blue and green and orange colour. Old crones, with silvery hair and faces creased like medlars, tottered along with baskets on their feeble heads ; by them went girls, tall and with heads erect, on which were supported jars brimming with water ; and slowly gliding in and out of the crowd were veiled Turkish women, muffled in white like ghosts, showing nothing but the gleam of their dark eyes, and attended some-

times by a negro black as ebony. Occasionally
the mass would be pressed together and parted
by a patriarch with a beard of snow solemnly
enthroned on a donkey between coloured saddle-
bags ; and occasionally through the reluctantly
formed opening a cart would come, drawn by
bullocks, with their huge horns swaying. Then,
as one watched and waited, other sights would
reveal themselves. Little brown - legged boys
would skip by with trays of coffee, which the
cafés sent out to the shops ; and bakers' men
would appear, going more circumspectly, carrying on their heads long trays like planks, each
with its row of loaves smelling fresh from the
oven.

Of Oriental bazaars that at Cairo is commonly
supposed to be the most interesting, and of course
in scale and in value and variety of merchandise
this of Nicosia cannot for an instance be compared to it. But if the two are judged by the
impressions they produce on the mind the advantage is the other way. In the bazaar at Cairo
the stranger perforce wanders, accompanied by a

banal consciousness of the neighbourhood of Shepheard's Hotel, or else at every corner he encounters the inhabitants of it. Cockney and Yankee accents clash in the air close to him, and hands in every direction are red with " Murray's " and " Bädeker's." The existence of the modern world is in no way eclipsed in his mind : the scene seems rather by contrast to bring it into jarring prominence. But in the bazaar of Nicosia everything conspired to make the modern world forgotten. In every sight, in every sound, in the very air itself, there was the flavour of another civilisation and of other centuries—one might almost say of another world. The men who passed were every one of them men who might have seen djins or effreets, have been wrecked on the Loadstone Mountain, or done wonders with talismans. There was not a face that might not have seen marvels, and probably not a heart that did not implicitly believe in them ; and the knowledge that this was so, through the quick action of sympathy, wrapped me round myself with the same mysterious atmosphere.

Cairo, again, cannot, nor can any other town that I know of, offer anything comparable to the following experience, with which my first day's visit to the Nicosia bazaar concluded. After wandering about with me for a considerable time, Mrs. Falkland paused before a low squalid-looking arch, which divided two shops, and said, "We will come this way." Plunging through the arch, we emerged under the open sky amongst some outhouses, in a passage which seemed to lead only to somebody's back door. At the end, however, it took a sudden turn. We advanced a few paces, we passed through another arch, and we found ourselves under the shadows of the flying buttresses of the cathedral. It seemed as if in a moment we had travelled three thousand miles. We were surrounded by a vision of silent mediæval Europe. The pinnacles soared above us and the coats of arms looked down on us.

To both these scenes I again and again returned, the imagination each time taking a fresh draught from them as from a well, and colouring my thoughts afterwards as I sat in my host's cloisters and watched his orange leaves tremble and heard his fountain splash.

Another of the sights of Nicosia — of the sights which the tourist would call such—was a ruinous pile of buildings, which is now called the Konak—thát is to say, the Turkish Government offices—but which was once a palace of the kings of the House of Lusignan, and earlier still of the Byzantine Dukes of Cyprus. Its principal entrance opened on a large irregular *place*, and the external view of it was not impressive or interesting. It consisted simply of a long blind wall, patched with mud and ragged at the top, in the middle of which was a tower with a Gothic doorway. The dilapidated doors were not fastened, and Colonel Falkland, who was my guide, unceremoniously pushed them open. Inside was a guard-room with a heavy groined roof, beyond this was another, and then came a long court, surrounded by crumbling buildings that had been used by the Turks as barracks. Of these a part was modern, and consequently already in ruins ; but amongst this, and under this, were many parts

that were ancient—solid stone staircases climbing to
roofless chambers, and halls with ponderous vaulting, of which some were Byzantine. Nothing,
however, retained any marked architectural
character. All beauties of form and proportion
had been lost, most likely for centuries. But the
extent still remained of the labyrinthine structure
—chamber after chamber, chapels, baths, and
banquet halls, faintly and plaintively proclaiming
to the eye what they had been, and reminding
one by their silence of the life that had for ever
left them. Oranges laid their cheeks against
walls where had once been frescoes, and the long
roofless corridors were carpeted now with violets.
I said that the place had no architectural feature.
As I was turning to leave it, however, I found
that it had one. This was the inner side of the
entrance tower. Over the door was a magnificent
coat of arms—that of the Lusignans—surmounted
by a crown and a helmet; and over this was a
window which, the moment I set eyes on it, gave
to the whole scene a new soul and sentiment.
The lower part was defaced, battered, and broken,

choked with bricks and ragged Venetian shutters,
but its upper part was as perfect as in the days
of its glory—a great Gothic arch filled with exquisite tracery.

The impression I took away with me was one
of confused sadness. I little knew what sadness,
of a very definite kind, had been near me all the
while amongst that desolation and silence, and
that I should see it face to face on the occasion
of my second visit.

And now that I have mentioned the Konak,
the ramparts, the bazaar, and the cathedral, the
tourist's sights of Nicosia have, I think, all been
enumerated. But the other sights—sights that
slowly showed themselves and gave the place its
character by a series of delicate touches, each
dependent for its force on its surroundings as
much as on itself—these were innumerable, and
can be described only by specimens. They were,
in fact, not so much sights as experiences ; and
every day yielded a fresh crop of them.

One afternoon, for instance, in a street that
was then strange to me I caught, through an

open doorway, a glimpse of a long cloister.
Slanting sunlight was coming in through its
arches, together with some orange boughs and
banana trees, out of an unseen garden. I ven-
tured in, with the feeling of a timid trespasser.
Directly within the entrance, dim in the vaulted
shadow, was a door, surmounted by a mass of
intricate carving. At each extremity of the
device was a quaint heraldic lion, and in the
middle I detected the heads and the wings of angels.
I advanced into the cloister. The sleepy garden
revealed itself, and on the other side a series of
whitewashed cells, each with a bed, a chair, and a
bare wooden table. I now realised that I was in
some Greek monastic establishment. Presently
an old priest, having a long silvery beard and
wearing a cassock and a high brimless hat, came
towards me, and asked me by smiles and signs if
I should like to visit the interior of the church.
I assented. He took me to the door with the
carvings over it. He pushed it open and I
entered. I started. The incense-smelling twilight in which I found myself was a-glimmer with

gold and paintings! The actual structure was
severely simple. It consisted of three aisles, of
which the middle one was lit by a low dome, and
the plain-cut stone-work was bare of all orna-
mentation. But the pulpit stood upon shafts of
brilliant gilding, and blue and crimson saints
looked down from its sides. There were rows of
stalls, with fantastic gilded canopies; and before
the unseen altar was a great towering screen, gilt
also, and gorgeous with the whole army of
martyrs. Overhead from the roof depended
antique crystal chandeliers, and on an illuminated
reading-desk were the Gospels, bound in em-
bossed silver. The priest had remained outside.
There was a profound stillness round me, and my
first impression was that I was alone. Presently
a faint sound called my attention to the chancel,
and I perceived that before the screen were innumerable hanging lamps, and that a silent
acolyte was lighting them one by one. I felt a
longing to linger; an influence in the stillness
detained me. The faint smell of incense, in the
strange way peculiar to it, filled the air with a

sense of contrition and sorrow and aspiration, of burdens taken away, and of hopes set free to rise again.   Are there no burdens borne by the modern world?   And if it has them where will it lay them down?

When I went out the old priest was seated on a bench by the entrance.   About him was a group of neophytes, who were being brought up for the priesthood.   Some of the young faces were commonplace and stupid enough ; but on others was the expression which once, with a fulness of meaning, deluded men were accustomed to call spiritual.   Happy, I thought, compared with the lot of many of us, was the lot that lay before them.   For them in this secret nook the ages of faith survived.   All their years the soul would remain a reality for them ; prayer would never seem to them a waste of despairing breath ; heaven would be near them, invisible saints around them, and life would still promise something beyond itself, until the day when (as men of science would tell us) death came to them quietly, bearing the incommunicable disillusion.

Nicosia as a rule, however, breathed lighter thoughts than these, distracting the mind from itself with a mirage of terrestrial beauty. Often I returned alone to the old Armenian house, and mounting to its flat roof looked round me at the city shimmering in the sunshine. Far away were the mountains, pearl-coloured with the haze of noon, and purple shadows, such as lie on a grape cluster, would come creeping down over them beyond the milk - white minarets. On occasions such as these to breathe was like drinking an elixir in which imagination and memory had both dissolved their pearls. It quickened every appetite for sensuous (not sensual) pleasure. The blue of the sky seemed to enter into one's veins ; even the crisp shadows in the cracks of the walls or the columns seemed to be things of beauty ; and one longed to do what the Devil says no man ever does—to say to the passing moment, " Stay ! thou art so fair."

But this is only one memory out of many. How many fresh houses every day did I pass whose antique doors gave glimpses of green and

black shadow, of glossy foliage, and blue, blinding
sky! What variety of detail in each of these
luminous pictures — cloisters, clambering stairs,
running conduits, and vessels of beaten brass!
And what changing pictures, dissolved as soon as
formed, in the streets! The brown brigand-like
shepherd, with the breath about him of the plains
and of the mountains; the old majestic Turk,
with his long robes with fur; the lean Greek priest,
with his unshorn, dangling hair, followed by a bevy
of boys with garlands for some saint's shrine;
buxom Armenian ladies, with bursting velvet
bodices and heart-shaped silver buckles; the
muleteer on his mule, with his long lance-like
goad; and again, strangest of all, the gliding
Turkish women, veiled from head to foot in their
flowing yashmaks, which were drawn in at the
back so as to show the outlines of the hips, some
of them white, and others of silk coloured brilliantly
—the meetings, the passings, the successions, of
figures such as these, as like and yet as different as
the waves of the breaking sea, were like the waves
in the pleasure they gave me watching them.

Another of my favourite walks was along the
ramparts. I reached them from Colonel Falkland's house by a lane I have already mentioned,
with a fountain in it, at which Greek girls continually were filling their pitchers. The ramparts
were only a few paces beyond, and every fine
morning on the gray mouldering battlements
Turkish women were sunning themselves, like
rows of ragged tulips. Nor must I forget another
thing, of which the mention of flowers reminds me,
and that is the Turkish children. Some of them
had their heads covered with shimmering grass-
green handkerchiefs, and their petticoats were of
golden yellow. Some had crimson head-gear and
petticoats of ultramarine. In fact they glittered
with all the colours of the rainbow. In the
unfrequented lanes of the Turkish quarter one came
round corners on little quiet groups of them,
sometimes toddling along, sometimes playing
together in the middle of the roadway. They
looked like bunches of anemones and daffodils,
dropped in the dust by some recent passer
by.

Again, to go back from human beings to buildings, almost every fresh ramble brought me to some new mosque, to the tree-tops of some new garden, embowering perhaps a gay pavilion, and to rooms with painted ceilings spanning the road on arches ; and, more curious still, amongst the by-lanes, in which I constantly lost myself, used as barns or stables, or places for dogs to litter in,· but still covered with carving and beautiful with their pointed windows, one after another I came on mediæval churches — remains of the three hundred for which Nicosia once was celebrated.

And over all was the living and liquid sunlight, sharpening every outline with its broad washes of shadow, filling here and there a window or arch with midnight and giving to every scene a con- stantly changing character. Sometimes a familiar wall would become a new thing, as a bough laden with leaves or with almond blossoms hung illumi- nated over it. Sometimes in the crowded bazaar, at the end of one of its dim passages, the eye would suddenly catch the crags of the far-off mountains ; and constantly in some narrow, shadowy street, where the tops of the houses were black with their projecting roofs, I stood arrested by the sight of the blue sky at the end of it—an oblong of lapis lazuli inlaid with a dark cypress tree.

I should, however, convey a very incomplete impression if I spoke of Nicosia only as it appeared on the days of sunshine ; for though certainly sunshine, at once soft and brilliant, was the rule, clouds and showers were exceptions hardly rare enough to be remarkable. But clouds in that wonderful climate seemed seldom to have any gloom in them. They were as fresh and warm in January as they are with us in June. They hovered over everything like the breast and wings of a dove, and from all the viewless gardens they summoned the smells of flowers. The gray, too, of the evening, into which the afternoons faded, instead of depressing the mind, as it sometimes does, into a mood of vapid dejection, carried with it its own subtle exhilaration. I often look back to a walk that I took along the ramparts with Colonel and Mrs. Falkland. We came

about five o'clock to what is called the Kyrenia
Gate.   Outside was the Turkish cemetery—a
bare enclosure surrounded by a broken wall.   Far
away over the great pastoral plain was a dying
line of sunset between two mountain ranges, and
a faint gleam rested on the leaning stones under
which the nameless Turkish dead were sleeping.
Within was the darkening town, with its Gothic
cathedral and its look of remote Damascus.
There was an odd pathos in the scene—a gentle
desolation touched with a certain wildness—which
caused the thoughts to enter tents and deserts,
and then sent them back to the music of Gray's
Elegy.   The moment was full of voices and of
melancholy with no pain in it.

Such, then, were the scenes amongst which my
life passed itself, varied by pleasant gatherings at
familiar English meals, and hours of conversation
in the evening.   But familiar though the household life of my host and hostess was, its details
were somehow transfigured by the sense of its
strange surroundings.   The English table-cloth
and the silver of English salt-cellars had in my

eyes a foreign glimmer when flecked by the
Cyprian sunlight ; foreign associations stole across
the palate at the taste of unknown wines and
fruits and cheese ; and phantoms of the East and
of the old Western crusaders hovered at night in
the drawing-room amongst the shadows of the
lofty rafters.

And once again I must say, what I have said
before, that the novelty of the place—the impression that it was a dream or an enchantment—
grew stronger instead of weaker as I saw more
and more of it. It was 'a dream still, but a dream
that was every day more wonderful, for it was a
dream that would not melt.

However, after a week of this delightful
idleness, conscience forced me to take some
further steps about the business which was by
way of having brought me to the island. I sent
Scotty to explore the mountains as I had resolved
to do ; and, after having been absent for some
twelve hours, he returned with the news that the
very place had been found—cave, cypress tree,
ruined church and everything. I instantly de-

cided on going there the next day but one, and
when I happened to mention this to my charming
acquaintance, Mr. Matthews, to my great pleasure
he offered to come with me.

CHAPTER X

MY experiences of a Cyprian mule had taught me one thing, and that was never to ride one when there was any other means of conveyance. It was accordingly arranged that we should drive as far as Kythrea and ascend the mountains on foot, accompanied, however, by a guide, and our two servants on mules, which would carry our luncheon, and I hoped carry back some marble.

I breakfasted at eight with Mr. Matthews in his old archbishop's palace. One entered the pile through a low-browed Gothic doorway, which admitted one to a vaulted hall, used originally as a stable ; and from this one passed into a court, surrounded with dim arcades, and full, in the usual way, of palms, orange trees, and bananas.

An old stone staircase rose through the air on arches, its balustrades brushed by the dark-green leafage, and brought one in two turns to an immense open loggia, carpeted with matting and surrounded by plain divans. Across the garden one looked at a medley of neighbouring buildings, partly Oriental, partly crumbling Gothic, which shone in the blue sky with a promise of perfect weather. Out of this loggia, besides various bed-rooms, opened three large apartments, whose decorations were of some interest. One of them —the largest—had at one end a curious niche, which might once have held a statue of a saint or the Blessed Virgin. The walls of all three were wainscotted, and adorned with some carved mirrors, and the ceilings were mosaics of coloured geometrical spaces, reminding one somewhat of a pattern in a kaleidoscope grown dirty. The house had been entirely altered, as well as halved in size, since the days of its episcopal masters, and the history of these decorations could not be arrived at accurately. The niche may have been mediæval, but the wainscotting and the ceilings

were Turkish ; and certain pieces of plaster-work
—flowers and bows and ribbons—evidently dated
from the earlier part of the last century, when the
taste of Paris not only governed Europe, but
actually penetrated to this remote corner of the
East.

As we drove out of Nicosia the same feeling of
freshness and primitive life saluted us which had
made my expedition on the mule and the feather-
bed so invigorating ; but on quitting the carriage,
where the road ended at Kythrea, we found our
feet in every way preferable to the mule. The
village, with its people, its watercourses, and its
gardens, again made a series of shining idyllic
pictures. The women had gay jackets and gayer
petticoats, and in their hair tiaras of brilliant
beads. The waists of the men were bound with
gaudy sashes. The horses, sheep, and cattle
stood, as formerly, knee-deep in the green grass
under the olive trees.

Our ascent through the mountains had only
two new features, neither of which was apparent
till we were nearing our destination. One of

them was the fact that, instead of being close
to Pentedactylon, the place in question was
at least three miles away from it. The other
was that during the last half-hour of our walk
the rude path which we followed was littered
with small fragments of the very stone I was
in search of. On the red ground, and amongst
the gray pebbles, they caught the eye with
their greenness as if they were dusty leaves.
Elated by this, we welcomed in good spirits
another mass of greenness which soon made itself
visible. This was the solitary cypress tree of
which we had heard so much. It stood there,
just as it had been described to me, large as a
churchyard yew; and the other details of the
scene equally answered my expectations. We ate
our luncheon in front of the cave and the fountain ;
the orange-coloured precipice rose like a wall
opposite to us, and above us the ruined church
showed its splinters of desolate masonry.

Our luncheon over, we instantly set to work
with our geologists' hammers, and began to look
again for the green marble masses. Our search

was, however, fruitless. Stone masses of some
sort were on all sides of us in profusion; every
slope was littered with them. But one and all
they had surfaces of silvery whiteness; and our
hammers showed us that they were nothing but
gray limestone. There were green fragments
everywhere, but none beyond the size of a pebble;
and we were obliged to content ourselves with
making a collection of these, when time warned
us that we ought to be turning homewards. We
had, however, hardly proceeded a couple of
hundred yards when something caught my eye
which made me stop short suddenly. On an
open plot amongst some myrtle bushes, that was
dotted with a few gray boulders, I saw amongst
these a large sombre something, which a second
glance showed me was a mass of dark-green stone.
We both of us hastened up to it. It was the very
thing we were in search of, except that in size it
fell far short of my expectations. It was perhaps
as large as a small pig, and was not wholly un-
like a pig in shape. I broke off what rudely
corresponded to the nose; and having hastily

looked in vain for anything else like it, I handed the specimen to Scotty, and we resumed our way, promising ourselves to return and continue our explorations in a day or two.

The journey home was interesting in several unexpected ways. We went down the mountains so quickly that we were again traversing Kythrea before the gold was gone from the afternoon sunlight. Presently, as we neared a poor isolated cottage, the prevailing quiet was broken by a singular wild moaning. " Listen ! " said my companion, pausing. " Those people have lost some one. That is the dirge which they always sing for the dead." We passed the cottage ; and, squatting against its farther wall, we saw two women with dark dishevelled hair and painfully strained faces, the one silent, but beating her breast rhythmically, and the other pouring forth a prolonged piteous wail, of which the words and cadences seemed constantly to repeat themselves. " Soon," said Mr. Matthews, " that one will be silent ; she will beat her breast, and the other one will take up the singing. The custom," he went

on, " is of extreme antiquity, and there is no doubt
that it comes from Phœnicia. It was expressly
condemned by a pope in the Middle Ages as
'that heathenish Syrian custom of immoderately
wailing for the dead.' "

Mr. Matthews was full of information like this ;
and for the rest of the way back he poured it
forth into my ear. He was the only person I met
during the whole of my stay in Cyprus who had
studied systematically its mediæval history, who
showed any interest in its castles and feudal life,
or turned to its past with a sense of romance or
sentiment. I had been debating for some days
as to what places in the island would best repay
a visit, my time being unhappily limited ; and on
this point Mr. Matthews was the very adviser I
needed. I found, in fact, after a single hour's con-
sultation with him, that my programme for the future
was taking a definite shape and including the very
things in it which I should probably value most.

In addition to his instructions about buildings
and architecture he helped me to understand the
existing scenery of the island. The whole of the

mountains, he said, with perhaps a few exceptions,
were at one time covered with forests. These
have, however, been constantly felled for timber,
from the days of Alexander the Great to the days
of the Turkish sultans ; and thus by a slow but
ceaseless process, in the course of two thousand
years, two-thirds of them have disappeared. It
is the slopes of the Pentedactylon range, looking
towards Nicosia, that have suffered most in this
way. The consequence has been that the soil,
in which once the trees were rooted, has been,
to a great extent, washed into the plains below,
and has in some places, within historical times,
raised their level by at least thirty feet. In proof
of this he told me that at a village, whose name
escaped me, there is a singular church, which
stands in a walled enclosure. The walls of this,
as seen from the outside, rise hardly more than a
few feet from the ground ; but one finds, on looking over them, that they sink to a depth so great
that the church within stands in a sunk basin,
leaving nothing visible from the neighbouring
fields but its roof.

The depth of soil, indeed, over a large part of
the island is astonishing. It is still abundant even
amongst the lofty crags of the mountains, and the
forests would again rise as luxuriant and green as
formerly if it were not for the peasants, who
cut every stick for fire-wood, and the ubiquitous
goats, who allow few sticks to grow. Certain
tracts, however, which belong to the State, have
been placed by the British Government under the
protection of foresters, who with some success
keep the goats and peasants away, and already
within their limits the slopes that were naked
yesterday are fledged with pigmy pines that
promise to make forests to-morrow. There seems
little doubt that if this change completes itself
the rainfall will be increased and the climate
modified, with results that can be foreseen by
anybody. As it is, wherever water is plentiful
the ground is a mass of greenness, as we saw it to
be at Kythrea. There is hardly a spring whose
presence is not signalised by an ilex or a sycamore,
towering like a sentinel over its source, and
whose banks are not fringed by olives, gardens,

and fruit trees. Cyprus, in fact, is really a
sleeping Eden, needing only the gift of seasonable
rains to awaken it.

From subjects like these my companion
wandered into history, and he told me a number
of quaint and humorous anecdotes, which he
himself, or writers like De Mas Latrie, had
unearthed from the dim chronicles of the Cyprian
Middle Age. Some of them, with their naïve
detail and vividness, lit up parts of the past on
which few eyes ever linger, like a match struck
suddenly in the passages of a forgotten crypt.
Most people know, for instance, in a dull, colourless way, that Richard Cœur de Lion made a
transitory conquest of Cyprus, and that this led
somehow to its possession by the Lusignans afterwards; but few people know the particulars of
this dramatic transaction—fresh to-day as they
ever were—which I must indulge myself by telling
the reader as I had them told to me.

As every schoolboy knows, and indeed as all
men and women know who are fresh, as very few
of them are, from reading a schoolboy's books,

in the year 1191 Richard Cœur de Lion was on his way, by sea, to the Holy Land. He had with him a considerable number of ships, and on one of them was his betrothed, Berengaria, whom it was arranged that he should marry at Jerusalem. Some way south of the island of Rhodes he encountered a violent storm, which scattered his fleet to the four quarters of heaven. Certain of the ships were wrecked on the coast of Cyprus, not far from Limasol ; and another, freighted with the precious burden of Berengaria, at last found itself rocking on the swell in Limasol roads. The sailors of the former, though the shore on which they had been cast was Christian, instead of receiving any help from the natives, were attacked and robbed by them ; they only reached Limasol with difficulty, and on their arrival they were seized and detained as prisoners. As for Berengaria, she fared very little better. She was, it would seem, extremely sea-sick, only, instead of being, like the others, ill-treated on landing, she was told insultingly that she must not land at all.

The explanation of these barbarities was as
follows.   Cyprus was at that time under the rule
of a certain Isaac Comnenus, who had lately
tried in Armenia to make an independent king
of himself, and, failing, had fled to Cyprus.   Here
he was more successful.   He arrived armed with
some forged imperial letters, on the strength of
which he was accepted as duke or governor.   He
at once set himself to wring, by taxes or otherwise, whatever treasure he could from his new
subjects.   By means of this he surrounded himself with a powerful band of mercenaries; and
he presently felt himself strong enough to pro-
claim himself emperor of Cyprus, openly defying
his imperial sovereign at Constantinople.   He
had already quarrelled with the crusaders in Asia
Minor, and was jealous of the ease with which,
in Cyprus, they had hitherto obtained provisions.
He began, therefore, by subjecting them to all
sorts of extortionate duties, and at length ven-
tured to say bluntly that he would not for the
future allow them even to land.   As to the
shipwrecked sailors, for whose landing the storm

was responsible, he would do nothing for them beyond keeping them still in prison ; but as to the Princess Berengaria, on reflection he changed his mind.

It suddenly occurred to him that it would be a magnificent stroke of state-craft to entice her on shore, secure her, and get for her some great ransom. Accordingly on the day following his first insulting message, he sent her another which was accompanied by presents and provisions, explaining away his discourtesy and begging that she would honour him by landing. There were, however, some experienced sailors on board who knew something of the person with whom they had to deal ; and by their advice the presents and invitation were declined, and nothing was asked for but a supply of fresh water. Isaac Comnenus, furious at his scheme failing, replied brutally that they should have no water from him, and for fear they should take it he choked up the brook at Limasol with blocks of marble and columns, taken from ruined temples.

The last block, however, had hardly been put

in its place when a number of sails rose in sight on the horizon. These proved to be the rest of the English fleet, with King Richard himself commanding it. He was making for Cyprus as a natural place of refuge, not knowing that the others were there before him and little dreaming of the sort of welcome they had experienced. The moment the news was told him, in a violent fit of passion he forced a landing with a body of his soldiers at Limasol, on which Isaac Comnenus in terror fled to the mountains. Where to find him and how to communicate with him was a difficulty, but Richard at last discovered two monks, through whom he sent him a message threatening war and naming his conditions of peace. Isaac sent, in reply to this, to say that he would presently meet King Richard at Limasol and discuss the matter with him in person. He was as good as his word. He arrived in royal pomp, with every preparation for receiving a brother monarch royally. When the meeting took place he set Richard at his side on a throne covered with silk, and standing before them was the interpreter. The first to speak was Richard, who addressed Isaac thus :—

" I am astonished, my lord Emperor, that a Christian prince like you, that a witness like you of the sufferings of that Sacred Land in which our Lord Christ was crucified, have made no effort to deliver it from the yoke of the infidels. You will not only not aid those who are now besieging Acre, but will not even give provisions to those who are coming to aid them from so far. In the name of God, in the name of our Holy Faith, I demand that you put an end to all the complaints that are made against you. I demand that you join us yourself, as you ought to do, with your own army, and that for the future you allow the crusaders freely to buy in Cyprus whatever may be requisite for their enterprise."

To this Isaac replied with a grave and regretful courtesy, " My lord King, I am well aware of the honour with which I should cover myself if only I could do as you advise me. But for me it is impossible, seeing I know this : that

if once I left my island I should never again
return to it. Nevertheless I desire to aid you,
so far as my means suffer me; and till Acre is
taken I promise to do for you this much: I
will send and will maintain for you a company
of two hundred soldiers; and any and every
crusader who comes to Cyprus for provisions
shall be allowed to buy them freely, and shall
pay no duty upon them."

Richard, accustomed to the rougher manners
of Europe, was not only pacified but charmed by
Isaac's Oriental courtesy; and he retired, after
many civilities, delighted with the results of the
interview. Nor was Isaac himself any the less
satisfied, though, as will appear presently, for
somewhat different reasons. His only object in
meeting Richard at all had not been to make
him a friend, but to gauge his character as an
enemy; and the conclusion he had come to with
regard to that point was this: he considered
Richard as a man absorbed by a single passion—
a desire to reach his destination and begin his
conflict with the infidel—and for this reason

unlikely, come what might, to waste his time
by remaining in Cyprus to assert himself. Accordingly the two monarchs had hardly retired
to rest when Isaac quietly rose, and not pausing
to dress himself, mounted a horse and galloped
off to Colossi. From this place, which is not two
hours from Limasol, he had the hardihood to
send a message to Richard, telling him and his
followers to ·be quit of the island instantly, " or
else," he said, " I will very soon let you know
how little I think of you and all your barbarous
Franks."

The result of this message was singularly
unexpected. Instead of pocketing the insult and
hurrying on to Palestine, Richard at once disembarked his entire military force ; and the clank
of Western armour and the tramping of Western
horses were soon spreading terror in the startled
streets of Limasol. Isaac, as best he could, got his
forces together ; but Richard, falling on them, put
them to instant rout, seized an immense treasure,
and returned to Limasol in triumph. Here he
was presently joined by Guy de Lusignan, who

in the most romantic manner imaginable had
risen to be King of Jerusalem ; and here Richard
was married in solemn state to Berengaria. Isaac
meanwhile had fled into the recesses of the mountains ; and thither Richard, as soon as his wed-
ding was over, accompanied by Guy, lost no time
in pursuing him. They at last drove him into
the open country, and joined battle with him
outside the town of Tremitus, which lay in the
central plain, some ten miles north of Larnaca.
Here Richard was again completely victorious ;
he took Isaac prisoner, and he found himself
master of the island. As for Tremitus, he
made it a heap of ruins. Near its site there
are still some broken Phœnician walls ; and
long afterwards the story lingered amongst
the islanders that these were the remains of a
town that had been destroyed by an English
king.

As a pendant to this story I must add that
of Guy de Lusignan. Some ten years before the
events just related Baldwin IV., King of Jerusalem,
was dying. His eldest child, who was destined

to succeed him on the throne, was a widowed
daughter named Sibylle, who had married the
Baron de Montferrat ; and at this juncture all
her near relations begged her for all their sakes to
marry a second time, and to marry some one
who would bring strength to the family. Sibylle,
however, if not extremely wise, was what excellent
people in these days are accustomed to call
unworldly. There happened at that time to be
a young Frenchman in Jerusalem—a penniless
member of a noble but unimportant family, who
had little to recommend him but his face and his
pleasant manners. To Sibylle, however, these
had for some time recommended him, not only
well but, if gossip said true, too well. When,
therefore, she was thus importuned to marry,
instead of turning her attention to the great
barons of the realm, she horrified her friends by
selecting this valueless, detrimental Guy, who
was merely a second cousin of a Sire de Lusignan, in Poitou. With much wifely tact she at
once made him independent, giving him the
countship of Jaffa and Ascalon ; and before long,

with his wife, he ascended the throne of Jerusalem.   How, after his wife's death, his position
grew precarious, and after various vicissitudes
Richard sold him the island of Cyprus for a sum
about equal to £200,000, need not be told here ;
and I will end his story with one delightful touch,
which shows that men, even in those far times,
were our kindred.   His brothers at home, when
they heard of his splendid fortunes, instead of
rejoicing in them, in that unnatural manner which
our friends the scientific altruists and Mr. Herbert
Spencer would suppose, were consumed with the
far more homely and human feeling of mortifi-
cation ; and one of them, Geoffrey, exclaimed
in words, which one feels must be authen-
tic, " If my brother Guy has become a king
he is perfectly certain to end by becoming
God."

Whilst I was listening to stories of this kind,
which made me forget the rough though rapid
movement of the carriage, dusk had insensibly
descended on the wide Cyprian plains, and the
figures of our attendants on mules were like

ghosts upon either side of us. Suddenly I saw the moonlight fall upon masonry, and we were entering Nicosia through the gloom of the Famagusta Gate.

CHAPTER XI

THE ETERNAL COMEDY

THAT evening I was somewhat late for dinner. Scotty having been absent with me, nothing was prepared for my dressing, and when I came to look for a white tie I was unable to find one anywhere. At last, after a desperate turning over of everything, I came on a collection of them in the strangest place in the world—in the corner of a cupboard, beneath my photographic camera ; and near them was another surprise, a number of my silk socks carefully sandwiched between some boxes of photographic plates. When I explained to Mrs. Falkland this mysterious incident, both she and her daughter at once broke into a laugh, exclaiming together, " That must have been Metaphora ! "

" And who is Metaphora ? " I asked.

" Ah," they said, " she is a specimen of a native Cypriote. She is one of our servants. You are quite sure to have seen her."

Then I too joined in the laugh ; for Metaphora, as I now divined, was none other than the curious bouncing creature whose grin and whose movements had already caught my attention. There are some people who are born to excite a smile. I at once seemed to recognise, by a flash of instantaneous insight, that Metaphora was a member of this class ; and the accounts I was presently given of her showed me I was not mistaken. Her manners, her English, and her impulses were all equally entertaining. I was gratified to find that, quite unconsciously, I had already aroused in her the liveliest interest in myself, that she had described me to Mrs. Falkland as being a "very pretty gentleman," that she had actually added, " He all the same as Vahly Pasha "—Vahly Pasha being the Governor, the most magnificent human being she knew—and that that evening she had given special attention to my room, "because the poor gentleman would be tired, having been all day on the roses." In Metaphora's language "the roses," I found, meant "roads."

I asked why her idea of making me more comfortable should have shown itself in hiding whatever I was most likely to want. "Ah," said Mrs. Falkland, "she is really almost half-witted. If I tell her to look for a thing she will often start off before she has heard what it is, and then she will come back to me saying, 'I not find it.' I say to her, 'How can you if you will not stay to hear what it is?' and then she answers, not so much to me as to herself, 'Fool Metaphora. She very fool girl. Poor nowti [naughty] Metaphora!'"

The following day I discovered the truth of this description for myself. Looking for some of my letters, which had been placed under a weight on my dressing-table, I found that they all were missing. At last, protruding from a packing-case, which, with an open end against the wall, was supporting a military chest, I espied the tips of a piece of foolscap paper and of a torn copy of an old *Evening Standard*. A near examination showed me that all my letters, my envelopes, and the waste paper used for my packing had been rolled up together into a tight ball and stuffed into this hiding-place. I asked Metaphora that evening what had induced her to do this. "Ah," she exclaimed with a long meditative breath; then her eyes shone as if she had solved a problem. "Nowti Metaphora!" she exclaimed. "Me nowti — me very fool girl!" And then putting her head down and giving a sort of caper like a colt, she bounded out of the room and rustled down the stairs like an avalanche.

The servants, Mrs. Falkland told me, were as much amused at her as anybody. One of her peculiarities was a horror of beef, or, as she called it, "bullock meat." It was a favourite practical joke with the Scotch cook, Fraser, to give her a plate of beef with some chicken bones stuck amongst the slices, when, thinking the meat chicken, she would swallow it all with gusto, exclaiming, "Good! oh! good! Metaphora, she like that."

Poor Metaphora! Though her mistress thought her half-witted she still was blest with illusions which for her made life beautiful. Her waist was like that of a barrel; her smiling mouth went literally from ear to ear; yet she was firmly persuaded that one of Colonel Falkland's secretaries — a good-looking young Englishman who was quite unconscious of her existence—had fallen in love with her one day when she opened the door for him. She was also persuaded that whilst *he* was in love with *her*, Fraser, the cook of fifty, was equally in love with *him*; and whenever Fraser thwarted any one of her wishes she set it down to the angry jealousy of a rival—or, as she herself expressed it, "Fraser, she jelly me."

She had also her aspirations, which are even better things than illusions, her "devotion to something afar from the sphere of our sorrow." The longing of her life was for a tight-fitting velvet dress like one made for the Princess of Wales as she had seen it in the pages of a fashion-book.

I have lingered over Metaphora not for her own sake only, but because from my introduction to her manifold excellences I date my insight into the comedy of Cyprian life. Colonel Falkland, whose sense of humour was keen, by what seemed to me an exceedingly natural transition, went on from Metaphora to something even more naïve and ridiculous; and that is the something which passes for the political life of the island. I had arrived, I believe from a study of *Whitaker's Almanac*, at what Cardinal Newman would call a "notional assent" to the fact that Cyprus possessed an elected legislative council; but I never vividly realised before that evening that this council, to me hitherto merely the shadow of a name, implied all the horrors of a modern popular franchise. At first this discovery terribly shocked and disappointed me. I felt as if suddenly I had fallen out of the clouds to the ground. Good heavens! I thought, and are all these enchanted creatures—these wild shepherds, these mysterious turbaned merchants, who move through an air that seems charged at once with wonder and simplicity

—are they really nothing but modern voters in disguise, with beliefs in the people, in the vices of the governing classes, in the popular conscience, and in the mandates of the constituencies? But, as I listened to my host a little longer, I found that my fears were needless. The blight of a constitution which was only inflicted on the islanders — I believe I speak correctly — as a sop to our English Radicals, has fallen on most of them like snow on a summer sea. With the exception of a small minority, drawn principally from the Greek shopkeepers, the glorious privilege of taking part in their own government touches them only as an occasional vague annoyance, which the moment it is over fades away from their consciousness. When the elections take place for the Legislative Council the difficulty is to persuade them to vote at all. The peasants indeed, even during the heat of a contest, are rarely aware of the names of either of the rival candidates. They have been constantly known to ask the returning officer to take their papers and do just what he liked with them. It

frequently happens also that the head man of a
village is begged by his fellow villagers to go and
vote instead of them, and let one piece of meaningless trouble do duty for them all.

No doubt it may be said that though this is
true of the majority there is still a minority which
understands its political privileges and uses them.
There certainly is, and it uses them too with a
vengeance, but it uses them in a way so delightfully simple and childish that, instead of infecting
the air with the prose of modern Europe, as a
corporate body it merely seems to the imagination to be playing the part of Bottom in *A Mid-
summer Night's Dream*. This minority is composed of perhaps a couple of hundred people, all
of them professional Radicals, and the greater
part of them Greeks. In almost every respect
they are ludicrously faithful imitations of their
engaging brethren in the West; only the imita-
tion has this great advantage over the original,
that it can hardly be called mischievous and is
infinitely more amusing. The professional Cyprian
patriot in the effect he produces on the mind is

very much like a monkey and a parrot imitating
Mr. William O'Brien, the parrot supplying the
voice and the monkey supplying the gestures.
Almost every device distinctive of the Western
agitator is employed by the Cyprian also, from
flattery of the people to abuse of the existing
order ; and his political arguments and exhorta-
tions have the same wide range, beginning with
lowly exaggeration, then rising to misrepresenta-
tion, and finally soaring into the thunders of
absolute fiction.

The *Daily News*, or even the *Pall Mall Gazette*
itself, might have envied the success with which,
shortly before my arrival, the patriots had collected
a few hundred women and children, had sent them
with a petition from Nicosia to Government House
—a pleasant stroll of little more than a mile—
and contrived to get the event described in the
English journals as a magnificent demonstration
composed of ten thousand persons.

I am going here to indulge in a half-minute's
digression. To the sober reason few things can
seem sillier than the proposal of professional

religion-makers to worship idealised humanity; and yet occasionally one can almost detect a meaning in it. For in humanity as a whole there is under the changing surface a persistence, an august immutability, which at odd moments is brought home to us, and is like nothing else in the world. What, for instance, can be more striking than this characteristic, the same always and everywhere : that the men who take the trouble to say they despise rank are men who inwardly grovel and cringe before it, and would wear it themselves, if they could, with the most arrogant vanity? Of this Cypriote patriotism afforded me a very pleasant illustration, and that is the reason why I have thus paused to moralise. During the first years of the British occupation one of the persons whom the Government found most troublesome, was a certain individual who rejoiced in the name of Palæologus. He was consumed with a passion for the people and for popular freedom. Every *demos*, he held, should manage its own affairs, nor submit its majestic self to any oppression but its own. The Turks, according to him, were indeed vile usurpers, but the English were viler still.   Cyprus was a Greek island ; it ought to belong to Greece.   As for himself, he declared with the eloquence of a Demosthenes he had in his own veins the blood of the Greek emperors, and he appealed to his compatriots to side with him as their natural leader ; and under his name as a banner to protest against the oppressions of England.   As often happens to agitators, his agitation landed him in a libel, making him amenable to the law, which the oppressors now administered.   No sooner had this happened than he triumphantly established the fact that he was not a Cypriote subject, that he was not even a Greek, but that his domicile was at Smyrna, and that his father was a Turkish tailor at Constantinople.

This story suggested to me a very natural question.   I asked what the oppressions were of which the English were alleged to be guilty. What a Radical calls oppression is generally some necessary act misrepresented, but still there must generally be something to misrepresent.

The most definite something in this case was, so I learned, taxation. It is the only political question which the people at large appreciate, and a reduction of taxes is the cry that most quickly appeals to them. That this should be so is certainly not surprising. They are most of them very poor, and they feel the slightest burden. It would, however, by no means suit the Radicals to make the existing taxes their only or even their principal grievance, for if these taxes were reduced the business of the Radicals would be gone. They are obliged, therefore, to supplement this one definite grievance with a number of others which are at once indefinite and imaginary, which being indefinite cannot be disproved, and which, as they do not exist, cannot be taken away.

Their success in this line is remarkable. I found, from what I was told, that they almost equalled the Irish leaders in what may be called the patriot's vision — that peculiar faculty by which benefits are seen under the aspect of injuries—and also in that faculty, peculiar to the professional patriot also, of frenzied indignation at events that have never happened at all. Thus I asked what the Radicals said about this fact: that the English had conferred on them one blessing at all events, by extirpating the locusts which once ravaged the island.

"Yes," I was answered, "that is a blessing undoubtedly, but the Cyprian patriots have been quite equal to dealing with it. True," they say, "the English have done this. Of course they have; but they ought to have done it sooner. Instead of thanking them for what they have done we have every cause to complain of them for taking so long in doing it, and, after all, who has paid for it? We have! Greece would have done the same thing, but have done it years ago; and Greece would have borne half, if not all, the expense of it."

This is good. Could a Mr. O'Brien, a Mr. Dillon, or a Mr. Davitt have done better? It is, however, outdone by the following burning sentence, with which one of the Cyprian patriots strove to arouse his countrymen: "Under the Turks,"

he said, "you were merely poor people. Under
the English you are helots!" All the logic of
modern agitation breathes in those few syllables,
which would have absolutely no connection with
facts whatever if they did not happen to contain
a vague inversion of them.

Let me, however, do the patriots justice. If
they are not very honest in the matter of means
they are perfectly sincere so far as regards their
ends. They do, no doubt, desire the substitution
of Greek rule for English, for the definite and
intelligible, if not well-founded, reason that they
see in it an unlimited prospect of Government
places for themselves. It would be cynical also,
and perhaps even disingenuous, with the knowledge
which I happen to possess, to deny that in some
cases their political animosity towards ourselves may
be due to feelings of a warmer and less calculating
kind. In one case at least this was so. One
patriot's wrath — I tell this for the honour of
patriotism — was almost epic and heroic in its
origin. The hero was a man renowned for his
probity, especially for the severity of what would

be called his moral character; and entering one night a certain house in Nicosia, the fame of which was hardly equal to his own, he was met at the door by a British soldier emerging, who, brimming over with zeal for the honour of England, hit him in the eye out of a sense of pure superiority, exclaiming as he did so, " You b——y Greek take that!"   The Greek's character was far too spotless to enable him to explain his grievance against the soldier, so he avenged his outraged dignity by opposing the British Government.

So much moral modesty will be thought doubly remarkable when the surrounding state of society and of opinion is considered.   Though the temples of Aphrodite are overthrown and her altars flameless, though shy professors grub in the dust of her scandalous courts and her very name is appropriate to alien Christian uses, the influence of the goddess is still immortal in the air, and the Bishop of ——, when I was in the island, was about, with a curious appropriateness, to figure as the co-respondent in a divorce case.   That, no doubt, was a scandal, but a mild scandal only. Another prelate, not very long ago, was said to have a child in every village of his diocese. Another was thought a model of decorum and discipline because he asked leave, instead of taking it, to keep a couple of mistresses ; and the present Archbishop of Nicosia who is really a respectable man, is regarded as an absolute saint because no such romances are connected with him.

The behaviour of the Turks is in many ways superior to that of the Greeks ; but with regard to the point to which we are now alluding I am not quite sure that their superiority is very decided. The following story makes me feel doubtful. During the early years of the British occupation it fell, Colonel Falkland told me, to the lot of a friend of his to superintend the collection of taxes in certain parts of the island. One day the person in question had been up betimes in the morning, and having visited already two Turkish villages, arrived about noon at a third. Here he was given breakfast at the house of the principal inhabitant, and while the meal was in progress an official report was brought to him of the taxes that still were owing there. Half the people, it seemed, had that year paid nothing. He asked why. He was told that the people were poor. "Who," he asked, "are the richest?" The names of the richest were read to him. "Have these men paid?" he asked. The answer was, "No, not one of them." "Well," he said to his subordinate, "we will begin with them. Make them pay first, and we will see what we will do afterwards." His host, who was foremost amongst those thus alluded to, heard this unwelcome order, but it did not diminish his courtesy. On the contrary, knowing that his guest would by this time be tired, he closed the shutters of the room for him and begged him to refresh himself with a siesta. The guest gladly stretched himself out on a low divan, and before long sleep was stealing over him. Suddenly a slight noise startled him. He opened his eyes, and soon, in spite of the darkness, he became conscious that some human figure was present. He saw at last that it was a female. He concluded that she was there by mistake, and he gave a slight cough as a hint that the room was occupied. Instead of retiring, however, the apparition glided towards him, stood at the side of the divan, and in silence bent slightly over him. He raised himself on his elbow. As he did so the figure let fall her yashmak and disclosed to his gaze a beautiful Turkish girl, who in another moment he saw was his host's daughter. He stared at her, speechless with astonishment. In answer she fixed her eyes on him, and he read a meaning in them—no matter what it was—which no well-conducted father, whether Christian or Turk, would approve of. For a second or two he was almost stupefied; then, as if by inspiration, a sense of the truth came to him. He suddenly sprang up, he threw the doors open, and there outside were all the chief Turks of the village, waiting for a sign from the girl that the collector of taxes had committed himself. Had the plot succeeded, as Colonel Falkland observed, needless to say that the taxes of those Turks would have been light.

This kind of discourse carried us far into the

evening, and a few days later the thread of it, which was now broken by bed-time, was taken up, not by Colonel Falkland, but by Mr. Matthews, who, true to his word, went again with me to look for the marble. As to the marble, the result of our researches was disappointing, and I came to the conclusion that it was worth no further trouble ; but on the way back such a trifle as the collapse of my whole practical expectations was quite put out of my mind by the series of stories that were told me. I can only repeat—indeed I can only recollect—a few, for even the best of stories often fade from the memory almost as quickly as happiness fades from life. It is true that in the *motif* of them there was a certain amount of sameness ; but so there is in most of Boccaccio's tales and in every French novel that reaches a tenth edition. In fact what a breach of the seventh commandment is to these, some attempt at evading the taxes was to the others.

Mr. Matthews, being connected with the assessment of taxes himself, was naturally on familiar ground. Two of his principal heroes were prelates. At the beginning of the British occupation the Archbishop of Nicosia came to the authorities and inquired with perfect gravity if it really were possible that he would be expected to pay his taxes. The answer, of course, was " Yes." " Very well," said the Archbishop, in a tone of obstinate meekness, " then you expect something of me that I am quite unable to do." Asked what he meant, he replied " I mean simply this : that my lands are assessed at four times their actual value." " Indeed," said the authorities. " If that is the case we will have your lands revalued. But we have gone by the assessment left us by the late Government, to which it appears you have never taken exception. Can you kindly explain this to us ? " " Heh ? " said the Archbishop ; " but that is explained easily." The Turks, it appears, had assessed him at this really exorbitant figure, with his own consent, but on this distinct understanding : he was never to pay a penny. Then, when any of the Greek peasantry grumbled, the officials would be able to say, " Look at your good Archbishop :

what are your burdens to his? And yet he never makes a murmur."

If the Government, however, has trouble in getting the taxes out of the bishops, the bishops in their turn have trouble in getting their own dues out of their flocks. "Ah," said one of them one day to Mr. Matthews, "dreadful, dreadful people in the village of Alitsópalo! They will pay me nothing! As soon as ever my collector goes to them all the Christians at once pretend to be Turks. The first cottage he enters, the owner, when asked his name, declares that he is Mohammed and his wife over there is Fatima; whilst the collector knows, though at the moment he may not be able to prove it, that this one is really George and the other is really Anna. Ah!" said the bishop, "dreadful, dreadful people!"

But this piece of ingenuity is crude and simple when compared with others which at times are resorted to for a similar purpose. In one town Mr. Matthews found that the amount of unpaid taxes was exceptionally and inexplicably large; and of these arrears he was told that the larger part was irrecoverable, and that he need not therefore trouble his head about them. The mystery was inquired into, and the names of the defaulters were produced. Then came to light this singular fact : all these men were aliens, and therefore were exempt from taxation. How, then did it happen that they had been assessed at all ? The answer was this : a certain gross sum was due from the town to the Government, and the townspeople, having engaged to pay this, were allowed to distribute the burden amongst themselves as they pleased. The lion's share had accordingly been at once laid on the aliens, who readily fell in with a plan from which they could not possibly suffer ; and in this pleasant way the liabilities of the natives had been halved.

Another town distinguished itself as follows. The inhabitants were desired by the Government to send in their own valuation of the house property that was to be taxed. A statement was accordingly presented duly to the commissioner. He looked at the total with astonishment. It was only £3000. He desired that the assessors should

be sent for ; and when they came he asked them
if they were satisfied that their valuation was
really correct. They said, " We certainly are. If
it errs at all it errs by being a little too high."
" Well," said the commissioner, " the matter is of
some importance. May I ask if you are prepared
to sign a paper to this effect ? " The assessors
drew themselves up with an air of virtuous hauteur.
" Sir," they replied, " on serious occasions like the
present, when we deliberately say a thing, we are
naturally ready to sign it." " Then in that case,"
said the commissioner quietly, again casting his
eye over the list of figures before him, " I shall,
under powers given me by the Government, take
over from you, for the purpose of public improve-
ments, a hundred of these houses ; and I will do
so at your own valuation, which you cannot complain of, as you have just told me that it is high
rather than otherwise. Here is the paper, gentlemen. Have the goodness to sign it." The
assessors started. For a moment they were
utterly silent. Then came a shuffling of feet, an
interlude of hemming and hawing, and then

stuttered excuses. "Well," said the commissioner blandly, "if you are not quite sure about the matter take a day to think it over. Come back to-morrow, and then you shall tell me the sum that will really satisfy you." The assessment by next day had risen from £3000 to £7000.

Some readers, perhaps, may think these anecdotes trivial. My own view is that they throw a great deal more light on that least trivial of subjects, the corporate character of the people, than volumes of scientific speculation on the future of man and of democracy. At all events here is one anecdote more, and it certainly can be called trivial by nobody. It is, indeed, hardly an anecdote; it is rather a piece of important constitutional history, which shows how democracy in Cyprus was within an inch of destruction, and how it saved itself.

The policy of the Cyprian patriots has been, from the beginning of the chapter, at once consistent and simple. It has been to oppose every scheme or suggestion, no matter what, that originated with the British authorities. The authorities for a long time had borne this treat-

ment with patience, when a measure was laid
by them before the Council which was not only
so obviously but also so urgently necessary that
no rational man could have two opinions about it.
When, therefore, the patriots, utterly undaunted,
proceeded to oppose it, just as they had opposed
the others, the Governor's patience fairly gave
way at last, and he told them plainly that if this
sort of thing continued he should be obliged to
appeal to her Majesty to reconsider the constitution. The patriots were staggered ; they could
hardly believe their ears. They were like dreaming somnambulists, marching to imaginary con-
quests, who had been suddenly wakened by coming
into collision with a wall. To reconsider the
constitution they knew could mean only to
abolish it. They saw, therefore, that in this case
there was nothing for them to do but to drop
their opposition with as good a grace as possible.
But how was this to be done with any grace at
all ? That was the question. They could not
make themselves ridiculous in the eyes of their
chief supporters by voting for a measure which

they had been calling abominable yesterday. They accordingly hit at last on the following plan. When the day came on which the fate of the measure was to be decided, a number of those who opposed it were to keep away from the Council, just sufficient to allow of its being carried by a majority of one, the rest of the party declaiming against it as formerly. Everything was settled; but on the morning of the eventful day the patriots discovered that somehow they were still one too many. It was necessary, therefore, that one more of them should absent himself. Their choice fell on a gentleman whose name, if I recollect rightly, was Picrides, and he was told to suggest some pretext by which his absence might be accounted for. "Come," they said, "you can easily pretend that you are ill." "No, no," he said; "that will never satisfy my supporters. I live in Nicosia and I am known to be in robust health." "I have it," said some one. "Urgent business summons you, and in half an hour's time you must be on your way to Larnaca." This suggestion met with universal approval, Mr. Picrides

himself being as well satisfied with it as anybody.
But presently recollecting himself, " Bah, my
friends ! " he exclaimed, " you have forgotten one
thing ; you have forgotten the expense of travelling there and back. The double fare by the
diligence will come to full five shillings. Do you
expect me to pay that out of my own private
pocket ? Never. I go for the sake of my party,
and my party must pay it for me." At this the
other patriots looked extremely blank. " Very
well," said Mr. Picrides calmly, if you will not
pay for me I remain, and my country must take
the consequences. Awed by so much firmness,
the others at last gave in. Mr. Picrides was
given the sum required. He went for the day to
Larnaca. In his absence the measure was carried ;
and he thus stands alone in the annals of the
popular cause as a hero who engaged to save, and
who did save, a democracy, for no other reward
than the payment of his own expenses.

Stories take a colouring from the scenes
amongst which one hears them. These I heard
as, for a second time at twilight, we were driving

home from the spurs of Pentedactylon and were
speeding across the plain towards the walls and
minarets of Nicosia. The last time I had done
this I had been listening to the romance of the
past. Now, with equal entertainment, I had been
listening to the comedy of the present; and this,
though many of its details were modern and
prosaic enough, and indeed called to mind the
paragraphs of our own newspapers, was yet for
the most part so naïve and so whimsical that,
under the influence of surrounding associations, it
seemed to become insensibly part of the romance
itself. If it suggested our newspapers it suggested
them only as a certain bank of clouds, which came
floating over the mountains, suggested to my eye
a phalanx of Irish members. For a moment I
thought I saw the features of Dr. Tanner, about
to provoke the censure of some unseen Speaker in
the firmament; but just as he seemed on the
point of calling the stars "liars" the noiseless air
transformed him into a dignified, silent Turk,
whilst the body of his supporters, all prepared to
cheer him, softly melted together into a single

monstrous griffin. Then up from behind the mountains, closely following after them, came a giraffe and a camel, with necks as tall as steeples and heads like cotton-wool, dipped in the light of evening; and the whole aërial medley slowly floated and vanished into the darkening depths of the sky, at the edge of which the sunset was burning. And thus the politicians of contemporary Cyprus, instead of breaking the charm or disturbing the associations of their ancient Oriental island, merely added to them a new element of unreality. Their antics and tricks seemed to me, as I heard of them, to harmonise completely with the dream-like evening that then surrounded me. I remember its aspect still. The dome of the sky above was a transparent Prussian blue; lower down in the east it was clear like alabaster. One by one the golden points of the stars began to show themselves suddenly, as if they were being lighted. In the west the sunset at first was a brilliant orange; then this darkened into a deep stain of crimson, and against it black from the plain rose clusters of far-off palm trees.

CHAPTER XII

THE ETERNAL TRAGEDY

I WAS sorry to disturb the placidity of my life at
Nicosia by even a thought of leaving it ; but, as
there were other places which I was fully determined to visit, I had already settled with myself
what these places should be. Three of them, so
I found, lay not very far apart—the town and
castle of Kyrenia, the mountain castle of St.
Hilarion, and the mediæval monastery of Bella
Pais, which report said was wonderful. Accordingly, in the course of the next few days,
Colonel Falkland, to whom I explained my
wishes, procured for me an invitation to stay
with one of the district judges, Mr. St. John, who
lived within easy distance of all the three places
I have mentioned. Mr. St. John's official duties

would be shortly calling him from home, so he begged that, if I came, I would come as soon as possible. I had not expected quite so much hurry in the matter ; but, as hurry was necessary, it was arranged by an exchange of telegrams that I should go to him as soon as I could get a carriage to take me.

Meanwhile, in the single day that intervened, I underwent an experience entirely new and unexpected. I came down to breakfast, idly thinking over the stories which I have been just confiding to the reader. Little did I know, whilst I was smiling at the comedy of the island, that I was going in an hour or two to be introduced to its tragedy.

There was an old building in Nicosia which had once been a caravanserai, and which, some one told me, the Turks had used as a prison. I had several times been struck by its picturesque appearance, by its external arcades, by its deep and shadowy gate, and by its gray mouldering walls. Mrs. Falkland this morning greeted me with the pleasant intelligence that a certain

Captain O'Flanagan, who occupied some post of authority, had promised to come at eleven o'clock to fetch us and show us over it, as it still was Government property. The Captain arrived duly—a tall, handsome Irishman, buoyant and almost bounding with the proverbial spirits of his nation. I was somehow disappointed to learn from this sprightly gentleman that the building was a prison still, and that a body of police were quartered in it. The rascality of the natives, so far as I had heard of them, was, it is true, almost as idyllic as innocence; so I had no fear of being introduced to an Oriental Newgate : but the sight of a sergeant and three or four subordinates, whom we found standing under the arch to receive us, quite dispelled my prospect of rambling over the precincts as I pleased. There was a good deal of military saluting, and then an unlocking of gates, and we passed into an open court, even more picturesque than I had anticipated. It was surrounded by two stories of cloisters, with the usual pointed arches, and in the middle was a miniature mosque with a cupola. The upper cloisters were reached by several graceful staircases; against the wall of the mosque was a fountain, gray with age; and quaint stone shoots for discharging the rain water protruded all round from the top of the walls like cannon. The ground-floor on one side was occupied by vaulted stables opening into the external arcades, which had originally caught my attention.

The imagination peopled the place with antique Oriental travellers; but I had soon seen enough of it, and I thought we were all departing when I found that, besides the prison, we were going to be shown the prisoners. I had myself no wish whatever to see them, but the others were more curious; and Captain O'Flanagan, whose hilarity rose with the occasion, seemed as anxious to show them to us as if they were pet monkeys.

Accordingly a gate was unlocked at the foot of one of the staircases, and we mounted to the upper cloisters. I had expected to find a few poor creatures in corners, far apart from each other and looking more like hermits than prisoners. To my astonishment the cloisters, from

end to end, were crowded. Rows and groups of
human beings, with the warm sunlight falling on
them, were standing or sitting, engaged in various
occupations. Some were boot-making, some were
rope-making, some were sewing soldiers' trousers.
They were of all ages, from the age of gray hairs
to boyhood; and the chief effect they produced
on me, as I watched them quietly at their work,
was wonder that such harmless-looking people
should be in prison at all.

I lost no time in inquiring what were their
offences. As to four men and two youths in
succession, I received the same answer, " Sheep-
stealing." That was just as it should be. It was
a pastoral and picturesque offence; and I was
glad to think that they were expiating here in
the sunlight instead of in their cells, whose dark,
grated apertures were gaping just behind them
like the cages of wild animals.

We had advanced some way, and I had been
standing still for a moment to watch a wistful-
eyed boy—a little fellow of fourteen—who was
working diligently with a sewing-machine, when,

turning to continue our progress, I saw something
move in the gloom of the cell close to me.   I
looked in through the bars ; but in a second I
withdrew my eyes, for they had encountered those
of a miserable human being.   I called to Captain
O'Flanagan, who was in the middle of an Irish
witticism, as, with another of our party, he was
peering into the cell adjoining, and asked him
of what the man I had just seen was guilty.   He
consulted a scrap of paper posted against the wall
with the prisoner's name and offence on it, and
placidly said, " Murder."   We passed on, and I
now began to realise that half of these cells, which
I had thought empty, were tenanted ; and we
were constantly invited to pause before this one
or that one, exactly as if we were being taken
round a menagerie.   Some of the forms within
looked hardened and desperate enough, and there
was a certain grim satisfaction in seeing that the
iron had closed on them ; but for the most part
it seemed to me, as I glanced reluctantly into the
shadow, that their aspect betokened a humble,
lamentable resignation, as if some weight had

fallen on them, they knew not how nor whence,
and they could only bear it with the amazement
of dumb animals. At these poor creatures I was
unable to look steadily. One instinctively turned
away from them with the reverence due to sorrow.
And yet from time to time I could not help
inquiring what this man or what that man had
done to bring him here. I could hardly believe
my ears when my questions, one after the other,
with a sinister sameness, met with the answer,
" Murder." Here and there was somebody who
had only robbed with violence ; in one cell was
a forger, and in another was a veteran pirate ;
but murder seemed to preponderate over every
other crime. I expressed my surprise at this to
the sergeant, an intelligent Englishman. He
answered, shrugging his shoulders, " I saw you,
sir, stop just now to look at a little boy. That's
one of our specimens ! He's here for murder
too ! " " That boy ! " I exclaimed. " I suppose
it was an accident that took place in a quarrel ? "
" Not a bit of it," said the sergeant. " He and
a friend of his, of the same age as himself, had

15

some grudge against another boy. They waited
for days and days, till that boy was alone, and
they strangled him with a couple of boot-laces,
which they had knitted together for the purpose."
As I listened to all this, whilst we slowly made
our progress, all the air seemed to grow sickly
round me, and to come to my nostrils tainted
with blood and sorrow. The prisoners at work
in the sunlight were most of them tolerable
objects; but these black cells, with the guilty
eyes within, which one felt, without looking at
them, were gleaming at one out of the shadow—
the sense that these were close to us became
soon intolerably painful. I drew a long breath
when I found myself once again in the street;
and I was glad to learn, since it seemed we were
to make a morning of it, that the rest of our time
was to be given up to the Konak.

As I passed again through its silent vaulted
guard-rooms, as I again looked at the beauty of
the crumbling window over them, and caught
through a broken arch a breath of the hiding
violets, I was conscious of an effect like that felt

by the nerves when something cool is laid on
a head that is physically aching. I mentioned
to Captain O'Flanagan that I had seen the place
before. " Ah !" he said, " but you couldn't have
seen half of it." I at once found that this was
true ; for whilst he was in the act of speaking
we were being introduced to a scene that was
certainly quite new to me. It was a small,
irregular yard, surrounded by mean outhouses,
much like the yard of a dirty farm-house in England. There was a pump in the middle of it ;
on the ground were some earthenware basins ;
here and there was a heap of kitchen refuse, and
our noses were soon saluted by an odour of warm
cooking. At the sound of our voices a door
presently opened, and a woman emerged, whose
proportions were those of a female Falstaff. With
a rolling gait she advanced a few paces towards
us, and then, perceiving Captain O'Flanagan and
the sergeant, she turned round and preceded us
into a kind of kitchen. Through this we passed
into a whitewashed passage ; the female Falstaff
opened a door at the end of it, and we found

ourselves in a bare room, with windows high up in the walls, confronted by a party of fourteen or fifteen women. I asked some one near me what these women were doing here. "Don't you know?" was the answer. "They are some of the female prisoners."

The horrors of the day, then, were not ended yet. We had left one prison merely to enter another. I faced the situation, however, and examined the faces before me. A part were young, but the larger part seemed old—wrinkled, and dejected, and suggesting nothing but compassion—all but one; amongst them was one exception. This was the face of a hideous, bleareyed crone, who was almost bent double, and, with hands pressed against her stomach, peered up at us, showing her red eyelids, with an expression of cringing wickedness. Never in my life had I seen a face at once so miserable and so evil. "And what," I asked, "has she done?" I anticipated the answer. It was the old story, "Murder." But there was more to follow. This old woman, I learned, had caused the death, not

of her victim only, but of two other men besides.
She had hired three to assist her in her deliberate
deed, and two of them had been hanged, whilst
the sentence of the third had been commuted.
The old woman's sentence had been commuted
also—perhaps in consideration of her great age
and feebleness—but if justice in this case demanded the extreme penalty the debt had been
paid practically not once, but many times.   At
the beginning of her imprisonment the old woman
had a fever; and in her delirious sleep she was
continually waking up, clutching her wizened
throat, and imagining that the rope was round
it.   Turning away from her, I saw amongst the
medley of criminal faces, a little creature looking
at us with soft coal-black eyes.   This was a baby
that had been lately born in the prison.   It lay
in its mother's arms, surrounded by squalor, and
by calamity ; but already its small nails had been
made pink with henna, and a rude care had
darkened it under its eyes with kohol.   Were all
the seeds of the full-grown evil near it, sleeping,
ready to sprout in this half-conscious seedling ?

There was one experience more, and the night-mare of the morning was ended. From this prison of criminals we were taken to an adjoining building ; and there, in a double row of sunless, silent cells, we were shown the lunatics. There were not many of them. One and all they were old. Each was alone, and if they had not moved occasionally they might almost have passed for parts of the dilapidated walls confining them. I could not learn anything about the past lives of any of them, but, judging from their battered aspect, all of them must have long been familiar with some form of misfortune. If this were the case, for one thing they were to be congratulated on their present condition ; for madness had taught them what sanity could not teach them —to smile.

At luncheon Colonel Falkland questioned me as to what I had seen. I was glad to thrust away from me the oppressive feelings that had been caused by it, and get about one or two points a little practical information. I remarked on the apathy with which the prisoners, those

even in the cells, seemed to bear their confine-
ment. "Yes," said Colonel Falkland, "and some
of them—though not all—go to the gallows with
as little apparent feeling. As for the mere con-
finement, so long as it is not solitary, I doubt
if they mind that. They like doing nothing, and
they are able to talk with their companions.
Solitude, without tobacco, is the thing that they
really dread. I suppose," he added, "that of the
prisoners you saw to-day, not more than one
or two, even if any, were solitary?" That was
true; and I asked why, if such was their feeling,
the worst of them were not given the only punish-
ment they could appreciate. Colonel Falkland
said that this was at present impracticable, for
the simple reason that the prison did not admit
of it. Packed as the prisoners were, even now
there was hardly room for them, and the Government had not a penny with which to enlarge the
building. "But why," I asked, "need they all be
sent to Nicosia? Are there no old prisons in the
other parts of the island? And does Cyprus,
with its handful of 160,000 inhabitants, really

contribute the whole throng I have been looking
at ?"   "Without a doubt," said Colonel Falkland,
"there are other prisons in Cyprus—a prison in
every district; but each of these is just as
crowded as this.   You ask if all the prisoners
you have seen come from Cyprus.   Every
one of them comes from the single district of
Nicosia."

Ever since that morning a veil had been drawn
across the sun for me; and now, as I listened,
the day grew darker still.   One of my Cyprian
dreams—of my happy dreams—had been broken :
and it was a dream which till to-day I had always
taken for a reality.   I had imagined that, in spite
of their petty, bizarre rascalities, these islanders
knew little of the more monstrous horrors of life.
I had taken pleasure in noticing the honest faces
of the peasantry, and their frank smiles, when
one exchanged greetings with them on the road.
I had heard much of their readiness to offer
hospitality or help to strangers, and of the firm
but gentle pride with which they always refused
any payment for it.   I now learned that in this

island of Cyprus there was more crime, in proportion to the number of its inhabitants, than in
any other known country in the world.

I asked from what classes the criminals mostly
came, in especial the murderers, and how the
murders arose. From what I was told I derived
a little comfort. In the towns the Turkish murders nearly always originate in some ordinary fit
of sombre but sudden passion, and the Greek
murders in some half-drunken brawl. A number
of these last have taken place at weddings. Wine
has flowed ; quarrelling has risen out of laughter ;
knives have flashed, and in a second or two one
knife has been red. In the country districts
the cause has generally some connection with
sheep-stealing, or disputes about boundaries and
water rights, or matters equally simple. I saw,
however, that this explained a part of the case
only. Blood was shed in ways that left darker
stains than these. One father whose son had
been sent to prison for stealing considered that
the lad had brought disgrace on his family, and
deliberately murdered him on the day he was set

free.   I had already seen a boy and an old woman whose crimes had been as cold-blooded and premeditated as crimes could be; and now Colonel Falkland told me that at this moment at Kyrenia three men were under sentence of death for a murder of which the only motive was robbery, and which had been planned for days and had been resolved on for weeks beforehand.

And yet, even among these dark clouds, a touch of whimsical simplicity stole like a faint thread of light, and relieved my mind by at last justifying a laugh.   One of the three men whom I have just mentioned fled, after the murder, to the hut of a lonely shepherd, and begged to be kept there in hiding.   The shepherd, who had only a slight acquaintance with him, asked why he wished to be hidden.   On this the murderer, more like a child than a man, explained everything in the most naïve manner possible.   The shepherd looked grave.   He said that this was a serious matter, and that under the circumstances his protection would have to be paid for.   The murderer replied that the booty had not yet been divided. "I have no money," he said, "but save me, and I will steal a sheep for you."

With this anecdote Colonel Falkland left me. He went to his office, and I sat in the garden alone, feeling as if the burden of life, which I thought I had left in England, had again laid its hands on me, like a bailiff on an absconding debtor. This mere dejection, however, which was after all useless, in time gave way to reflections that were more profitable. I thought of our modern Radicals, of our sentimental believers in the natural goodness of man, and of what a lesson these people might learn from Cyprus. Here were no wicked plutocrats, no hereditary aristocracy. The merchant princes and the nobles of the Middle Ages had gone. They had not left even the memory of their names behind, and modern times had produced no class to replace them. The larger part of the population owned the larger part of the soil. They worked by themselves and for themselves. They had no example except their own to corrupt them, and no oppression except that of the necessary tax-gatherer. They lived, in fact, under the Radical's ideal conditions; and yet crimes, which included crimes of the most brutal and degraded character, occurred amongst them with a frequency not to be matched in any country of aristocratic and capitalistic Europe. Surely this in itself is enough to show how false, or at best how insufficient, is the theory, that the wickedness of the many is caused by the artificial oppressions of the few.

If a man wishes to ensure the bad opinion of others, his best course probably is to be honest about himself. At the risk of achieving this result, though I do not profess to be anxious for it, I am going to indulge in a piece of honesty here. I am going to confess that the foregoing obvious moral, being at the expense of people with whom I specially disagree, if it did not exactly reconcile me to the miserable facts that suggested it, at least made me look at them in a less lugubrious light. In the middle of this mood a slight sound disturbed me. I looked round, and there—with her feet on a bed of violets—was poor Metaphora, blowing her nose in her petticoat.

Poor Metaphora! She seemed to reconcile me to everything. She again supplied us at dinner with unfailing amusement, and afterwards Colonel Falkland, when we were smoking our cigarettes together, asked me if I ever had heard this strange creature's history. I had not, and so he told it to me. "Metaphora was once in prison," he said. "Metaphora was tried for murder. Yes," he went on, "I can see what I say surprises you. What happened was this. Some years ago, just before we came here, she— she was hardly fifteen—was seduced by a Turkish official. She had twins, and both of the twins were murdered. She was accused of the crime and tried for it, but medical evidence showed her to have been at the time so weak that she could not have committed it—it was a physical impossibility. The real criminal was most probably her mother. Anyhow, the event for the time—and I am sure it is no wonder—quite deranged the poor girl's faculties, and to this day she has never quite recovered them. So the other night," he added, "when Mrs. Falkland called her half-witted, what she said had more truth in it than perhaps at the time you thought."

This was enough, and more than enough, to make the morbid clouds of dejection, which had only partially lifted, once more descend on me. "And so," I said to myself, "this delightful city of Nicosia—this city of dreams and peace—is haunted by all the plagues and all the sorrows of London, and the lightest and silliest laughter to which one goes for refuge has its hidden roots in an unnatural pool of blood." As I went to bed, and for some hours tried vainly to sleep, the air seemed heavy and oppressive as if charged with thunder, and I was pleased to think that on the following day I was going to escape to new, even if not very distant, scenes.

CHAPTER XIII

A VILLA AMONGST THE MOUNTAINS

OUR generation, accustomed to rapid travelling, is apt to think of the times when railways were not as if they were divided by some great gulf from our own. My own impression is, that if railways vanished to-morrow we should, as mere travellers, soon become reconciled to the change. In Cyprus I was able to put this impression to the proof, for the conditions of travelling there are just what they were in England, I do not say merely before the first railway was made, but a generation and a half before the first railway was thought of. The roads for the most part are such that, except for the shortest journey, an ordinary carriage requires from three to five horses, and the distance, reckoned in time, from one place to another is just what it was in England in that seemingly remote period when Reading was as far from London as Edinburgh is now.

This was all brought home to me vividly the following morning. Mr. St. John's house was hardly sixteen miles from Nicosia, and yet the coachman had sent me a message, to say that with four strong horses we should be four hours in getting to it. I had arranged accordingly to start as early as possible. The air, as I came downstairs, was fresh and crisp in the garden, and touched my face with the effect of a mental tonic. I had only half done breakfast when Scotty came to inform me that the carriage was at the door, and that all the luggage was in readiness. The entire household assembled to see me start, including Metaphora, who frisked, and grinned, and giggled. There, in the narrow street, was the battered and dusty vehicle with my portmanteaus tied behind to it like a lady's dress-improver, and a tribe of Turkish children staring at the imposing spectacle. It was a vehicle of curious pattern. It resembled a barouche, surmounted by the

canopy of a four-post bed, the curtains of which
were drawn close at the head and foot, and tied
back with ragged tape at the sides. As I entered
it I had a glimpse of four sinister horses ; Scotty
climbed laboriously to a high seat by the driver,
and we started to the sound of a whip that made
all Nicosia echo. Our pace was surprisingly—
indeed I thought dangerously — good, as we
whirled round corners and sent goats and
Oriental figures flying, and before many minutes
we were out in the open country.

There, under the blowing breath of the wide
Cyprian morning, the last remnants of dejection
fluttered away like cobwebs. I have already
spoken often of the magic of this marvellous air,
and it is tiresome to be speaking of the same
thing continually ; but, though the air may be the
same thing, the effects of it were never the same.
Every landscape in the island it made like a live
chameleon, always iridescent with melting and
changing colour ; and what it did to the mind
was every bit as various. To those who despair
of ever being really happy in life—by which, I

16

suppose, I mean two classes of men, those who are familiar with thought, and those who are familiar with pleasure—when at any time thought or pleasure has taught its lesson to them anew, to such men I would say : " Try breathing the air of Cyprus." As for myself, what I felt when I submitted to its charm that morning was a buoyant calm, on which complaisant meditation floated, and in which the immediate future cast pleasant reflections.

The road, it is true, was at first not interesting, as for many miles it lay over a perfectly dead level, with hardly a cottage or a palm tree to break the monotony of the prospect. For a mile or two outside Nicosia it was in very tolerable order, but after that it rapidly got worse. In several places it was little more than a track only too well indicated by ruts in the hardened mud, and then from hardened mud it would change to shelving sand. The movements of the carriage changed their character accordingly. The commonplace briskness and smoothness with which we started now became a slow laborious jolting,

or else, where the sand was, a kind of muffled
crunching and plunging that was slower and more
laborious still. Then it was that thoughts of our
old-fashioned English travelling came crowding
into my mind ; and I had the satisfaction of feeling that, so far as travelling went, I was living in
the England of eighty or a hundred years ago.
I asked myself how this affected the aspect of
daily life. Did it make me conscious of any
want—of the loss of any ordinary convenience?
Not in the least. The very idea of railways had
almost faded from my mind, and without any
regret, or comparison, or sense of irksomeness,
I had come to regard post-chaises as the most
natural means of travelling. And how did this
affect my conception of distance? Did it make
near places seem remote and remote places inaccessible? No—not in the sense of producing
any feeling of practical helplessness. I felt as
able as if I were in England to get from one
place to another. The only difference was that
it seemed to me as if the landscape were larger
and all its far perspectives were softly and inde-

finitely deepened. Railways and steamers may
perhaps widen the mind, but they do so at the
cost of making the world smaller.

This train of reflection was in due time interrupted by our arrival at a village, where the horses
stopped to rest themselves ; and in place of reflecting I now began to observe. All the boys
and the dogs assembled to stare and bark at me ;
and presently there came to my ears, I could not
tell from where, a sound which I recognised as
the Syrian wailing for the dead. Beyond the
village a quite new sight presented itself, and this
was a green common dotted with clumps of rushes,
its grass being as close and fine as any that could
be found in England. Here and there about it
ran a few little threads of rivulets : it was another
example of the power of water over the Cyprian
soil.

Beyond the common I found myself at the
base of the mountains, or rather of a number of
low outlying hills, which resembled nothing so
much as so many heaps of mud shot here at
random by the carts of Titan scavengers, and

which not even the air of Cyprus could prevent
from being frankly hideous. Up these and
amongst these we now began to toil. The road
itself was little more than a ledge, rudely cut
along the sides of intricate slopes, and was constantly dangerous, without ever being impressive.
But at last we rose to the slopes of what may be
properly called the mountains ; and high in front
of us a gash in the gray sky-line marked the pass
which looked down upon Kyrenia. And now
beauty began once more to show itself. To the
left were peaks upon peaks whose forms and
names were unknown to me, and some twelve
miles off to the right were the familiar summits
of Pentedactylon. The road now was in far
better condition. Huge limestone boulders glittered on either side of it, between them were tufts
of myrtle ; and soon, as we mounted higher, all
the stony slopes and scarred sides of the gorges
were green with the fairy spires of a far-reaching
infant pine forest. The ascent was so slow that
I got out and walked some way. New aromatic
smells seemed to be abroad in the air. I looked

back, and below me were the plains of Nicosia like a sea, with Nicosia itself like a vague dim circle in the middle of them. Short as the distance was that I had really travelled, I had all the sensation of approaching a fresh country. The variety of travel is in the inverse proportion to the speed of it.

At last I topped the hill. I was there before the carriage, and I stood in the pass surveying the scene on the farther side. Its beauty exceeded every expectation I had formed. Some of its features indeed I had seen before on the ever-remembered day of my first search for the marble. There was the blue sea and the Cilician coasts beyond it; and nearer at hand was Kyrenia at the water's edge, like a water-lily. But there was another beauty which completely took me by surprise. This was a sudden luxuriance, a sudden exuberance, of vegetation. The pines were no longer saplings. There were strong and stalwart groves of them; nor was theirs the only foliage that filled and fascinated my vision. To right and left the mountains from their topmost pin-

nacles fell in a succession of varied and indented
slopes to shadowy valleys a thousand feet below
them ; and all the steep sides of these silvery
amphitheatres were dotted with a multitude of
dark-green climbing caroub trees.   Before me in
crumpled curves was the road descending into the
distance, sometimes hidden in a cutting, sometimes
by a projecting rock, and again reappearing on
the brink of some folded hollow; and every
hollow and valley, so far as my eye could distinguish, was green and soft with a crowd of
various leafage.   Near me in a gorge were the
tops of a thicket of oleanders, on a ledge a little
way off was a large slender acacia, and on the
lower levels, though all details vanished, I recognised the green of grass and a medley of terraced
olive-yards.

Mrs. St. John's house was, I knew, some way
out of Kyrenia, but I knew no more than that
either of its locality or its situation.   Scotty,
however, with a wag of his head towards the
coachman, had already said to me, " Right, sir.
This fellow, he know."   So when, overjoyed with

the prospect, I again entered the carriage, I re-
signed myself without anxiety to the passive
pleasures of expectancy. We had not, however,
proceeded for more than half an hour—we were
still amongst the mountains, and Kyrenia was still
far below us—when the coachman stopped his
horses, and Scotty, scrambling down, came to me
and said with a certain air of apology, "This
fellow, he ask is it this house you want to go to?"
"What does he mean?" I exclaimed, when I got
out and looked about me. "Where is the house?
I can see no house anywhere." The road at the
spot where we had halted was beginning to grow
steep, and was curving round the sides of an
acclivity which below lost itself in a gorge, and
above, covered with myrtles, seemed to rise to a
lofty plateau. Here a sandy and most uninviting
track branched off, and at some impossible angle
ran upwards and lost itself in the leafage. "Where
is the house?" I repeated as soon as I had looked
round me. Scotty pointed to the track and said,
"This fellow say it there." Seeing me look incredulous, he added with more firmness what he

might, one would think, have as easily said at the beginning, "That where the judge lives; the driver, he know it well." "Can he drive up?" I asked. "Yes, sir," said Scotty. "Get in, sir." I got in, still feeling somewhat doubtful, and the four horses, in a way that was truly marvellous, took the ascent with the activity and enterprise of goats. Their pace, however, was soon quenched by the sand, and a moment or two later I heard Scotty's voice calling to me, "I think, if you please, sir, the gentleman he here."

I got out, and there, sure enough, to my great relief, was my host advancing to meet me. He was a youngish man, with all the air of a sportsman, and his smile was already a welcome, even before he opened his mouth. But the curious thing was this: in the place where I might have looked for a house I could see nothing but a white circular tent, which was shining and swaying on the very brow of a precipice. Mr. St. John directed the coachman to stop at this flimsy structure, and he and I began to walk up towards it. "Do you see that?" he said, with an air of enthusiasm. "There's not another like it in Cyprus. It's a real Damascus tent. Just wait till I show you the inside of it."

I went with him, hardly knowing if I were standing on my head or on my heels.

"If you'd only come," he resumed, "an hour earlier you'd have seen my tandem—two thorough-bred Arabs. That's right," he shouted to Scotty, "down with the luggage! and let him turn his horses there; it's the only place where he can turn." In another moment we were at the tent ourselves. My host lifted the hangings. "Look!" he said; "do you see the lining?—blue, crimson, orange. They only do that work at Damascus. Go inside; I'm quite sure you'll be pleased."

I entered, and he followed me. "Well," he exclaimed, pointing to what confronted us, "don't you call that perfect? To my mind it's beauti-ful!" I said that it was, and eyed it slowly and carefully. The object of our attention was a new English-built dog-cart, which had only arrived a few days ago, and which, together with the two thorough-bred Arabs, formed, for the present, the joy of their owner's heart. " Just now," he said, " I am rebuilding my coach-house, and meanwhile I keep this trap in the tent. The drive in front of the house is so blocked up by the masons that carriages can't turn there, and so they must stop here. Come, let us go up. I hope you don't mind a climb. It's nearly two o'clock ; I think you must want some luncheon."

Everything now wore quite a different look for me, and I felt that I was once more in a world of calculable circumstance. The ascent of my host's road was indeed an affair of climbing, and I shuddered at the thought of a carriage coming down round its frightful corners. Some twenty paces or so brought us in sight of the house. It stood on a height above us, surrounded with gorse and myrtle ; a habitation absolutely solitary, in a scene of leaf and precipice. In appearance it was a cross between a white English villa and a brown Swiss cottage, having the solid core of the first and the surrounding balconies of the second. It was a strange object in such a

place, but it was strange in a piquant and agreeable way, filling the air with a swarm of far-
fetched and subtle associations, which made one
feel bewildered as to where one was. The interior
completed this peculiar mental effect. The white
pavement of the passage, the walls, the chairs—
everything, instantly suggested the daintiest civilisation of England, simplified and etherealised by
the air of these lonely mountains. At home the
simplicity would have been probably called bare-
ness, but here it was exactly what the conditions
demanded. The carpets, from Karamania and
Smyrna, covered but half the floors; the beautiful
coloured matting in the bedrooms might have
seemed rough in London; but here such asceti-
cism of taste was the very refinement of luxury,
and harmonised, as none of our more elaborate
comforts could, with the flowers, the books, the
blue Vallauris vases, and the cascade of fairy-like
notes that chimed from a Bond Street clock.
Cyprus, in fact, gave a sense of remoteness to the
house; the house gave a sense of elusive civilisation to the mountains; and the warm air which

floated in through the windows seemed at once
as much at home and as strange in this exotic
dwelling, as if its walls had been the petals of
some unknown anemone which from some foreign
seed had blossomed up there out of the soil, half
a native and half an alien.

Such were the impressions which formed
themselves in my mind as I sat at luncheon, and
to which the luncheon contributed by its own
delicate simplicity, by its cold meats, its goats'-
milk cheese, its conserve of golden apricots, and
its jug of Cyprian wine. My host and his family,
of whom he presently spoke to me, had already
had their meal. The children, he said, under the
charge of the governess were somewhere in the
neighbourhood amusing themselves. Mrs. St.
John had gone out to look for them, and would
soon be back with the eldest two of the four. " I
tell you that," he proceeded, "because we have
been thinking this. You want, I know, to see
the Castle of St. Hilarion. It is on the mountain
directly behind the house. You can go there
easily this afternoon, and spend an hour there,

and, if you like it, Mrs. St. John and one of the boys will come with you. I have things to do myself, or else I would come also."

No proposal could have been more charming than this. Needless to say I jumped at it, and I was still expressing my satisfaction when a shadow darkened the window, and gliding past it was Mrs. St. John herself. She will, I know, not think it an impertinence if I venture to speak of her as slim and graceful, and to say that she seemed to me the moment she entered the dining-room like the embodied spirit of her house, as I have just tried to describe it.

CHAPTER XIV

THE CASTLE IN THE AIR

OUR expedition was soon arranged. Mrs. St.
John and her eldest boy would ride. I was
offered a mule, but I greatly preferred to walk.
In a quarter of an hour we were all of us setting
out, the boy on a white donkey, his mother on a
white horse. We scrambled through a breach in
a wall from the yard behind the house, up a
shoulder of hill, which at first was rough with
brushwood, but which higher up was under some
rude cultivation. Beyond this was a table-land,
also cultivated ; then a thicket of gorse ; then a
dip in the ground, ribbed with curving furrows
and crowned with a further thicket. The same
alternation went on repeating itself of rocky, bush-
grown ridges and rudely-cultivated hollows ; but

all the while we were, on the whole, ascending.
At last there opened before us a great gash in
the mountains, which showed us the sea and the
coast-line far below, and made us feel that already
we had climbed high into cloud-land. Our real
climbing, however, had not yet begun. On the
farther side of this opening rose a stupendous
cliff, which looked as though it were dizzy at its
own altitude and were on the point of hurling
itself down through the depths of the unobstructed
air. Scaling the side of this, amongst endless
rugged projections, there could just be traced a
pale faltering line, looking like an impossible
goat-track. I found it in another ten minutes to
be the track that we were to traverse ourselves.
On foot certainly it proved to be easy enough, but
it was so steep at its turnings, and everywhere so
rough, so narrow, and so littered with rolling stones,
that as I looked down into the aërial abysses
below me I confess I felt glad that I was on my
own feet, which were prudent, and not on those
of a horse like Mrs. St. John's, which pattered and
clambered upwards with an almost criminal levity.

When we reached the summit the view before us was this. The serrated summits of the mountains were running like a wall to our left, rising above us some four or five hundred feet ; and under their shadow, for several miles in front of us, there extended a sheltered valley, of which certain parts had been ploughed. On the outer edge of this, forming a sort of gorge, about half a mile off, rose a huge isolated rock, shelving in a savage abrupt way towards the mountains, but dropping towards the sea in a single appalling precipice. At a first glance its form struck me as curious ; at a second glance I saw that it was covered with masonry. What I had at first taken to be a number of natural crags, I found to be a row of towers, rising one above the other like a break-neck garret staircase, from a wall that climbed the eminence at an angle of forty-five. From the lower end of this wall other walls extended themselves, with other towers, enclosing a vast sloping area. On a shoulder of the rock towards the sea was a crowd of confused buildings, whose dark windows showed that the

17

interior was still not roofless ; and high above all was the summit, over whose seemingly inaccessible ledges crenellated walls peered, crowned with yet loftier towers.

And so this was the Castle of St. Hilarion ! I looked at it speechless with gratification. It could not have been better if it had been built after one of my own dreams. Indeed, as we traversed the valley, and came more and more nearly under it, what it suggested to me, with greater and greater vividness, was the fancy that it had been built after a dream of Gustave Doré's.

From the bottom of the valley up to the lowest buildings was a climb amongst clods and rocks of at least two hundred feet. This brought us to a line of long gray walls, broken at intervals by semicircular towers, and at one point flanked by a sort of out-work or barbican, through which we entered under an arch that had almost fallen. Wading through weeds, between broken walls and turrets, we presently found ourselves in the court, if that can be called a court which was so steep that it seemed about to fall on us. It was

mottled everywhere with thick brushwood and
gray stones that looked like natural boulders, but
which I saw presently were fragments of fallen
buildings. Then here and there, in lines that
were half obliterated, I detected amongst the
brushwood traces of broken walls; and it was
presently plain to me that what I have called
the court must originally have looked like a town,
built on a steep hillside. I had arrived at this
conclusion, when Mrs. St. John, who knew the
place, began to call my attention to one or two
of its details. She pointed out to me two dark
apertures, one in a level plot, the other in a bank
of rock. I examined the first, and I found that
a stone staircase led down to a series of vaulted
rooms. I examined the second. It led into a
great gallery, partly cut in the rock and partly
the work of masons. Here Mrs. St. John followed me, and high up in the walls she pointed
out to me a long series of rings. According to
architects, she said, this was the stable for camels,
and those were the rings to which were fastened
their halters.

Our next move was to clamber somewhat higher and make our way to the buildings below the summit. The approach to them was curious. It lay along the foot of the overhanging precipice, between the natural rock and the ruins of a lofty wall, which together with the rock had once formed a gallery. At last a small doorway admitted us to a vaulted vestibule, with stairs in it leading to upper and lower chambers. The disposition of these it is impossible to describe to the reader, for this reason if for no other, that I could not master it myself. I began my explorations by mounting. I came to a curious loggia, which exhibited three natural pictures through its three open arches—silvery mountain slopes on which pine trees showed like pigmies, the sea, and the unfathomable depths of country lying below. Then through some crooked passages and up some winding stairs, straying fortuitously, I came to a small chapel, with fragments of frescoes still clinging to the apse and with two priests' chambers leading out of it. Retracing my steps, I discerned, in spite of the twilight, that there were frescoes in

the passages also. Then there came more stairs,
more rooms and passages, and then I began
descending. At the door where we had entered
Mrs. St. John was waiting for me; and we now
took the steps that led to the lower regions.
Here was a crowd of heavily-vaulted rooms, with
small chinks for windows, through which the daylight glittered. Their number and variety of level
was all I had time to remark about them; and
then down some more steps, through a narrow
pointed doorway, we issued into the open air, and
I found myself on the most singular spot I ever
remember to have visited. It was a little grassy
triangular space of ground, bracketed out, on the
enormous seaward precipice, and seemed to have
been once a garden. Beyond it, also hanging on
the brink of the precipice, was an oblong building
with a flat grass-grown roof and an arched doorway; and again beyond this, on a sharp, projecting crag, was a mass of masonry, roofless, but
absolutely perfect, which a second glance showed
me was a colossal cistern. I entered the first of
these structures through some brushwood that

choked the doorway, and I found myself in a
suite of chambers with Gothic windows and beautiful groined roofs.   They had originally been six
in number, three above and three below ; but the
intermediate flooring had long since given way,
leaving, however, all the way round the walls a
ragged fringe of mosaic, eloquent of unknown
occupants.

When I came out, I seated myself with my
companion on the ground, and we looked about
us, contemplating the strange scene.   The part of
the castle through which we had reached this solitude now revealed to me a number of architectural
features—chimneys and gables, and traces of
high-pitched roofs, which reminded me of many a
baronial ruin in Scotland ; but what struck me
most was what I saw as I looked upwards.   The
sides of the rock above us, which seemed to rise
to the clouds, on every ledge showed fragments of
windowed walls, as if half of its sides had once
been cased with chambers, and over the brink
at the summit appeared an arch and a few
battlements.

I looked up at these last as if it were hopeless
to reach them, for the face of the cliff showed no
mode of ascent except the line of a sheep path
just traceable intermittently on masses of headlong
débris which had fallen amongst rocks and saplings. My surprise therefore perhaps exceeded
my pleasure when Mrs. St. John in the quietest
way in the world pointed to the very path and
proposed that we should go up it—a path on
which, so far as the eye could tell, a single false
step meant a helpless fall into eternity. Under
the circumstances, however, I put my fears in
my pocket. I was also intrepid enough to burden
myself with my camera, and with all the heroism
of which false shame is so prolific I proceeded to
lead the way. As for Scotty, poor man, climbing
was not his forte, and he looked so exhausted at
the very gates of the castle that I left him behind
to amuse himself by making tea for us, and several
times I had taken a backward glance at him
lighting a fire and wiping his brown face with his
jacket.

The ascent we were now engaged in, though

not less steep than it looked, was easier. At the summit we found the arch, whose top we had seen already, and this admitted us into a spacious quadrangle, of which two sides were formed by buildings, and two by natural rock, capped by towers and battlements. All the ground was a chaos of fallen building stones, amongst which were standing some fig trees, with far-spreading twisted branches, whilst grass grew with a soft luxuriance that surprised me, and massed in various groups was a sisterhood of secluded anemones. Across all this we passed to the farther side, as my companion had said that the sight of the place was there. And there I found it was. It was a long banquet hall, about seventy feet by twenty, of which both ends, vaulting and all, were perfect, but the middle completely ruinous. This hall formed the whole of one side of the quadrangle, and its outer wall was on the very brink of the precipice. Below were the tops of pine trees, that clung to ledge and crevice, and it would not have needed a strong arm to throw a stone that would have fallen 2,500 feet. Presently, looking

up through the broken roof, I saw that above it
was an upper story, roofless. "Come," said Mrs.
St. John, "you will like to examine that. Local
tradition calls it the Queen's Lodging." She took
me into the court, and I saw—what I had not
before noticed—a wide external staircase, by
which this upper story was reached. We
ascended the weather-worn stairs, which yet had
mouldings on their edge, and reached the broken
floor of these broken upper chambers. Overlooking the precipice there still remained several
of the beautiful windows by which they once were
lighted. The mullion of one and the tracery
above it were entire ; the others reared in the air
nothing but branching fragments: but each retained entire two stone seats in the recess formed
by it in the thickness of the wall, and in one of
these recesses Mrs. St. John and I sat down.
Leaning from the window, I examined the face of
the rock. So broken and irregular was this that
in many places the walls rested on arches flung
across rifts and chasms. The masonry seemed
like a chamois leaping from crag to crag, and

the whole place for a moment or two was like one of those dreams which end with the sleeper falling from some frightful and unimaginable height. I felt that it must all give way and send me descending into space with it.

By and by Mrs. St. John said meditatively, " What a work it must have been to build this ! It is supposed that the stones were brought up on the backs of camels, and the workmen must most of them have been slaves." As she said this a host of thoughts and images, which had been long latent in my mind, now made their shapes visible. I bethought me of the little I knew of the castle's history—that it was founded in the twilight of early Byzantine times ; that it was an ancient stronghold in the days of Isaac Comnenus ; that at his orders it surrendered to Richard Cœur de Lion ; that since then, as its architecture plainly showed, it had been enlarged and embellished by the kings of the house of Lusignan; and that finally the Venetians had, for strategical reasons, destroyed its strength by shattering its towers with gunpowder. Then came thoughts of what a life,

during the days of its glory, had been lived in it,
what a strange, hybrid civilisation had blossomed
here in mid-air. I seemed to see on the turrets
the banners of Western chivalry, with the lions of
the Lusignans and the sign of the Cross undulating on them, and then at the windows the flicker
of silken Asian curtains. I had visions of
Christian ladies going softly in a heathenish
splendour, which the Europe of that day would
have hardly credited ; of knights in velvet
doublets or flashing armour ; of priests and
princely bishops. Here from a chapel floated
a scent of incense, there from a balcony came
the sound of a tender lute and a love - song
in mediæval French ; and mixing with all these
images were others of an alien kind—strange
dusky forms in Oriental habiliments, some waiting like genii to do the bidding of their masters
in court, in ante-chamber, or on staircase, others
leading up the mountain pathways winding trains
of camels. Finally, my thoughts came winging to
the spot where I myself was seated, and busied
themselves with the dim forgotten queens, who

from the very seat I occupied, and out of that very window, must have often gazed down into the stupendous depths below.

The view was towards the sea, and beyond the lilac waters there were my friends the mountains of Asia Minor, which each time I looked at them had maddened my imagination. Framed in this Gothic window, cut by their Christian mullions, they seemed to me now to assume a new aspect. They were like the pagan world seen through the eyes of the Middle Ages and heard with its ears; and mixing with its litanies, psalms, and knightly love-songs came wafted across the waves the pipings of Pan and Marsyas.

Cilicia! Phrygia! As I looked I repeated the words to myself. In the smallest fragment of matter which the imagination can represent to us we learn from science that there are unnumbered atoms, and that these atoms are all of them in unceasing movement. So in some simple words there are tribes of meanings and of memories.

"We ought to be moving," said Mrs. St. John at last. "It will never do for us to be benighted

in these mountains." Her words restored me to
the present, with all its silence and solitude, and
put an end to that revel of dreams which had
just been making my mind a Field of the Cloth
of Gold.

But the waking was merely the waking from
one charmed existence to another. Far underneath us, between the mountain base and the sea,
lay a belt of groves and olive-yards, dotted with
gleaming villages, and fringed with little promon-
tories that ran into the waves like mulberry leaves.
From amongst these, as if from some submerged
world, up through the air came a musical tinkle
of goat bells and the miniature shouts of undistinguishable human beings. Around us the
ruined masonry enclosed an enchanted quiet.
Near us on the floor, which the queen's feet once
had trodden, lay the bleaching bones of a kid,
the remains of some vulture's feast. Nothing
that we could see moved, except the bells of some
near anemones, and a vulture itself overhead,
wheeling in slow circles.

We remained for a few minutes longer, that I

might take a photograph, and we then descended. In the lower court was Scotty, who had some tea ready for us, and having drunk it we made haste to be gone, as the light was already waning. We had reached without difficulty those lower regions of alternating thickets and plough-land which I have already mentioned, when suddenly, on a level space littered with stones and bushes, Mrs. St. John checked her horse and said we had missed our path. Scotty maintained that we were on the path we had come by; Mrs. St. John, however, remained certain of the contrary. We discussed landmarks and looked for them, and as we did so we realised how quickly the evening had fallen with its bewildering twilight. We retraced our steps for some distance; we tried another path, and then again another. For some time I had faith in Mrs. St. John's knowledge of the locality, but presently this failed me. There was indeed little to guide her. The mountains were nothing but dim, mysterious masses; the shape of the ground near us was all but lost in the obscurity, and all we could see was the shadows of dark bushes and endless multitudes of pale, glimmering stones.

"Come," said Mrs. St. John at last, "we must take the path by the valley. There is a mule track, which we are certain to find, leading down to the Kyrenia road." I had noticed this track as we went, and I willingly agreed to her proposal. It lay now about half a mile behind us; so we turned back towards it with all the expedition possible, I walking in front to examine the nature of the ground. Before long I heard a slight sobbing in my neighbourhood, and also a sound like the bleat of a plaintive sheep. I turned round and discovered that they both proceeded from Scotty. He was thoroughly frightened, and thought that we should never reach home again. "Sir, sir," he cried, "this is not the right way. The other I know he right. You and me, sir, we will go back by the other. Come, sir—you come, sir!" "What!" I exclaimed; "and, even supposing it is right, do you think that we can go and leave this lady and her little boy amongst the mountains?" "No, sir," said poor Scotty collapsing, " it is true, sir ; what you say is true, sir."

The mule track at last was reached. We were just able to distinguish it, but its headlong course gave it the aspect of a precipice. However, we went down it, though not without great difficulty, Mrs. St. John's white horse at the angle of every zigzag threatening to fall with its rider crashing into the darkness. At last our course became easier and more level, and at the same time came the first glimmer of moonrise. " Sir," exclaimed Scotty, "I know this mule path now. It take us, if we go with him, half way back to Nicosia." I too began to realise something of our whereabouts, and I could well believe that what Scotty said was true. The Nicosia road, which I had traversed only that morning, I could see like a dim line on the far side of the valley ; so, thinking anything better than a prolongation of our present ex- periences, I proposed that we should try to reach it by diving into the intervening hollow. I scrambled down the slope myself, feeling my way with my stick. The ground was better than I expected. I called to the others to follow. They did so. We had to explore every yard of the way ; but at last, after half an hour of wandering, stumbling, and considering, the road was reached, and we felt that practically we were at home again. In one sense we were not ; for we had still three miles to go. It was nearly nine before we were in-doors, and Mr. St. John, though by no means a nervous man, would hardly have been human if he had not felt anxious. But dinner and lamplight were all the more grateful after the toil, the solitude, and the dim bewilderment of the mountains, and we were all in excellent spirits when George, the Greek butler, whose English was remarkably good, brought the following news to his mistress : "You can," he said, "now have as much milk as you want. Achilles tells me that all the goats have kittens."

Achilles was the cook : Euripides blacked the boots. I heard both these facts before I retired to bed, and I believe that when I went to sleep I was still smiling at the thought of them.

CHAPTER XV

AN OLD-WORLD FORTRESS

WHEN I awoke next morning the breath of the spring breathed on me. My bedroom windows admitted me to a balcony, the roof of which hid from view the summits of the opposite mountains. All around was a multitude of green valleys and gorges, and below, at some two miles' distance, were the walls and windows of Kyrenia. Mr. St. John told me at breakfast that he was going there presently on business, and offered to drive me down with him, that I might look at the town and castle. I was delighted with this arrangement till the moment came for starting, when voices called to me to come down to the tent, and I not only recollected but actually saw the tandem. From the tandem I glanced at the road

—steep, with sharp curves, and bordered by a precipitous slope; and though Mr. St. John was really an excellent whip, I had not at that moment the least reason for knowing it. However, any fears on my part would have seemed to any one present not only a folly but a rudeness, so I took my place behind the two thorough-bred Arabs with the calmness of a French aristocrat starting on his way to the guillotine.

I derived some comfort from the fact that we went with extreme slowness, and that a groom walked in front to take care of us round the corners; but when we were once in the public road, and the leader's head was satisfactorily turned towards Kyrenia, this guardian genius jumped up behind, and it seemed, as I looked before me, as if we had nothing between ourselves and eternity. The road was a steep zigzag, which no English coach would have descended without necessity. It was formed in many places by blasting the sides of a precipice, and below it all along were the abysses of a deep ravine. The appearance of it was hardly, in my eyes, mended by my host's conversation. "Just look at that leader," he said as the animal gave a frisk. "He was never in harness till ten days ago. He's a very high-couraged horse, but see how steady he goes. Whoa, boy! whoa, boy! Where are you going, stupid?" This last exclamation was caused by a sudden bolt which the high-couraged horse made towards the edge of the precipice. "Ah," said Mr. St. John in explanation, "just there is a mule path, and whenever he sees one he's sure to try to go off on it." Whilst I was mentally congratulating myself on this escape from destruction the genial voice at my side kept begging me to confess that "after all there was nothing like a tandem;" and for the third time I was assenting, when, turning sharply round a horrible corner, we found ourselves confronted by a straggling procession of camels. The high-couraged leader shied across the road; the idiotic camel-driver shouted and brandished his long pole, and danced about madly like a cross between a child and a devil. The groom jumped down, and rushed to the leader's head, and treated the camel-driver to what I trusted was a volley of oaths. The camels defiled past, and presently we were on our way again. " Capital ! " said Mr. St. John. " Did you notice what luck we had ? If we had not happened to be on the wrong side of the road, ten to one that fool with his pole would have sent us bundling over. Now," he continued, " we're almost down on the level. From here — you see — I will spin you into Kyrenia in no time."

To my great relief the road was from this point admirable. A gentle incline led to a long straight avenue, bordered with olive trees ; and the fields on either side looked like a succession of fruit gardens. At the end of the avenue was the court-house with a sycamore tree in front of it, under which were a number of people waiting for the doors to be opened. I trust our arrival created a deep sensation amongst them. If it did not the fault was, I must say, wholly theirs.

Here Scotty was awaiting me ; and leaving Mr. St. John to a morning of official duties, I wandered off in the direction of the sea and of the castle.   My way took me past a ruined church and a mosque, and brought me to a wall overlooking the town and harbour.   The town was little more than a single esplanade, curving prettily round a miniature port.   The houses were all of stone, and were most of them neatly whitewashed, and had it not been for several strange features, I could almost have fancied it a fishing town in Jersey or in Cornwall.   One of these features was the collection of outlandish craft in the harbour, little lean misshapen schooners, mostly from Asia Minor ; another was a Greek campanile ; and another, which I might not have seen if I had not already been told of it, was a row of white posts on the quay, for securing the ships' cables.   They were columns of snowy marble, taken from a temple of Venus.

Whilst I was studying this scene, the castle was directly behind me, separated from the road on which I stood by a deep artificial ditch.   It was the last building at that end of the town, and its sea-ward walls had their base splashed by the breakers.   I had already seen it from a distance,

and its aspect I had not thought interesting. It
was simply a square, plainly of great size, with
bastions at three of its corners, and a round tower
at the fourth. It seemed, indeed, to be less a
castle than a fortress. But, now that I turned to
look at it near at hand, I found it impressive in
a way I had not expected. I knew that it dated
from the days of the Byzantine emperors, and
that, though since their time it had been enlarged
and altered, the last hands to touch it had been
those of Venetian masons, four hundred years
ago. Such being the case, what first struck me
with wonder was the utter absence of any sign of
decay; and then my mind was filled with the
mass and the perfection of the masonry. The
walls, from the ditch to their summit, were seventy
feet in height, and from bastion to bastion their
length was four hundred feet. In the whole
expanse there was not a single window. It was
perfectly blank except for one rib of moulding,
for a multitude of loopholes pierced at the top
for musketry, and for an ominous line of rare
oblong apertures, with low arches like half-lifted

eyelids, behind each of which a cannon once was vigilant.

Besides these, there was but one other opening —a single narrow door not far from the sea, reached originally by a drawbridge, but now by an arch of stone. The English Government has used the castle as a prison ; I had therefore been obliged to provide myself with an order to visit it. This was inspected by a sentry, who was basking on the bridge ; and Scotty and I passed on into the building. The door admitted us to a dark vaulted passage, about twelve feet in height and perhaps of equal breadth. For the first twenty feet it was level, then it turned an angle and ascended for sixty feet by a gentle slope towards the light. Midway was a locked iron gate, by which sat a man whose face and whose European clothing plainly bespoke him some one of superior station. He asked me, in perfect English, if I wished to see the castle, and called a sentry, who promptly gave us admittance. I had not expected to find there an official of so much education, and was greatly pleased when he put himself at my disposal as a guide.

The inclined passage had brought us into a a small court, surrounded by massive buildings in a state of excellent preservation. On one side of it were two arched recesses, large enough each to shelter a couple of large waggons; opposite to them another incline led to some upper chambers; before us was a Gothic doorway, which admitted us into a shadowy hall; and through this we passed into the central court of the fortress. The general plan of the whole was now at once evident. Halls and chambers originally had extended all round it, touching the outer walls; but on two sides they were partly ruinous. The ruins, however, were of a very instructive kind, for they showed one a section of many of the old interiors. The whole of one side had been built in high compartments, with thick walls and heavily vaulted roofs, and each compartment had been divided by wooden floors into three stories. These, my guide told me, had been the mediæval barracks. I asked

him if the place had been simply a place of
strength. "No," he said, "it was a palace also;
and that stone staircase, which now leads to
nothing, is said originally to have led to the
queen's quarters." When he said this we were
on the ramparts, and the great court was below
us. He pointed out to me some enormous sub-
terranean cisterns, which a number of prisoners
were clearing of ancient rubbish that had choked
them, and also the foundations of buildings by
which formerly parts of the court must have been
occupied. Amongst these was a great hall of
state, of which one wall, with its corbels, was
still existing. I was then taken to some of the
prisoners' cells, fortunately empty, and then to
the prisoners' kitchen. The lofty mediæval groining was here perfect and beautiful, and the ribs
sprang from shields carved with the lions of the
Lusignans. "And now," said my guide, "you
would like to visit the chapel. It is Byzantine
and very curious." We crossed the court to an
opposite angle of the castle, and entered a quarter
full of ancient chambers. The chapel was reached

by a dark stair and a passage. In form it was a stunted cross, with four semicircular apses, and it was lit by an aperture in a dome that covered the centre. There were traces of frescoes still on the broken plaster, and the floor was still half covered with the old tesselated pavement.

And now there awaited me sights of a different order. I had heard already of the galleries which used to contain the cannon; and when I mentioned them to my guide, he at once said he would show them to me. When we regained the court, he called to a sentry for a candle, and, furnished with this, he took me to a black arch in a wall, which proved to be the mouth of a steeply descending tunnel. At the bottom of this was one of the galleries in question. The floor was slimy with mud, which had been washed down the tunnel from above; but this mud was the only sign of disuse—I might almost say the only suggestion of antiquity. The buildings I had just been visiting had the brown tints of time on them; age had written its wrinkles on corbels and arch and column; and there were everywhere traces of mediæval irregularity in the architecture. But here the cut stones were smooth as the brow of youth. The pointing was perfect; four hundred years had done nothing to it; every arch was symmetrical, and the gallery ran straight as an arrow. Nothing was wanting but the cannon, and a sufficient ignorance of engineering, to make one suppose that one was standing in some fort just built by the English, and just described by Mr. Labouchere as a waste of the people's money, and not under arches that had echoed their last to gunpowder before the Spanish Armada ever set sail for England. The castle above, like most ancient buildings, carried one away out of the present into the soft mystery of the past. This gallery, which was only one out of many, seemed to summon the past into the hard light of the present.

And yet, when I rose again to the brilliance of the blue Cyprian sky, and saw around me the silvery Cyprian mountains, and near me the bloom of the sea from whose foam Aphrodite rose, the charm of dreamland fell again over everything;

and I said to the passing moment again, "Stay, thou art so fair."

It is true that I could see near me the unhappy prisoners at their work. But I could do no good by thinking of them, so I did not let them trouble me, and I had forborne purposely asking my guide any questions about them. This visit to a prison was, I said to myself, very different to the one which had darkened for me a whole day at Nicosia. Care, however, in one form had been dogging my footsteps even here, and the form it took was doubt as to this delicate question —Was my guide a person who would expect what is vulgarly called a "tip"? Or was his position so high, that even to offer it would be an insult? Having been troubled with this problem for some considerable time, I at last determined to solve it in the following way. I intended, if possible, though this intention was not fulfilled, to pay another visit to the castle; so I told my guide to expect me again shortly, meaning meanwhile to inquire how I should treat him. " I hope," I said to him at parting, " I shall find you here on my return." In his melancholy refined eyes I saw the dawn of a smile. "Certainly, sir," he said, "you are sure to find me. I am a prisoner."

Mr. St. John, whom I asked about this gentleman afterwards, told me that he was the nephew of a rich Greek merchant in Liverpool; that he had been in his uncle's office, who had privately dismissed him for embezzlement; that he had then run off with the wife of one of his friends; that then he had come to Cyprus, where he had got himself employed by the Government; that presently he took to embezzling money again; and that the Government, not deterred by any uncle's tenderness, consigned him without mercy to the sort of quarters which he ought to have occupied seven years before. And yet, poor devil, I could not help liking him, and he looked as if butter would hardly melt in his mouth.

For the moment, however, as soon as I left the castle I forgot him with a heartless celerity, which I did not then know he deserved. He was completely put out of my mind by an exquisite

Corinthian capital and a marble slab covered with Greek inscriptions, which as I passed out over the bridge at once caught my eye, shining forlorn on a rubbish heap and facing the Gothic fortress.

I lunched with the commissioner of the district, a Scotch gentleman, who occupied a Turkish house overlooking the harbour. I washed off the dust of antiquity in a quaint Oriental bedroom, with a ceiling painted like those in the palace of Mr. Matthews. My entertainer received me in a large hall, spanned by pointed arches and strewn with light - coloured carpets. We looked out of the window at the pillars of the Temple of Venus, and then we quenched imagination in a dish of excellent curry. When I returned to Mr. St. John's, however, my imagination was once more craving. He and I made a second excursion to St. Hilarion. I drank the romance of the past like a glass of mental absinthe, and I arranged to go next day to seek for a yet deeper draught of it at the ruin of ruins, the wonderful Abbey of Bella Pais.

CHAPTER XVI

THE ABBEY OF HAPPY PEACE

FROM a distance I had already seen it, lying low on a spur of the mountains—a gray mass, embosomed in vague foliage. It was visible from the balcony in front of my bedroom window. It was barely four miles off, but Mr. St. John told me it would take me two hours to get to it, a fact I could hardly credit till experience showed me the reason. The reason was that the only road to it was a mule track, which traversed a series of deep ravines or valleys, and climbed amongst rocks over the steep ridges that separated them.

Yielding to advice, I again had recourse to a mule, Scotty and a guide accompanying me on two others. We took the road I had descended with the tandem yesterday till we came to the

spot where the leader had first shown a liking for
the precipice ; and there the guide did what the
horse had mercifully forborne to do ; he rode, as
it seemed to me, like Marcus Curtius, directly
over the brink into the chasm. I saw, however,
on looking down, not his shattered remains, but a
few rough rocks, like steps, descending some
thirty inches at a time ; and then came traces of
a narrow winding path. Most of man's finest
heroism is merely disguised necessity. So was
mine, and I am certain so was Scotty's as we
committed our destinies to the descent and
followed our apathetic leader. But, after the first
uncomfortable plunge, I felt as a diver might feel
when he opens his eyes on the world of waves
and shells and sea-weed. The world in which I
found myself was just as surprising and beautiful.
I was in a valley scented with myrtle and
thronged with thickets of oleander, and at the
bottom of it across the path a clear stream
went murmuring out of the green shadow. As I
was crossing it I stopped short, as if I had seen a
ghost. It was not a ghost I saw, but a sudden

mental vision of the world of bowery paganism seen by the eyes of Keats. I had a vision of shy nymphs and naiads ; their limbs glimmered and their eyes peered through the oleanders ; and I felt that somewhere on some neighbouring slope, a white sylvan altar was beginning to steam with incense. My mind's eye, it is true, saw this for a moment only, but it left the valley haunted with the air of the old mythology.

We all know with what rapidity in fairy stories the wandering hero passes from one king-dom to another. Quitting this valley, I passed with the same rapidity into scenes which, for some subtle reason, breathed a wholly different sentiment. Here, too, as I looked at pine-grove or rock, or at small rudely-terraced vineyard, bodiless presences showed themselves to that organ of sight which sees them. But they were not nymphs or naiads ; they issued from a different stratum of history. Sometimes a knight in armour flitted like a shadow through the brush-wood ; sometimes in front of me plodded a mediæval pilgrim ; once or twice I heard the

voice of a troubadour ; and near the vineyards I
saw Provençal peasants dancing. No doubt my
imagination committed many anachronisms and
confused together many incongruous centuries ;
but the wayward pageant for me had a perfect
inward congruity ; nor could the spectacles of any
professor of history — not even those through
which Professor Freeman makes faces at Mr.
Froude—have shown me anything fit, for pleasure's
sake, to be compared with it.

Nor were the real sights that saluted me less
delightful than the visions with which they
blended. The way continued to dip into rivulet-
haunted dells, to climb bushy banks, and to skirt
luxuriant slopes. Here and there through the
world of greenness a living peasant came, with a
sash like a red poppy, and sometimes a goat or
two or a couple of desultory bullocks. The
greenness was of all kinds and shades. Tall
reeds grew by the shadowy rivulets ; glossy caroub
trees dotted stretches of sun - warmed soil ;
cypresses and poplars towered in slender companies ; and here and there was the stem and

spreading plumes of a date palm. Then, too, in
constantly recurring patches, the earth was sprouting with all kinds of vegetables ; and through the
trunks of the trees shone the greenest and most
luminous of grasses, responding to every slightest
breath of the air, with a shiver of tremulous emerald.
The sky and the distant sea, both of the dreamiest
blue—two shades of the same cloudless turquoise
—added their magic to the scene. On the Asian
coast there was a faint delicate haze, behind which
the line of mountains was lost ; but now and
again, high up in the sky, there appeared the
flashing of some Cilician summit. The flowers,
the wild thyme—— But I stop. Could my words
be what I wish them, every one of them would be
fragrant with thyme and myrtle ; the margin of
every page would be a margin of breathing
flowers ; and could I only convey to the reader
the truth about this short journey, I should have
planted for ever a new garden in his memory.

Hours like these — should we be grateful to
them ? or do we owe them a grudge for mocking
us ? That is not a senseless question. For half

the charm of them lies below the sensuous surface
and beyond the luxurious meditative stir of the
imagination.   It lies in suggestions of some
elusive blessedness which might be ours if——
Who shall finish the sentence?   Could life give
to us all that life suggests to us, there are
moments when one might fancy that its chief
evil was death.

Minor evils, however, would probably irritate
us even in that case.   A minor irritation was not
wanting to me that morning.   It took the shape
of poor innocent Scotty, who, whenever I was in
the middle of some dialogue with myself or with
nature, was sure to interrupt it with some irrelevant
observation.   When I was saturating my mind at
one place with the romance of a hanging pine-
wood, he turned round in his saddle and said this
to me : " Once in a wood like that I shoot with a
English gentleman.   He was captain of English
ship, and I there for interpreter.   That was in
Karamania.   In Karamania are many wild pig."
This is a mere Liebig's extract of a good five
minutes' discourse which buzzed round my ear

like a bluebottle, and which I had not the cruelty
to kill.   In another place we came to a roofless
chapel—a little plaintive ruin still containing an
altar.   I was pausing to look at it when Scotty,
seizing the opportunity, pointed in the direction
of the sea and said, " There, sir, are many tortoise,
but these fellows here are stupid ; they never
make no soup of him." *Tortoise* I saw was
Scotty's version of *turtle*.   For a moment a vision
of green fat and Madeira crossed my mind like a
swallow : I then dismounted and examined the
broken walls.   On the far side of them some
young trees, sprouting on the brink of a precipice,
made a gray cloud of foliage ; below was a deep
valley with reeds and a stream at the bottom of
it ; and not a quarter of a mile beyond, glimmering amongst orchards and cypresses, were the
traceried windows, the cloisters, and the flying
buttresses of Bella Pais.

The Abbey of Happy Peace !   If peace of any
kind were an affair of locality, never was name
more aptly bestowed than this.   On the slopes
behind it, also thick with cypresses, a village of

white houses shone, embowered in gardens, which
crept caressingly close to the abbey walls.   The
abbey itself stood on the brink of the cliff
some hundred feet in height ; and below it was a
valley of palms, acacias, and oleanders.   Our way
lay through a straggling lane of the village.   The
houses were of stone and were neatly whitewashed,
and many of them were fronted with picturesque
arcades.   The whole look of the place was somehow inexplicably superior to that of the mud-
built villages in the neighbourhood of Nicosia.   In
all directions was a babble of running conduits,
and women were passing with jars of water on
their heads.   One of these, of whom Scotty
inquired the way, pointed an old man out to us,
who kept the keys of the building, and we presently
reached it through an ally between two orchards.
We entered by a gateway in a square Gothic
tower, the upper part of which had disappeared
and had been replaced by a tall Greek campanile.
Within was a sunny orange garden and a dark
fraternity of cypresses, and through the leaves and
stems was a glimpse of pillars and pointed arches.

From each side of the entrance-tower lofty and massive walls had evidently once extended, surrounding the whole abbey with a considerable fortified enclosure; but of these there remained only a few fragments, and their place was taken by the walls of neighbouring orchards.

Before inspecting the abbey itself in detail I hastily walked round it to arrive at its general plan. This was simple and can be described easily. It consists, or consisted, of a quadrangle, with the buildings ranged round it thus : The church occupied one side, the abbot's lodging another, the refectory a third, and the kitchen and the dormitories a fourth. Of these the abbot's lodging has entirely disappeared ; but the church is perfect, the refectory is perfect, and so are the kitchen and dormitories, excepting the roof and floors. Round all these ran an internal cloister, and this on three sides is absolutely perfect also. As for the church, it has now been appropriated by the Greeks, and is served by the parish priest ; and Greek screens and galleries and second-rate garish gilding mar the solemn

effect of the old Catholic columns. But in front
of the west door is a beautiful arcade or portico
like that which so much struck me before the
cathedral at Nicosia ; and there the only gold is
the gold of the shining oranges, seen in the sunlight through arches of slender shadow. I sat
down there on a crumbling seat of stone and ate
a frugal luncheon, at which no monk need have
been scandalised.

Then I explored carefully all the rest of the
building. It was surprise on surprise of delicate
spiritual beauty. As for the cloisters, through
which I passed to the kitchen, they were much
like those of Magdalen College, Oxford, and,
excepting on one side, were almost as well preserved. The kitchen was half-choked with the
fallen vaulting of its roof, and a crooked fig-tree
grew in it. Perhaps the reader will think that in
the kitchen, even of a monastery, spiritual beauty
is hardly the beauty one would find ; but the
prevailing sentiment of the building penetrated
every part of it, as its spirit was meant to penetrate every act of its inmates' life. And above

was the floorless gallery, where once its inmates slept, with a small window and a little cupboard in the wall at each place where had once been a brother's bed. Where are the brothers now? Where are their prayers and their vigils and their souls, of which some at least the most cynical charity may presume to have been white and taintless? Modern science would answer, in the words of Villon—and it is the only answer it *can* make—" Where are the last year's snows?"

Quitting this side of the building, I sought out the refectory. Its door opened from the cloister on the side facing the precipice and opposite to the church. I entered. I was in a magnificent hall more than a hundred feet in length, more than forty feet in height, and in width more than thirty. Nowhere a stone was chipped, nowhere an angle obliterated. Not York Minster nor Westminster Abbey could show, in all their roofs, groining whose ribs rose and met more gracefully, or more complete preservation of the over-arching stone. To another feature they could show no parallel at all—to the palms and oleanders on

which the windows opened, and which, seen
through this Gothic framework, looked like the
work of sorcery. Presently I espied a passage
leading to some regions beneath. I descended
some broken steps which led me into a dim
twilight, and, advancing a little, I came upon two
crypts, perfect as the hall above, but not a third
of its height, and sustaining their ponderous vaulting on low hexagonal columns.

Reascending, I again betook myself to the
cloisters. Having seen the rest of the building,
I could now devote myself to these ; and for the
first time I fully enjoyed the fascinating strange
effect of them. I have already compared them
to those of Magdalen ; but for me they had
suggestions not of Magdalen only, but of Melrose,
of Dryburgh, of Fountains—I need not prolong
the list. They were all Gothic cloisters in one ;
they were all the spiritual seclusions in which
mediæval northern piety had ever walked and
meditated ; only they were sublimated into something lighter and more aërial ; the shadows clung
to their carvings with an unnatural crispness ;

and the scene outside, which filled every arch
like a picture, dazzled and bewildered the fancy
till it seemed to be seeing double.   Orange trees,
palms, cypresses, the spires of silvery mountains,
shining under a sky that gleamed like a single
jewel—how should northern arches look out upon
these ?   And that marble cistern sunning itself
opposite to the door of the refectory, what was
that ?   How came such an object here ?   It was
a Roman sarcophagus, florid with the sculptured
festoons of paganism.   The sunshine and shadow
slept on the silent floor, and I slowly for some
time paced to and fro, trying to fix in my mind
the shifting meanings of the place, which were
making my imagination flicker like mother-of-
pearl.   It all seemed unreal, and yet at the same
time so real that, as I looked up at the tangled
arching roofs, whose ribs sprang from their
columns like the curved stamens of flowers, it
seemed as if they would compel the life they
once sheltered to return to them.

At last it was time for me to go.   I shouted
for Scotty, who had considerately left me solitary.

Where he had secreted himself I have no means
of knowing ; but he appeared from somewhere, in
response to my voice, with such promptness, that
I seemed to have created him myself out of some
block of masonry. The mules were brought to
the gate, which the old man locked as we passed
out ; and at a slow pace I rode away in the sunshine, and left the Abbey of Happy Peace behind
me. Warmth and sunshine followed me all the
way home again — an emblem of the hours
through which I had just passed, and over which,
though melancholy had cast a shadow, it had
cast a shadow only like that of a summer cloud.
Experiences like these are always fresh to look
back upon ; one takes them away with one not
dead but living ; and memory, when it broods
over them, is like the air of spring, every time
opening new flowers.

It was five o'clock when I reached Mr. St.
John's house again. The family were at tea in
a room scented with violets ; and there was present an afternoon caller, whose personality and
conversation at once surprised and interested me.

He was a man of forty or so, the owner of a fine
estate in Scotland, who had taken a fancy to buy
himself some land in Cyprus—a considerable area,
not far from Kyrenia. He had built himself a
hermitage on it, consisting of a few rooms only ;
and he spent there four months each year, amusing himself with what he hoped were improve-
ments. For these he wanted a large amount of
stone ; and it was in connection with this want
that the interest of his conversation revealed
itself. He told me that he had taken the advice
of several natives as to how stone for building
could be procured most easily ; and the advice
given him had in every case been as follows—to
buy house property on the Asian coast opposite,
to pull down the houses, and ship the stones to
Kyrenia. It appeared that what his advisers
meant was this—that on the coast opposite there
were ancient Roman towns, desolate as Pompeii,
but apparently less dilapidated ; that the ruins
could be bought for a song, and, though fit for
nothing else, were the best material in the world
for building cheap pig - styes. My informant

added, " I have every reason to believe that such towns do really exist. A year or two ago I had here a Scotch mason and carpenter, and took them to the opposite coast with me for a cruise in a Greek caïque. On that occasion I went nowhere on shore myself, but these men did at one place, in the neighbourhood of which there was said to be a ruined city. They came back to the vessel in the evening, telling me that the whole of the day they had been walking amongst friezes and architraves, columns, and plinths, and capitals—a wilderness of old carved marble."

Will the Protestant reader be shocked when I make to him an abrupt confession—that this day, which I had profaned by a pilgrimage to a Papist abbey, was Sunday ? He will, of course, infer— and rightly—that I did not go to church ; but there was an excellent reason for that—there was no church to go to. In the evening, however, I at least made a good end—and an end which at once befitted the Island of Flowers, the Island of Greek Poetry, the Christian Sunday that was ending, and the Catholic centuries that had ended.

Mr. St. John, who was familiar with both ancient and modern Greek, had been telling me at dinner that in this part of the island the language of the peasants retained words and phrases not to be found elsewhere, as old as the days of Homer. One example of them he gave me has alone stayed in my memory — and that is the word νόστον, meaning "a return home." Even that I should probably have forgotten, if he had not added further that the adjective νόστιμον, or "homeward-going," stands to-day in their dialect as a synonym for "lovely" or "desirable." A new pathos seemed, as I heard this, to gather round the νόστιμον ἦμαρ, which Fate took from Achilles. From topics like these we strayed to modern Greek generally; then to the modern Greek Bible, and from that to the Septuagint, and the differences between the two. There were copies in the room of both versions. We put them side by side, and set ourselves to compare their respective power and beauty. Two books occurred, as test cases, to both of us—Ecclesiastes and the Song of Solomon. We picked out such verses and chapters as had stamped themselves most vividly on our memories, and verse for verse we read the old Greek and the new. It was a fitting end to a fitting day. As we read of the Rose of Sharon, of the myrrh, of the pomegranates, and of the gardens, the flowers in the room and the air that stole in from the mountains made me feel that my host's house was a lodge in a garden of spices, a garden enclosed, fanned with the winds of Lebanon ; and then again, when we turned over a few pages, and gave our attention to the other Book we had fixed upon, another voice stole through that of the Song of Songs, and whispered to the Mystical Rose the secret that all is vanity.

CHAPTER XVII

BEHIND PLATE-GLASS WINDOWS

THE following afternoon I was to go back to
Nicosia, where I was to spend two days more
with my kind friends the Falklands, and after
that I was to migrate to Government House.
The same carriage which brought me had been
already ordered, and I was to start soon after
luncheon. Meanwhile the man whose mules I
had hired yesterday was coming up to be paid
for them, and I asked Mr. St. John at breakfast,
as I had not made a bargain, what was the price
which he thought I might be fairly asked. He
told me, and then, anticipating that I might be
asked more, and pursuing a train of thought
which the reader will easily follow, I resumed our
last night's topic — that of the modern Greek

language—and begged him to teach me the most
blackguardly oath contained in it : an oath which
would have on an exorbitant muleteer the same
effect that a stone has on a cur.   He supplied me
with what I wanted.   Its sound was all that my
fondest fancy could have painted—it was a mouth-
ful of crunching syllables ; but its meaning disappointed me by its mildness, as it merely expressed
a wish that the object of the malediction might
have the burial of a dog.

I found, when the time came, that I had not
thus armed myself for nothing.   The muleteer
asked at least three times as much as law, reason,
or custom gave him the smallest right to, and
though Mr. St. John, who was with me, kept
telling him this, he, with dogged persistence, kept
reiterating his demand.   I now recognised with
delight that my opportunity was come.   I loaded
my mouth with the oath and discharged it in the
rascal's face.   But alas ! despite all my efforts, as
soon as I opened my lips it emerged in the form,
not of an imprecation, but a laugh.   At last, on
Mr. St. John's advice, I produced what was

properly due, deposited it on a stone, and said to the man as I walked away that there was all he would get; he might take it or leave it, as he pleased. He left it with some threat; but I learned subsequently that as soon as I was gone he returned and went thankfully off with it.

When the hour for my departure arrived though I was full of regrets at leaving, I felt a sincere satisfaction, as I got into my carriage and settled myself in comfort amongst a number of furs and rugs, that I was not going again to encounter the perils of Mr. St. John's tandem. I had with me a book with which to beguile the way (Professor Thorold Rogers' *Six Centuries of Work and Wages*), and as we quietly climbed the mountains to the pass above Nicosia, I was so much absorbed in it as to have almost forgotten the scenery. Some readers will possibly not think much of me for not having felt a like tranquillity in the tandem. I will, however, brave their further contempt by admitting that when my present driver began to trot down-hill I was not only annoyed by the jolting and swaying of the carriage, but was convinced that so rapid a descent on so bad a road was dangerous. I was just going to tell Scotty that I wished we should go slower when his voice, anticipating mine, called something out to me. I could not hear what he said, but by instinct I divined his meaning. I rapidly seized one of the iron posts of the awning. At the same instant there was a lurch, a plunge, and a swerve, and the next half-second the world was topsy-turvy, as carriage and horses reeled over the edge of the road and fell with a crash on a slope eight feet below.

Had the accident happened thirty yards farther on our descent would have been, not eight feet, but eight hundred. As it was, the iron rod to which I had held had enabled me by its elasticity to break my fall so completely, that when I crept from under the awning, I did not even feel that I had been shaken. The horses were lying in a heap together; the driver was stupidly staring at them; and Scotty was crying like a child, though he was evidently quite unhurt. This being the case, I examined my camera and my dressing-bag; and, finding that neither had suffered, I had leisure to devote myself to my emotions. Scotty was expecting to see me storm at the driver, who, I afterwards learned, had, when one of the horses shied, jumped off the box, and quietly left us to our fate. Not knowing this, however, I found myself too much annoyed to be angry; and leaving the two men to look after the horses and the luggage, I walked five miles ignominiously back to Mr. St. John's to seek assistance. Mr. St. John welcomed me with equal surprise and cordiality; he at once despatched assistance to the scene of the accident; and the following morning, three mules were procured, on which I and my belongings were safely transported to Nicosia.

When the day came for me to quit Colonel Falkland's roof, though I had known its shelter for so short a time, I felt something of the sorrow of a boy who first leaves home for school. The impressions with which I associated it had been so many and vivid, that it seemed as familiar to me as if I had known it for a life-time. I was, however, only migrating from one scene of hospitality to another ; and the hospitality in this latter case was made additionally pleasant from the fact that I found it amongst surroundings of an entirely fresh character.

Government House, as I have already mentioned incidentally, is outside Nicosia—about a mile and a quarter from the walls. It is not only entirely modern, but it will never become old. It will never become old, for it will have fallen to pieces first. It is in fact an enormous wooden shed, surrounding three sides of a court, and consisting of a single series of rooms, with a verandah on either side of them. It was made in England for use in some totally different region, where it proved not to be wanted, and so it was sent here. It has been erected, or rather one may say pitched, on a dwarf eminence, overlooking a waterless river, and the plains stretching to the mountains ; and its boarded sides, and its red-tiled roofs, are by this time embowered in thickets of pines and eucalyptus trees. The court within has a fountain at the open end, a lawn-tennis court in the middle, and flower-beds round the borders, from which breaths of mignonette, when I was there, came wandering.

My first evening, though agreeable in itself, I felt rather flat as an incident of life in a remote country. If the rooms had not all of them opened into a verandah, and their ceilings risen at a sharp angle into the roof, I might almost have fancied that Cyprus had been a dream, from which I had just awoke and found myself disappointed in England. The walls were covered with familiar English papers. The carpets, though Eastern, had been most of them bought in London, and suggested nothing but civilised English life ; and the chairs, the sofas, and the books that littered the tables, had somehow an air of being within a day's journey of Piccadilly, and the Governor himself too, whom I will speak of under the name of Sir Robert—I had last seen him in Curzon Street, and Mayfair seemed to enter the room with him ; whilst one of his two aides-de-camp, having been absent on leave for a month or two, had only returned the night before my arrival, and had brought with him news which generally evaporates in crossing the Channel, of balls, beauties, and marriages, and of one or two of those characteristic absurdities by which some people well known in society, so often endear themselves to their acquaintances. There was also staying in the house a smart young officer from a regiment quartered at Limasol, with his pretty Canadian wife. They had lately been in Egypt and were full of the gossip of Cairo. It all disturbed my sense of visionary seclusion. Finally, the dining-room and the dinner —English in every particular, excepting the presence of two Oriental footmen—came like a veil between me and the city of minarets, and the myrtle-scented mountains whose breath I had been breathing above Kyrenia.

But the following day Cyprus reasserted itself, still looking strange and remote, though seen across London sofas, and touching the mind with a subtle change of aspect. That morning I enjoyed a new experience. About a mile off on the plain, amongst a grove of cypresses and

sycamores, stood a Greek monastery, which I had
often wished to visit. I happened to mention my
wish to the pretty Canadian lady. The idea of
it delighted her; she said she would come with
me; and for the first time since I had been in
the island I found myself setting forth, not as a
meditative pilgrim, but in the mind and mood
proper to a visitor at a country house.

The monastery itself was a square mud
structure, surrounding a court that was half
blocked up with a church. The monks' cells and
refectory were simply whitewashed rooms, opening
on untidy balconies; and they suggested nothing
but farm-buildings out of repair. The suggestions of the court were similar. There were heaps
of manure and puddles in it; and the monks
themselves, who flocked out to inspect us, had
about them a pathetic air of the furrows. The
faithful Scotty, who had tramped after us with
my camera, induced them to stand in a group,
whilst I took a photograph of their church. I
then realised that there was an old woman amongst
them, who so far as I could see must have been

the monastic char-woman. I know the reader
will not be shocked at this. Scandal itself would
have been silent had she lived alone with St.
Anthony. The photograph taken, several of the
younger monks came peeping through the lens,
expecting to see the picture. Meanwhile, the
senior members of the fraternity pointed to the
church, and invited us to enter it. We did so.
It was a plain building, with whitewashed sides,
and a heavy rounded roof; and, except for a
screen at the end, was bare as an empty barn. I
knew, however, beforehand that here, surrounded
by puddles and whitewash, was preserved a certain
treasure unrivalled in Eastern Christendom. I
soon saw where it was. The screen I have just
mentioned was covered with saints painted on
gilded panels: but one of these panels was only
half visible; it was draped by a jewelled curtain
of faded but rich embroidery, and hanging before
it were two burning lamps. Coming close to it,
I saw that the panel, in place of a picture, contained a relief, in beaten gold, of the Madonna,
the neck, the wrists, and the aureole being studded

with precious stones.   This was merely the veil,
however, the outer covering of the real treasure
—a thing far too precious for exposure : for
behind that plate of gold was, or was supposed to
be, the picture of the Madonna painted by St.
Luke the Evangelist.   Whether the relic is genuine
it is not my province to discuss.   Millions of
Christians at least believe it to be so ; and for the
whole body of the orthodox it stands, as an
object of pilgrimage, second only to the holy
places of Jerusalem.

When we went outside again there was a
certain stir in the court.   From a stable door
which I had not before noticed there was being
led out a long train of camels.   They gave to
the scene an odd patriarchal character, as they
passed through the gates, driven by a brown lay-
brother ; and when presently we followed them
out ourselves, we saw them by some trees at a
distance, drinking out of a stone cistern.

Before dinner that day I made another excursion—but where, or in what direction, it is
quite beyond me to say.   Sir Robert, who was

generally busy the whole of the afternoon, was accustomed to take a constitutional as soon as his work was over, and at six he and I sallied forth together. The way to the monastery had lain over rich ploughed fields. Our present course took us over stretches of rugged moorland. The evening fell with its soft mysterious dimness, making the gray boulders glimmer, in vague shadow, and giving the low horizon an aspect of incalculable distance. Here and there we passed by a small eminence, whose sides were honey-combed with a number of black caverns. These, my companion told me, were rifled Phœnician tombs. By and by, far out in the solitude, like a sail at sea, we sighted a pale object; it was a forlorn Byzantine church, standing altogether alone. It proved to be a landmark, which showed we had walked far enough. We arrested our steps. I asked what the church was. Sir Robert knew nothing of its history; but at times, he said, there was still service in it. After a pause we turned. A soft wild wind sighed in our faces across the furze; and we retraced our steps

over ground that was now hardly distinguishable.

A walk of this kind, and at this hour, with
Sir Robert came to be a daily feature of my life
at Government House. Another feature, almost
equally regular, was a corresponding walk with
him after breakfast about the garden—a walk
which was constantly enlivened by patches of
local colour. The colour in question was for the
most part contributed by beggars, or at any rate
by petitioners, with some want or grief or grievance. The rags of the men, and the robes and
the veils of the women, looked in the sunlight
as brilliant as Joseph's coat; and their strange
forms, as Sir Robert appeared in the verandah,
would begin slowly to glide towards him, over
the asphalt floor of the lawn-tennis court, as if he
were a Sultan with power to right everything.

The rest of the day I had usually to myself;
and I rarely found that my lonely hours were
vacant. Not to mention other occupations and
amusements, I had plenty of work cut out for me
in developing the photographs I had taken, and

in exploring the innumerable pages of De Mas
Latrie's *History of Cyprus.* Amongst these,
shortly after my visit to the Greek monastery, I
was delighted to find the history of the renowned
relic I had seen there. I hope the reader will be
as much pleased at it as I was.

In the year 1090, Manuel Voutoúmitis, then
Duke of Cyprus, was one day hunting amongst
the mountains of Myriánthoussa. There, in the
midst of forests full of wild animals, at that time
dwelt a large number of anchorites—some in
communities, some as hermits in lonely oratories.
One of this latter class, by name Isaiah, was so
shy and bewildered at sight of the duke coming
that he scuttled out of the path into the bushes,
quite forgetting to salute him. This scandalous
conduct was more than the duke could stand.
"What do you mean, sir," he shouted, "by not
touching your hat to me?" And, rushing after
Isaiah, he seized him roughly by the collar, called
him all the names which his command of bad
language supplied him with, and finally inflicted
on him a chastisement so undignified that I will

leave the reader to arrive at its nature from the
sequel.   The duke's foot miraculously withered
up on the spot.   Isaiah turned and looked at
him.   The duke looked at Isaiah, and became
convinced, possibly for the first time in his life,
that he had made a serious mistake.   In that
extreme state of discomfort which often passes
for repentance, he acknowledged his fault to his
victim, and to all his spiritual advisers ; and at
last it was announced to him that he might be
cured upon one condition.   This condition was
that he should procure and bring to Cyprus the
picture of the Blessed Virgin painted by St.
Luke, which the emperor Alexis Comnenus kept
in his palace at Constantinople.   To Constantinople the duke accordingly went, and Isaiah
went with him.   Both told their story, and begged
for the precious gift.   The emperor, however,
though he did not refuse point-blank, kept putting
them off from month to month with excuses, and
at last offered them some money and two other
pictures instead.   Isaiah's patience was by this
time exhausted.   The duke, he said, might do

what he pleased himself; but, as for him, he should at once go back to Cyprus. No sooner had he announced this resolution than the foot of the emperor's daughter, and, directly after, the foot of the emperor himself, withered up exactly like the foot of Voutoúmitis. Then the emperor saw that he too had made a mistake. He hastened to do what had been asked of him. The three sufferers were cured; the relic was brought back in triumph to Cyprus, and the monastery of Kykko, which exists to this day, was built to receive and guard it. Kykko itself is amongst the mountains—a two-days' journey from Nicosia; but the monastery which I had visited belongs to the same foundation; and the relic had been brought down to it only last summer, with extraordinary solemnity, that it might procure rain for the plains, which were suffering from a disastrous drought.

The mention of monks, especially the monks of this monastery, reminds me that one morning I saw one of them on the lawn-tennis ground. What he could be doing there I at first could not conceive, and I thought of the ghost of the "black friar" in "Don Juan." A second glance, however, showed me that this excellent man was really painting afresh the white lines for the game, by which he earned, I believe, about one and eightpence a day. Who shall venture to call the monastic orders useless?

In fact, in spite of its English architecture, Government House abounded in quaint sights and incidents. Chief amongst these were some I have not mentioned yet—certain formal banquets given to the prominent natives. A few English officials were always invited also; but they only heightened the bizarre effect of the others. Sometimes there was a Turkish night, sometimes there was a Greek night, and alternately the table seemed to flicker with turbans and to be surrounded with fez caps like a border of scarlet poppies. As few of the Greeks, and not one of the Turks, were able to speak a single word of English, it might be supposed that conversation would not flourish. On the contrary, I have rarely known it busier, and for this reason: half the remarks made had to be committed to an interpreter, who first understood them wrongly, then had them explained to him, and finally passed them on to the person to whom they were addressed. Thus one platitude about the weather did duty for several, and the loaves and fishes of small talk which each guest brought with him, by this happy arrangement were multiplied threefold. As for the interpreters, they cannot be praised too highly. They were seated at the sides and the two ends of the table, like croupiers at Monte Carlo, and whenever an observation was hazarded or placed, so to speak, on the cloth, they raked it in, making it sound as they did so, and adroitly transferred it to the person to whom it was addressed.

Meanwhile various letters had reached me which warned me that my time in Cyprus was fast drawing to a close. I was expected, at the beginning of March, by some friends who had a villa near Florence ; and it had become necessary for me to settle the day of my departure. There was one difficulty, indeed, in the way of doing

so, and this was the fact that not a soul in all
Nicosia knew anything about the homeward
steamers beyond Port Said or Alexandria. At
last, however, I got some information from a
Government functionary at Larnaca, which showed
me that if I started in ten days' time I should
just catch at Port Said the homeward mail to
Brindisi. This accordingly I had arranged to
do. My days in Cyprus being thus unhappily
numbered, whatever I meant to see I should have
to see quickly ; so of all the sights which I had
once contemplated exhausting I found myself
obliged to select and be contented with two.
One of these was the mediæval sea-port of Famagusta ; the other was a castle about ten miles
distant from it, as interesting as St. Hilarion, but
of a totally different character, which was one of
the things about which Mr. Matthews had spoken
to me. Such being the case, Sir Robert had
written to recommend me to Captain Scott, the
commissioner of the Famagusta district, who
replied, naming a day on which he would be
happy to receive me.

The day arrived. Famagusta was nearly fifty miles distant; I had been told I should allow about nine hours for the journey, and Sir Robert himself assured me that this was none too much. My carriage was therefore ordered for half-past nine—a different carriage from the last, and happily with a different driver. This time it was a regular old-fashioned landau, which age and exercise had reduced to the colour of an unblacked boot. But it was not uncomfortable; its size made it imposing, and when it rumbled sedately off with its four dejected horses I felt like my own grandfather beginning the grand tour.

CHAPTER XVIII

THE GLORIES OF FAMAGUSTA

To any one looking at the map of Cyprus it would seem that the road to Famagusta, which is situated on its eastern coast, lay over a dead level. I had studied the map myself, and been delighted with this conclusion. I found, however, that it was not wholly correct. It is true that, regarded as a picture, the whole country I passed through was a plain; but it was a plain that would rise for miles in imperceptible slopes, and then descend abruptly in steep and dangerous banks. There were, therefore, some bits of exceedingly nasty road, which, after my late experience, might have made me uneasy if it had not been for Scotty, whose nerves were far more delicate than my own, and who, whenever we came to the slightest dip in the road, forced the driver to go at a foot's pace.

Landscapes, even when their general type is similar, are capable of as many expressions as the same type of human face, and, without our being able fully to tell why, affect our spirits as we look at them with as many moods and meanings. I have said already that in my morning journeys to Kythrea the plains conveyed to me a sense of the patriarchal ages. Plains to-day which were bordered by the same mountains made me feel that I was travelling through Arcadia. Far and near over pale rocky expanses, green in the sunlight, rose the leaves of innumerable asphodel, and vaguely here and there flocks of sheep were wandering. For the first part of the way I could distinguish Kythrea to the left of me, eight miles off or so—a straggling blot of green, lying at the foot of the mountains. Then it died out of sight, and the wonderful mountain ranges shifted their peaks into a new succession of citadels, and reached away like a tapering purple spear into the distance.

We arrived about one o'clock at a long, mud-built village ; and at the door of a courtyard belonging to some house we halted. Almost instantly an old bearded man, very dirty, but, despite the dirt, very dignified, made his appearance at the side of the carriage and bowed. At the same time Scotty explained to me, " Here, sir, we stop for one hour. The luncheon you bring—you eat it in this house." " No," I said, " I should prefer eating it in the carriage." " But, sir," said Scotty, " this is the head-man of the village. All English gentlemen eat their luncheon here. Upstairs he has nice room ready for you." Unwilling to wound the old man's feelings or disappoint what I presumed were his hopes of earning some trifle by his civility, I followed him across his court and up a species of step ladder, and was shown by him into a room, bare but scrupulously clean, furnished with a table and a few rush-bottomed chairs, and adorned on its whitewashed walls with a lithograph of the Prince of Wales. Here Scotty laid out the cold luncheon I had brought with me, and the old man, before I had half finished it, em-

barrassed me by adding some further refreshments
of his own. Some meat and some oranges I
civilly but firmly declined, but I took, in order to
please him, a tumbler of his Cyprian wine. To
my surprise it was excellent. I say "to my
surprise," because though most of the wines
of the island might be excellent if made
properly, they are generally spoilt for the European palate by the skins they are kept in and a
villainous taste of resin. But here of this taste
there was no trace whatever, and I wished for a
competent friend who might have shared and discussed the draught with me.

Luncheon over, I strolled out into the village.
I looked at the brown farm-buildings and at two
old Greek churches. The air flowed through the
streets like currents of tepid water. Presently I
saw that the door of one of the churches had been
opened. I entered and looked about me. The
gilded and painted screen was, as usual, the only
noticeable feature. Whilst I was looking at it I
heard a voice at my ear. I turned and saw that
an old man was addressing me. I concluded he

was the priest, though it was too dark to see much of him; and to avoid being absolutely silent, or making only inarticulate sounds to him, I mustered enough of his language to ask for the New Testament. He took me behind the altar to a little twilight sanctuary, and showed me a thin quarto bound in velvet and silver. I opened it at St. John's Gospel, and began reading aloud to him, appealing to him by a look to set my pronunciation right. He seemed delighted at thus playing tutor, and I was wondering that so small a village should have a priest so cultivated, when, passing with him into the daylight, I saw that he was my dirty old host. There now revived in my mind the same dreadful perplexity which had annoyed me in the castle of Kyrenia with respect to my friend the thief. Ought this old man to be paid? And if so, what? I began to fear that he would be too grand to accept anything, or—worse fear still—anything not exorbitant. I consulted Scotty. Scotty said, "Give him nothing, sir. He the head-man of the village. He like doing this. He do it always for English gentlemen.

No, sir, you give him nothing." That was an
idea, however, which I could not tolerate, so I
postponed the difficulty by saying I should be
returning in a day or two, resolving meanwhile
to consult Captain Scott on the subject.

Another three hours of travel through similar
scenery brought us to another village—a mere
cluster of cottages, close to which was a beautiful
farm or villa, belonging, if I recollect rightly, to
a Levantine banker in Nicosia. The house, which
I could hardly see, was secluded in a luxuriant
garden of orange trees and huge cypresses, shoot-
ing up from the plain like a dark volcano of vegetation. A wall of reeds was round it, twenty feet
in height, and the life of the oasis flowed to it in
a long aqueduct. In view of this garden we
halted, that the horses might rest again ; and by
the time we again started there were already
symptoms of evening. Evening was full of suggestions of the nearing end of my journey, and
set me thinking over what I expected to find at
it. Of the past history of Famagusta I had learnt
quite enough for the imagination to work upon.

I knew that it had been fortified by the Lusignans, and probably strengthened by the Genoese, who seized the town at the end of the fourteenth century and held it for ninety years as a kind of commercial Gibraltar. I knew also that Venice had left her mark on it. Again, I knew that during all these periods it had enjoyed a commerce and an opulence which is generally little realised. The merchants of Famagusta were then amongst the richest individuals in the world. The jewels, for instance, belonging to the wife of one of them, were so renowned and splendid that a Sultan desired to buy them, and at a fabulous price he did so ; but the lady and her husband, afterwards regretting their loss, offered half as much again in order to buy them back. Then too I had heard about splendid palaces and two hundred churches—about one church in particular, which was built by one of the merchants entirely out of the profits of a single voyage to Syria. But all my knowledge was vague, and I felt its vagueness most with regard to the present state of the town and the preservation of its ancient build-

ings. I had seen some photographs of it. They
showed me some old walls and a cathedral, a study
of a Gothic window, and some miserable mud-
roofed houses. But there was no general or intelligible view of the place, and these fragments of
it had bewildered rather than enlightened me. I
was glad that this was so. It gave me the more
to think about. In fact my mind was so well and
so fully occupied that I had hardly had leisure to
feel impatient when darkness had descended on
the plains, and there were still no signs of our
destination.

Suddenly, however, without any apparent
reason, the carriage came to a standstill, and a
boy who had been brought by the driver—I
could not conceive why—jumped down from the
box. The lamps had already been lighted ; the
boy took one of them and ran on as if to explore
the way. To me nothing was visible, as I looked
out, but bare rocky ground, whose ridges gleamed
in the lamplight with so wan a brightness that I
felt convinced there must have been a shower of
rain. Scotty presently came to the window and

said to me, "The boy gone on, sir, to find out the way. The driver he not see it. The ground here covered with snow." I looked again, and so it actually was ; and the air, which at one o'clock had been like July in England, smelt and felt as keen as an English February. In time we began to move again, but at a foot-pace only, the boy with the lamp preceding us. This lasted for something like twenty minutes. Then all of a sudden the snow ended like a carpet. The ground on each side was dark again ; the road was a dim glimmer, and the horses resumed their trot. On we went, and as I looked out occasionally I could see no reason why we should not go on for ever. We did not as a matter of fact go on for even half an hour. We abruptly stopped again. Again the road was invisible, and this time because the country was under water. The wretched boy, who was unembarrassed with boots, got down with the lamp again and paddled in front of us like a marsh sprite. We crawled after him and at length regained dry ground. The driver's patience now seemed exhausted, for he

whipped his horses up and we started careering
wildly over what seemed to me to be trackless
open fields. Could we possibly, I asked myself,
be on the highroad to Famagusta? In reply to
this mental question the carriage soon ceased to
jolt, and began to wade and labour through something that seemed like sand. It was an hour
past the time when I ought to have been at the
end of my journey; and I should now have been
in positive despair if at this precise moment there
had not come to my ears the clear notes of a
bugle. I looked out on the side from which the
sound came, and saw in the darkness some huge
shapeless building, which I knew must be part of
the fortifications of Famagusta. But I had not
much time to look at them, for the carriage turned
sharply round, and to my surprise began to drive
straight away from them. At the same time we
were again on a hard road.

I knew that Captain Scott did not live in the
town. No one did, I was told, but a small body
of Turks. He lived in a suburb called Varoshia;
but it seemed to me a suburb that was at an in-

terminable distance.   At last, to my great
pleasure, we passed a few roadside houses, and a
minute or two later we were in a street lit with
lanterns.   I was surprised at its length and its
picturesque appearance.   On either side of the
way there were quaint arcades at intervals, and
here and there in open spaces were piles of
pitchers, huge jars, and all kinds of pottery.   At
the end of this street was, at last, the end of my
journey.   We drew up before a door something
like Colonel Falkland's, and presently came a
man with a lantern, followed by Captain Scott.
The house, I saw at once, was of the regular
Cyprian type.   There was the same court or
garden, the same cloisters, and the rooms were
spanned by the same pointed arches.

I need hardly say that dinner was an exceedingly welcome sight.   I discovered during the
meal that my host, like myself, was a photo-
grapher, and Famagusta naturally had supplied
him with a number of subjects.   During the
evening he showed me a collection of views he
had taken of it ; but he had confined himself

almost entirely to isolated architectural details ; and the general aspect and the general condition of the town was still left to my imagination, like a sort of changing cloud. I took it to bed with me in this state and dreamt of it ; and I rose next morning with all the greater zest ready to find out the truth of the matter for myself.

Once more I realised, when, under the cloudless sunshine, I started after breakfast, the faithful Scotty guiding me, that Cyprus was a land of many climates, all delightful and all having the soft blandishment of a siren. The street of Varoshia by day was as picturesque as it was by night. The shops were like those of a mountain town in Italy ; and the pale collections of pottery, stacked in the open air, gave it in places the look of a sculptor's studio. It died away into a sort of open common, bounded on the right by green gardens and olive woods, and beyond them was a sea, which recalled the hues of the Riviera. Crossing this common, on whose edges the sky rested, I paused on a low ridge to take in the scene beyond. What I looked upon was a shining

22

meadow of asphodel, with a bevy of Turkish
women in white yashmaks, moving across it
slowly like a living cluster of lilies.   To the right
of me still, was the sea and a belt of gardens; to
the left on the horizon were the grave-stones of
a Turkish cemetery; and in front of me the
asphodel swelled like a hardly perceptible wave,
till its crest approached and very nearly eclipsed
a stretch of interminable masonry cutting the sky
like a ruler.   I need hardly say that I recognised
the ramparts of Famagusta.   At first nothing
struck me but a single straight line.   Then I
perceived that here and there were bastions, and
to the left, away from the sea, a cluster of sombre
towers.   Towards these towers it was that the
road conducted me, and just opposite to them it
entered a shallow cutting.   Reaching this spot, I
perceived for the first time that before the walls
there ran an enormous fosse, cut in the solid rock;
and here a causeway crossed it, which led to an
arched gate.   In all directions the walls were
scarred and seamed with the marks of former
gates, older even than this one; and this one

must have dated from the days of the Venetian conquest, whilst one of the others had been the work of the engineers of Genoa.

But before I explain any further details of this singular town, at whose threshold I was now standing, let me say a word about its general plan and situation. It will help the reader better to understand what follows. Famagusta is, roughly speaking, a square of about a mile, and is surrounded by walls of which every yard is perfect. These walls are about fifty feet in height, and are, on an average, twenty-seven feet in thickness. One of the four faces the sea and harbour; the three others overlook an immense plain, parts of which are barren and strewn with sand. Round the whole of these landward walls the fosse runs continuously. There are only two gates—the water gate, opening on the harbour, and the land gate, whose outer aspect I was a moment ago describing.

When I reached this gate I stood for some time on the causeway, wondering, before I entered, what I should find within. Not a sound broke the stillness ; not a soul seemed to be stirring. The place might have been a tomb, or a city in an enchanted sleep.   At last in the darkness of the arch I saw a figure that seemed a negro's, lean and in tattered clothing, which peeped at me and then vanished.   A minute or two later there emerged an old man with a donkey.   They passed me slowly and drowsily, and nothing else moved.

" In this ditch, sir," said Scotty, " they often shoot many snipe—game, sir, much game.   My brother he tell me that.   He live here.   He belong to the coastguard."

" Is your brother a poacher ? " I said, annoyed at this inapposite interruption.

" Yes, sir," said Scotty, who understood the question but imperfectly.   " He shoot much.   My brother a poacher—yes, sir."

Happily here the conversation dropped.   I crossed the causeway and entered the dark portal.

For forty feet or more I traversed a vaulted passage, with a sharp bend in the middle of it and just wide and high enough to allow of a waggon passing. In the gloom as I went by I noticed some ancient gates leaning, half unhinged, against the wall, and two places where a portcullis once descended. Then the passage widened into an open cavern of masonry, as big as a baronial hall, and at the end of this was the interior of the town like a picture. Facing me in the foreground was a poverty-stricken café, with a porch in front of it, supported on tottering columns and festooned with onions. To the left a lane, narrow, dirty, and tortuous, lost itself amongst a collection of hovels. To the right, built against the towers that reared their masses over me, was a little house in ruins, with the plaster of its rooms showing; and beyond it I saw beginning the long lines of the ramparts. Between the ramparts and the café was a gap, littered with rubbish, which seemed to give access to some open space beyond. I passed through it. A paved incline led me up to a bastion, and from thence I saw something of what the town, as a whole, was. I saw that about a quarter of it was occupied by a drowsy village, rudely built of stones that had once been parts of

palaces; and above the sea of their miserable
mud-roofs rose two great churches, one of them
evidently a cathedral. As for the rest of what I
have called a town, so far as I could see from
that spot, it was a desert. In all directions the
grass was growing, on soil uneven and mounded
with fallen and shapeless buildings; hillocks of
gray stones were scattered about like hay-cocks,
and amongst them, here and there, was a palm
tree, or group of palm trees, watching by the dead
like their brothers in far Palmyra. But what
gave to the scene its most peculiar character still
remains to be mentioned. It was a flock of
churches, most of them almost entire, which were
standing in this solitude, like a flock of scattered
sheep. Wherever I looked a fresh one caught
my eye. Some of them were hardly twenty
yards from each other. When I entered the
town my thoughts had been of Venice and
Genoa; these churches took me back to the
crusaders. The sight, as I realised it, affected
me like a burst of devotional music, vibrating far
off from the lost ages of faith, distinct, and yet so

faint that it made me hold my breath to hear it. It surrounded me with a new atmosphere, in which new thoughts were whispering; and amongst other things it occurred to me that outside of Palestine this was the most eastward town of all the crusading world—the town nearest to the Holy Sepulchre.

I descended from my elevation, and stumbling over the uneven ground, I made my way to the church that happened to be closest to me—a plain structure externally consisting of three aisles. I entered by a side door, the principal one being closed. I shall always remember that moment, when I found myself in the hollow shade, in the faintly echoing silence, of the interior. The floor was covered with refuse and drifted sea-sand ; a mud pen for cattle obstructed one of the aisles, and shadows of faded frescoes were glimmering on the walls all around me. Of these the most distinct was a group of the twelve Apostles, which still made round the chancel a continuous company of colours ; and as I tried to follow the details of limb and drapery, and to

decipher the expressions and features of the half-
obliterated faces, the light fell on a scroll, still as
distinct as ever, letting me see that it was held in
the Saviour's hands, and that on it was written, " I
will give you bread from heaven." It had only
taken a single glance to show me that the whole
of the building must have been gorgeous with
painting once ; but except in the chancel I had
at first detected nothing beyond stains of pigment,
and here and there an aureole. Now, however, as
I grew accustomed to the gloom, row upon row
of figures became discernible, till I seemed to
be surrounded by an army of saints and angels ;
whilst as if to connect all these with the world
of men still struggling, at the top of the pictures
ran a curious and graceful border, consisting of
flowers alternating with coats of arms. As I
lingered I felt that the walls were alive with
worship, with the creed that men are rejecting ;
and the naked sky stared in at the empty
windows, and through them, unnoticed and
unobstructed, the drifting sea-sand entered.

I went from this into several smaller churches

all standing so near to each other that they
might have been in one large field. The structures of these were somewhat more ruinous, but
the frescoes in one of them at least were more
distinct and brilliant. There was a perfect St.
George plunging his spear into the dragon, and
a Madonna whose robes were as blue as that
morning's sky : and in all was the same sound-
less echo of prayers long silent. It may be
thought a piece of empty sentimentality to say so,
but these churches seemed to me to be embodied
prayers in themselves. There they stood, looking
towards Jerusalem, broken but still steadfast, like
the forlorn hope of a world.

But I was not all this while forgetful of other
things. Quitting the churches and climbing a
mound of stones, I saw at a far corner of the
fortifications some low round towers overlooking
the sea. I knew that somewhere or other Famagusta possessed a castle, and at once perceiving
that these towers must belong to it, I set off over
the grass and ruins towards them. As I walked
my mind still went back to the churches, especi-

ally to the one in which the frescoes were most
brilliant, and more especially still to two inscriptions I had noticed, the one on the dragon's
scales, the other on the Madonna's robe. The
first of these was a man's name, Demetrius Something, followed by a date. The second was a
man's name also, with a date which was only
a few years later. I recall this distinctly, though
I forget the other. It was " B. Barker, 1808."

The distance to the castle, could one have
reached it in a straight line, would have been
about half a mile, but I found unexpectedly that
to reach it thus was impossible. When half-way
towards it I came on a sunken lane, with a wall
on the far side, and this I was obliged to follow.
It led me by a long circuit amongst some of the
Turkish dwellings. Wedged in between them I
came upon more churches, with straw protruding
from under their rude doors and mules' noses
poking out of their windows ; and in one place I
passed a beautiful carved fountain, just such as
one might see in an old town in Italy. The
castle turned out to be an oblong, irregular build-

ing, with outworks facing the town ; so that it, if the town were taken, would still remain defensible. Nowhere externally was there any trace of a window. There was nothing but straight blind walls and squat bulging towers. The only detail by which the eye was arrested was a square white patch directly above the gateway : it was the lion of St. Mark, which had been let into the wall by the Venetians. And now let me tell the reader that this dark and forbidding building, in which perhaps his fancy detects little to interest him, is really connected with a set of names and with a story almost as familiar to every one of us as if they had been facts of our own lives ; for in this castle is a tower still named by tradition *Torre del Moro*, from having once been the lodging of one of the Venetian generals, Christofero Moro, the original of the Othello of Shakespeare ; and it was to this castle, if anywhere, that Othello must have brought Desdemona.

As I passed in through the long dark entrance the figure of Iago seemed to lurk in the shadow.

As I climbed to the battlements by an external staircase Othello himself came with me, speaking familiar language, and all the place was filled with a well-known company, which the reader can imagine without my being at the trouble to describe it to him.   I was, in fact, almost as much at home as if I had been sitting in the stalls of the Lyceum Theatre.

And yet here, though it was hard to believe it, was not pasteboard but reality.   From these embrasures, whose stones were still so keen though grass trembled along their crevices, cannon once thundered.   The genuine sea-wind was at this moment breathing on them, and at the bases of their walls the live waves were splashing.   The various views of the town from this position were extensive, in especial those of the harbour with the walls and the quay facing it.   This harbour, so engineers say, might without any great expenditure be made one of the finest in the Mediterranean ; but now on its glassy waters only a few boats were rocking.   Nothing larger could enter ; it is almost silted up, having been left to complete neglect since the days of the Turkish conquest.

As to the castle, half of the rooms, it seemed to me, were walled up and utterly inaccessible. I certainly saw along one whole side of the court a row of windows which had no corresponding doors. I made my way, however, into a number of vaulted chambers—prisons, guard-rooms, and magazines for powder—and at last I discovered a great echoing hall, roofed with Norman arches that rested on heavy pillars, evidently, I said to myself, the very hall where Iago and Cassio had "made the canakin clink."

On mornings like these one loses count of time, and my watch now gave me a start by telling me that my host's canakins would soon be awaiting *me*; so I tore myself from the past and regretfully walked back to the present.

I did not remain there long, however. In the afternoon I came back to Famagusta, and Captain Scott came with me. The day had clouded over; some soft rain was falling, and I saw the place under a strangely new aspect—an aspect to my

English eyes not of deeper, but as it were of homelier melancholy.   Just as we entered the rain became heavier, and we sheltered ourselves for a time under an enormous arched recess which in the morning I had not noticed.   Captain Scott pointed out to me the arms of Genoa on the walls, and then a niche some six feet in depth, from whose sides depended a few poor rags of clothing. " There," he said, " lives a curious negro beggar; " and the apparition that had greeted my first approach was explained.

As soon as the rain had abated we again set forth, and wading along through the tall weeping grass we made our way towards something which I had heard of, but not yet seen, the Venetian arsenal and cannon foundry.   It had for a moment crossed my thoughts in the morning, but I could discover nothing that in the least suggested its whereabouts ; and indeed now, as I went with my companion, I was equally unable to conjecture where it was.   Nothing was before us but the long line of the ramparts, which showed us little but slopes covered with vegetation.   By

and by, however, in one of these slopes we came
to an aperture like the burrow of a Titanic rabbit.
As we entered it I saw that it was vaulted with
beautifully cut stone-work. We advanced a few
paces ; then the burrow widened, and we found
ourselves in a crypt of broad, curving galleries.
They were sufficiently lighted from a small court
or well, and the windows showed us the enormous
thickness of the masonry. They showed us also
the perfection and the wonderful preservation of
it. Here and there, in a corner where once must
have stood a furnace, the low, incumbent arches
were still stained with smoke, but everywhere else
the stone-work was so raw in its freshness that
one felt inclined to look for the masons' tools at
the foot of it. Departing by a passage like that
by which we had entered, I saw that the whole
was contained in a thickening or excrescence of
the ramparts. We reached the world outside
through a bed of untrodden weeds.

Captain Scott, having heard what I had seen
in the morning, had promised to show me such
other objects as would, he thought, be most likely

to interest me. He now therefore took me to a house—or rather to a shed—where some fragments of armour, found amongst the ruins, had been collected. They were too much broken, however, to be of interest to any one but an expert. So far as my eye could tell me they might have been pieces of rusty biscuit-tins. We were now in the inhabited quarter, amongst the tangled alleys. They were wretched beyond description, but after leaving the armour a walk of a couple of minutes brought us to an open space, whose spruce and orderly aspect struck me with some astonishment. Perhaps its condition was due to the fact that some few Government officials, including a body of *gens d'armes*, had their quarters on one side of it. On another side was the cathedral, with the ruins of some contiguous buildings, and opposite to the cathedral was a ruin of a different character—the ruin of a palace which the Venetians had built for their governors. A stately Renaissance gate gave access to a spacious court, flanked to right and left with the remains of what once were offices, and having at the end the body of the palace itself, a high roofless shell with a multitude of square windows. The court was gravelled with an almost meaningless neatness, considering how few eyes ever looked at it to whom neatness meant anything, and it was garnished at intervals with pyramids of old stone cannon-balls.

Having seen the palace, we turned next to the cathedral. It dates from the fourteenth century, and its style is so English that many authorities have supposed it the work of English architects ; but it struck me as like an English flower that, bewitched by a strange climate, had opened wider than it ever would have opened at home. The west front, which faced the gate of the palace, was a lace-work of doors and windows, the central window, which rose nearly to the roof, having in its tracery a large and beautiful wheel. All was practically perfect, it being now used as a mosque, except two decapitated towers, on one of which was a minaret. As I wandered round the building at every step I took I was more and more surprised at the grace and the exuberance of its ornament. From the bottom to the top it was rough with flowers and mouldings. As we lingered looking at it we felt that the light was failing, and we presently turned away and proceeded to one of the bastions. Here Captain Scott showed me a deep well or opening, at the bottom of which is now the tomb of a Turkish warrior, painted red and green like a child's toy locomotive; but tradition says—a tradition which is alive to-day—that the Venetians during the siege had in it a revolving wheel armed with knives, on which they threw the Turks as they scaled the wall, till the hollow below was choked with dismembered bodies.

From this spot I turned to take another look at the cathedral. I saw it under a new aspect. It rose out of a wilderness of desolate stones and grasses into the wan dimness of a weeping English evening, making me notice for the first time its colour—a curious tawny yellow, like the reddish parts of a lion. The broken towers, the pinnacles still perfect, the long line of carved windows and of buttresses—close to these, under their shadow,

were dwellings and human beings ; but it seemed
to the imagination as if this strange and yet
familiar building were utterly alone in the heart
of some endless solitude.

The landscape of the mind, against which our
thoughts and expectations move, when the wind
of the imagination is active, changes as quickly as
the clouds ; and indeed it consists often of several
landscapes, semi-transparent and showing through
one another. A few minutes later I had a curious
illustration of this. Instead of returning home
through the gate of the town we descended a
flight of secret stairs in the wall, and through an
aperture, that might once have been a drain, we
struggled out into the fosse. I had seen in the
morning that the rock here was covered with
asphodel. It seemed asphodel now no longer ;
it was northern docks and nettles. There was
here and there a pool of standing water, with tall
grasses near it, that took the likeness of reeds ;
and as we went along our coming disturbed some
waterfowl. How or why I am not prepared to
say, but a sense came over me that I was in some

marshes in the East Riding of Yorkshire. I felt
that in front of us must be the broad-shouldered
keeper, with his leggings and his velveteen jacket ;
and I fancied that soon I should be nearing the
lights and the avenues of a house which, except
in memory, I had not entered for years. Rooks
cawing in the elms, grooms in the stable-yard,
figures standing about the fire in the hall or in
the drawing-room, of whom half are dead, and
every one of them changed—all these too came
flitting across my mind ; and then presently
through the unsubstantial pageant, solid and
strange, the walls of Famagusta asserted themselves, and the abandoned towers built by Venice
and Genoa.

CHAPTER XIX

"VELUT UMBRA"

THAT evening at dinner I made a very pleasant acquaintance in the person of Mr. Guillaume, a distinguished naturalist and traveller. He had contrived to find in Varoshia bedrooms for himself and his servant, but so far as meals went he was the guest of Captain Scott. Excepting myself he was the only stranger in Cyprus who was thus at a loose end, as it were, and not on some professional duty. What castles and ruins were to me birds and beasts were to him; but he had no objections to taking a castle by the way, so when I told him what were my next day's plans he offered me his companionship, which I very gladly accepted.

My next day's plans were these: I have

already mentioned that I had heard of another
castle, which I had wished to see during my visit
to Captain Scott. The name of this castle was
Aya Napa, and Mr. Matthews had described it to
me as the best specimen he knew of a country
seat of a mediæval Cyprian noble, in which the
feudal fortress had softened into an Oriental
pleasure-house. Its original lords, in common
with the whole Western *noblesse*, had long since
wholly disappeared out of the island. Since then
the building had been a monastery ; at the present
moment it was a farm ; and though some parts of
it were gone, much of it was in good preservation.
Such was the information I was able to give to
Mr. Guillaume when, at the hour appointed, our
mules—we were to ride on mules—assembled at
Captain Scott's door, and thrilled the street with
excitement. We had two muleteers, two servants, and a *zaptieh*, or mounted *gendarme*, whom
Captain Scott sent with us. I forget why
or how it was supposed he might be of use to
us, but he at all events gave our cavalcade such
an air of dignity that the street boys cheered

us as we started as if we had been a coach and four.

Our road lay over a perfectly flat country, some of which was grassy like an English common, some ploughed like fields in Essex or Lincolnshire, and some a waste covered with bog - myrtle and boulders. The first .special feature that caught my eye in the landscape was the presence of several churches, evidently long abandoned, standing on the plain amidst the plough - land, with no habitation near them. There were three of them in a single field, as lonely as three crows. I took them to be one of the many indications remaining, of how densely the country in former times was populated. By and by we passed by a large lake—large at least in proportion to anything I expected to come across. It was several miles in length. A fringe of reeds was round it, and water birds flew and flitted over its smooth surface. Just beyond this we passed through a mud - built village, called Paralimni, or in plain English Lakeside. One thing made it peculiar : it was a village of dyers and the only dye used was black, or an inky purple. We saw the liquid simmering in smoky caldrons at cottage doors, over fires on the bare ground; blue-black washings meandered in streams along the gutters, and dyed material hung drying over garden walls and over currant bushes. After this we met nothing but open country, on which, like breath on a glass, spring was breathing a faint mist of greenness.

The last two miles of our ride were down a gentle stone-strewn slope, with the sea in front of us, fretted by low gray rocks. At the lower edge of the slope, between it and the sea, was a straggling village, built on a level belt of land, and at one end of it was a grove of sycamore-figs and olives. The *zaptich*, who preceded us, trotted on towards this, and presently disappeared behind a ridge of rocks and a cottage. We followed in his track, and as soon as we had surmounted the ridge the castle of Aya Napa, before completely invisible, was straight in front of us, not thirty yards away.

It was a square building, surrounding a court-

yard. It had been originally two stories in
height, but the second story remained over the
entrance only. It was pierced externally on the
ground-floor with small square-headed windows
about eighteen inches in width, and also with a
line of loop-holes. The upper windows were of a
very different character, the two that remained
having graceful pointed arches, and their height
and width being nine feet by five. The entrance
was much like the entrance of an ordinary
mediæval castle—a vaulted passage fronted by a
ponderous archway, which was still ornamented
with the arms of its original owner. Within the
scene was curious. In the middle of the court,
which was shady and green with orange trees,
was a marble fountain, surrounded by Gothic
arches and roofed over with a low stone cupola.
Round two of the four sides ran cloisters with
similar arches, singularly slender and graceful,
enriched with mouldings and built of carefully
hewn stones. On a third side were the stables,
and on the fourth were two chapels. Of these
chapels one was still in use, and I discovered on

entering it a very singular thing. On this side
of the castle was a low bank of rock, which
formed a wall of some fifteen feet in height :
against this rock the chapel of which I speak was
built ; and the chancel was formed, not out of
masonry, but out of a crooked cave, which averted
itself from the nave at an angle. Over both of
the chapels there had once been an upper story,
the floor of which must have been level with the
ground outside. The fragment of the upper story
which still remained over the entrance contained
three rooms, reached by an external staircase.
They were whitewashed and weather-tight, but
had no noticeable feature—at least they had not
till we ate our luncheon in one of them and they
thus became part of a very agreeable memory.
Beneath these rooms was a vaulted kitchen, again
beneath this a place that was once a cellar ; and
close by, in the wall, was a shadowy conduit,
bubbling and echoing with the noise of unseen
waters, which discharged themselves into a trough
of greenish marble, through the quaintest spout
in the world—the nose of a marble pig. The

boughs of the trees, as I remained looking at this
object, made on the wall a wickerwork of light
and shadow, and flickering in it was standing a
group of girls with hideous faces, but unconsciously draped like statues, and filling pitchers
that belonged to the Heroic Ages of Greece.

The rooms on the ground-floor I examined
one by one. They were dark and heavily vaulted ;
they were now used for farming purposes. In one
were some broken ploughs ; in one was an old
olive press ; and in one I came on a milk-white
Corinthian capital, with a small cavity about the
size of a basin on the top of it, in which some one
had just been washing the lid of a tin saucepan.

Thus making my rounds, I discovered a back
gateway, on the opposite side of the court to that
on which we entered. I passed through this, and
found myself in the grove of trees, the rich greenness of which I had admired already from a
distance. The scene was beautiful. Under the
boughs the grass was the tenderest emerald ; and
a furlong beyond it, between the dark stems,
shone the fresh levels of the sea. Presently I

was conscious of a sound like the splashing of a
small stream ; and I saw that, just under the
shadow of the castle wall, was a cistern or artificial pond, full of green reflections—reflections
troubled at one spot only, where issuing from one
of the walls a thread of water fell into it.   As
Moses brought water out of the rocks in Arabia,
so one might fancy that water brought trees out
of the rocks in Cyprus.   By the side of this
cistern stood a colossal sycamore-fig, almost a
grove in itself, and neighboured by several others.
As I rode away from the place, I noticed that for
miles over the plain there came to the castle
from somewhere a now broken aqueduct ; and it
cannot be doubted that when in this way the
supply of water was doubled, the sycamore-figs
and the olives grew over a wider area, and embowered the castle in green and silvery shadow.

It was a pleasant place to think about—this
secluded feudal dwelling, with all its piquant in-
congruities and all its obscure associations.   The
count or baron, its owner, with the name of some
Western family—we know how in the feudal ages

his counterparts in the West lived. We know
what gloom, we know what roughness of life, was
found within the walls of even the largest and
most important castles. But he, the Cyprian
lord, in an air scented with orange-blossom, was
moving luxuriously in the cool of his calm arcades,
which were bright with Eastern carpets, sweet
with Eastern perfumes, vivid with fountains—let
the reader complete the picture. It filled and
amused my mind for half of my ride back ; and
was only obliterated by the fact that for the last
five miles of the journey it was dusk and then
was dark, and I had to look where I was
going.

My stay with Captain Scott was to last for
one day more. I was to return then to Sir
Robert. This one day more I resolved to devote
to Famagusta. It often happens that a place
which, when first visited, has surprised the spec-
tator's eye, and deeply stirred his imagination, is,
on a second visit, found to have lost its charm ;
and he wonders—as some men wonder in connection with some women—how he could have

ever been fool enough to feel so much and so
deeply.   Such was not my experience in connection with Famagusta.   It impressed me the
second time even more than it had done the first.
The air no longer was of a soft familiar gray, it
was now clear like crystal ; and the scene, which
the other evening seemed to have been transplanted to England, had floated away again into
the fabulous distance of the East.   But the
melancholy of its meaning was now even pro-
founder.   It affected me, in spite of myself, like
some deep personal sorrow, which I could not
understand till I had sat down alone, and thought
over it.   I did sit down on the slope of the silent
ramparts, and waited for my impressions to separate
themselves and become distinct to me.   The
general aspect of everything I remembered so
vividly, that it no longer distracted me by the
details of its unexplored novelty.   The consequence was that a number of new impressions,
which I had not before been sufficiently at rest to
realise, one by one became clear to my consciousness.   Clearer than ever was the sense of the life,

the strength, and the splendour—layer upon layer
of civilisation—of which this town was the tomb ;
and along with this sense there now came another
—a sense of its present stillness, so deep that
one's ears tingled in it. I then became aware
that moving about the solitude, here and there,
were some sheep with a Turkish shepherd, and
that a few Turkish children were playing on the
fallen palaces. Now and again came a faint
human voice, and once the bark of a far-off
solitary dog ; but clearer than all, and more
eloquent than all, and seeming as though it were
the silence itself speaking, over fallen palace and
over dismantled rampart sounded at long intervals
the rustle of the breaking sea.

I roused myself by and by ; I rose, and moved
towards the cathedral, wishing to take a photograph of it. As I approached it I became in-
volved again in the sunken lanes with which I
already had made acquaintance ; and had some
difficulty in discovering any near view of it. At
last I lit on one—a view which was a perfectly-
composed picture, seen through the gate of a

poor cottage garden. I sent Scotty in to inquire if I might enter. He presently produced from the cottage a tottering, forlorn old woman. Not being veiled, she was, I suppose, a Christian ; but we could hardly be quite certain of her sex, much less of her religion. She said I might do what I pleased, and retired within her door again. Merely looking in from the road outside, I little thought what a scene that garden would present to me. Half of it was green with some carelessly grown vegetables, interspersed with weeds; the other half was occupied by heaps of ancient building-stones. At one corner of it was a broken Persian water-wheel, and one of its boundaries was a ruinous Gothic church; and it was over a gap in other ruins that the cathedral showed itself.

And now in all its intensity my experience of the former morning repeated itself. The whole desolation seemed to turn into music, and fill my ears with a sound overpowering and yet faint, as if it came from the violin-strings of a thousand distant orchestras—a sound which seemed to re-

cede in shadowy bewildering vistas, far away into
the heart of the irrecoverable centuries.

> Heard melodies are sweet; but those unheard
> Are sweeter.

In this melody, in this harmony, everything
round me joined—not only the objects on which
my eyes at the present moment rested, but all
the ruin which I knew was in my neighbourhood—
Othello's Castle, the Venetian arsenal, the palaces
fallen shapeless, and the forlorn chancels of the
crusaders. As my wandering consciousness went
from one of these to another, each time it seemed
that a new violin sounded; and as, for the practical purpose of choosing a position for my
camera, I scrutinised the details of the actual
scene before me, all this music took an articulate
meaning. Through the empty trefoil arches of
the small church close to me was a vision as of
desert palm trees; on its roof were clustering
weeds; unnaturally perfect, the west window of
the cathedral soared with its Christian tracery by
the minaret that had supplanted its towers; and
a few yards away from me, lying close to the

24

well, were the fragments of a broken water-jar.
Was not this, in absolute, in literal truth, the
embodiment of those words of the Preacher by
which many best remember him? The pitcher
was broken at the fountain, and the wheel was
broken at the cistern. Everywhere around, where
once was life and pride, the silver thread was
loosed, and the golden bowl was broken ; all the
daughters of music were brought low, and not
even the mourners were going about the streets.
This was the theme which the whole city of
Famagusta took up and prolonged like a fugue,
in endless variations, constantly gathering to itself other thoughts as companions. Of all the
energy, of all the hopes, of all the splendour of
the world, as the world has been in the times
that have preceded ours, might not Famagusta be
taken as in some measure the symbol? And
what was Famagusta now? Its beautiful cathedral, on the breast of a dead Christianity, itself no
longer Christian, was a part and parcel of death, re-
posing there like a useless forget-me-not on a coffin.
And for the rest, what remained of it? Only its

prayerless churches, which sheltered nothing but beasts, and the huge shell of its forgotten towers and ramparts, which resisted now no enemy but Time.

And yet, in spite of their melancholy, the suggestions of a place like this have a comfort for the mind in some of its moods, deeper than any hope. To a man, whatever may be his creed, they bring images and promises of rest; whilst for one who has taken his creed from modern science, and has logic enough to understand it with scientific precision, their suggestions, whether of comfort or not, are suggestions of a profound truth—the burden of the whole new gospel, a burden in every sense—that all effort and that all achievement is a delusion, and what unites us at last to reality is not life but death.

It is strange to look back on what were the world's hopes once; and then to think that " to this favour they may come." Lord Beaconsfield makes one of his characters say that " the age of ruins is past." It may occur to some minds, as they look around them now, to think that the age of ruins is only just beginning.

CHAPTER XX

THE BEGINNING OF THE END

THE following morning, by half-past nine, I was briskly driving away from the scene of all this sentiment ; and having yesterday been inclined to think that the best things in the world had grown old, the breath of the spring taught me that one thing at least was young. For miles and miles, on each side of the road, lines of tremulous anemones shone and smiled at me as I passed ; and finally, I do not know why, they gave place to continuous asphodel. We stopped again at the village I have already mentioned, with the green garden and the aqueduct. Whilst the horses rested I sat down by this last, and watched the life of the quivering water flowing. Clear as crystal it hurried along its channel, carrying tiny leaves and sticks like microscopic boats with it. I felt as I watched it as if I were fifteen again, and the future, for a moment, renewed the aspect of glory which once was daily visible to the happy eyes of inexperience.

At the other village, too, we also again stopped. I was again forced to accept the old man's hospitality; and this time he perfectly overwhelmed me by bringing me a plate of roast lamb and potatoes. As I strolled into the fields, in order to digest this banquet, I saw about half a mile off a curious arched structure, like the low roof of a waggon, planted flat amongst the furrows. When I came up to it, my surprise and pleasure were great. It was the identical church which Mr. Matthews had described to me as half buried by the extraordinary rise of the soil. It stood in a sunk enclosure, which was fenced round by a wall, and only its roof rose above the level of the surrounding country.

When I came back to the village the question finally presented itself, of whether the old man should be paid, or should not be paid; I had spoken to Captain Scott on this subject; and his answer was this—That the old man himself did just what Scotty said he did: he refused to accept anything in payment for his hospitality; "but," added Captain Scott, "his wife generally stands in the background, and when her husband is not, affects not to be, looking, you may slip into her hand any sum you please." From this I concluded that the old man himself, if the money were given him delicately like a physician's fee, would not be too delicate to take it; and as, when the time came for starting, his wife did not seem visible, I endeavoured, when I said good-bye to him, to press some coins into his palm. With a pleasant smile, however, and a gesture of real dignity, he gave me to understand that he expected and wished for nothing. I believed him, and believe him still; and it went to my heart that I had eaten his lamb so thanklessly. Just as I was starting a woman made her appearance, who I think was his wife; but I had no means of approaching her; and I could not then with her husband's eye upon me, offer her publicly

what he had just refused. I therefore went away
paying them with nothing but thanks, which
pleased one of them better than money, and I
could only hope, though I had some doubts about
it, did not please the other very much less.
Thinking the matter over as I went along, I
called to Scotty, to make myself quite sure, and
asked which the old man's wife was. " Sir," said
Scotty, " he has several woman there. I not
know which his wife."

By and by, in the middle of the lonely plain, we
passed a solitary chapel, standing close to the
roadside. I had not noticed it as I came, so I
stopped for a minute or two and examined it.
Inside it was smirched and blackened with smoke.
Shepherds must have used it for a shelter and lit
their fires in it ; but here and there were visible
glimpses of brilliant colour, especially blue and
carmine, which seemed to have hardly faded ; and
I saw that the whole walls had been originally
covered with frescoes which once must have made
this nameless forlorn building glow like a bed of
flowers. It was dusk and nearly dinner-time

when I reached Government House, and having been living amongst ruins till they seemed to have become a part of me, I hardly knew where I was when through several modern reception rooms I presently went to dinner with Sir Robert and his two aides-de-camp. The following morning I woke with a gathering sense of sadness. In a few days my present life would be ended, and no further event, no further expedition, intervened now, so as to hide the end from my view. And yet this state of things brought with it its own compensation. It suddenly opened my eyes to new beauties which I had not remarked when I felt they would greet me every morning. I remarked them now—configurations of rocks near me, and shades of colour on the mountains far away. I remarked them now as I felt them say good-bye to me.

Not only the landscape but Government House itself assumed a charm which I could never have suspected it of possessing, though this, perhaps, may have been simply due to the fact that I had by this time come to associate them with the companionship of my host, Sir Robert. Anyhow, such was the fact, and often as I stood at the window by a writing-table, well provided with the inkstands and the paperknives, and the ormulu candlesticks of London, and through the plate-glass of civilisation looked out upon savagery, nothing, I said to myself, is so charming as a simple life, provided only that one is not asked to live it.

One incident, and only one made any definite mark on those few days that were left to me. On a certain evening there was a succession of thunder-showers, then all the night a heavy and ceaseless downpour. " This," said Sir Robert in the morning, " ought to bring down the river. " I asked what he meant by this. He answered that the river below us was rarely anything more than a dry bed of pebbles, just as it was now. But generally once—sometimes three times—in the year, it would suddenly fill with water, flow for an hour or two, and again become dry and silent. I felt that the sight must be curious, and wished that I might be able to witness it. About four o'clock in the afternoon a servant came to my bedroom and asked me to go into the garden. There I found Sir Robert with an opera-glass, standing on the bank. " Look ! " exclaimed he, pointing ; " it is coming. Listen ! you can hear it." I listened and I looked. Very faint and uncertain I at last caught a sound like leaves rustling in a dream. Then suddenly far away on the plain I saw something flash, like the head of a pointed spear. Gradually this prolonged itself into a slim shining line, which presently took a curve. For a time its course was straight, then it curved again. In ten minutes, over the brown surface of the fields the water had stretched itself like a long silvery snake, and the sound I had heard, growing momently more distinct, explained itself to the ear as the voice of the stirred pebbles. The river channel skirted the bottom of the garden, and thus as the flood went by we had every opportunity of observing it. It pushed forward with a mass of bubbles and scum heading it ; it split itself into fierce rivulets, which a moment later were drowned in the body of the stream ; it gurgled against banks, it circled into transitory whirlpools. Gradually, as we watched it, its volume seemed to diminish, and in an hour's time there was only a trickling rill, over which a child of five years old might have stepped.

The following morning my eyes, as soon as I opened them, fell upon packed portmanteaus and closed boxes, and a writing-table bare of all those little possessions which turn in a few days a strange room into a home. An hour or two later the act of parting was over ; I was on the way to Larnaca, which I reached about three o'clock. I was to stay there for two days as the guest of Mr. Orford, one of the district judges, with some of whose family I was acquainted ; and he and Mrs. Orford did the honours of the afternoon by showing me the sights of the town—such sights as there were.

Larnaca proper is merely a large mud-built village half a mile from the sea, and having, as I found afterwards, nothing in it remarkable but a modern Catholic convent. The part where we were now (the part I had seen on landing) was a suburb stretching along the sea, distinguished by the name of the Marina.

Of the sights I have alluded to there is not much to be said. The most remarkable was a white Byzantine church standing in a court, surrounded by white cloisters. Within were the gorgeous screen and the glittering chandeliers to which my eye had already grown accustomed, and there was a little cellar in the rock, somewhere below the chancel, in which, by the light of a flickering tallow candle, the sexton showed me the second tomb of Lazarus. Outside, in a corner of the surrounding enclosure, were other tombs of a less equivocal character—marble slabs, enriched with bodiless cherubs, which looked as if they had strayed from a parish church in England. This strong resemblance was neither fanciful nor fortuitous, for these were the tombs of such English consuls and merchants as had lived and died at Larnaca during the last and the preceding century.

Having seen all this I was next taken through the bazaar, picturesque in its squalid way, but uninteresting after that of Nicosia. Then we adjourned to the esplanade by the sea, along which I had taken my first walk in Cyprus, when Scotty was guiding me to the scene of my first breakfast in it. The place to me now wore a very different aspect. The mixture of Gothic arches and flat Oriental roofs had come by this time to have a familiar meaning to me ; but the difference I was conscious of did not lie only in that. Larnaca, the first time I saw it, was the threshold of what was remote, and strange, and ancient ; now it was the threshold of everything that was familiar, and modern, and prosaic ; and the life that I had so happily escaped from stared me again in the face, as I saw, on the doors of two of the seaward houses, the words, " Messageries Maritimes " and " Austro-Hungarian Lloyd."

I had not, however, even yet quite done with Cyprus. I have said that the sights of Larnaca were not peculiarly interesting ; but one sight it had which attracted me more than I can say. This was a mountain, situated about ten miles inland, crowned with a mass of building, which

at once roused my curiosity. I asked Mr. Orford
what the building was; and he told me that it
was the monastery of Stavro Vouni, or the Holy
Cross. He had himself been there; he said it
was very interesting. It consisted, he told me, of
a court, surrounded by rooms, and a chapel of great
antiquity, containing a large cross. In the middle
of this is inserted a piece of some other wood,
and that is said to be a fragment of the Cross of
Calvary. More curious still was an account he
gave me of a series of vaulted rooms, which are
under the court and chapel. Their existence had
been forgotten for ages; and they were only discovered accidentally, by some robbers who visited
the place, hoping to find some plunder in it.
Five hundred feet below, there is another and
more accessible monastery, still tenanted by
monks; but the upper one is occupied only on
the occasion of an annual pilgrimage. Unhappily, to visit it would occupy two days, and I
had only one day to spare. I longed, and I half
resolved, to put off my departure, and to go back
again to the magical voices of the wilderness.

But common sense prevailed, and my longing remained a longing only.

Mrs. Orford, I think, sympathised a little with my feelings. She had never been herself to the monastery, the ascent being difficult ; but it had always stimulated her fancy ; and my last dinner, and my last evening, she beguiled with stories, which I wished I had known before, of the customs and superstitions that colour the life of the islanders. Most of these have by this time escaped my mind ; but I remember her telling me that the coin for Charon's ferry is still religiously placed between the lips of the dead ; and that a priest is buried with a lighted lamp on his breast—just such a lamp as our excavators find in the ancient tombs. I remember her telling me also that the two saints of the island are St. George—our own St. George—and St. Helena, the mother of Constantine. It is still told of St. Helena that, going from Jerusalem to Constantinople, she stopped in Cyprus, which she had heard was suffering from an unexampled drought. Many of the people had been forced to quit the country; more still were there, in a state of lamentable privation. St. Helena came, laden with alms and pity; and no sooner had she set her foot on the soil than rain began to fall, which presently formed a river. It was called the Queen's River, and it still flows to-day. As for St. George, the memory of him is just as green; indeed, it mixes more constantly with the daily thoughts of the people. Every night, mounted on a gray horse, he is said to ride to Larnaca over the sea from Beyrout; and any malefactor on whom he sets his eyes he seizes by the hair of the head, and drags through the sea after him. Only three years ago it is said that a man was found at sunrise on the roof of a house in the Marina with all his clothes dripping; and, whatever may have been the real history of his appearance, the people believe to this moment, with the most absolute faith, that he was some thief who had suffered St. George's chastisement.

Next morning, as I was dressing, I looked out on the sea—the very sea over which the saint rides nightly, and there I saw something that had traversed it in the night likewise—not, however, anything miraculous ; it was the very incarnation of modern prose—it was the long gray bulk, and the graceful lines and masts, of the Messageries Maritimes steamer that was to take me away from dreamland. It seemed to me almost as strange an object as the first sail from the West must have seemed to the natives of America. It seemed still stranger when, late in the afternoon, Scotty took me on board, performing for me his last service. The windows of the saloon on deck, the glimmer of brass fittings, the agile French of the sailors, and the slight smell from the lifted skylights of the engine-room, all affected me like the most unreal thing in the world—the forgotton voice of a friend, with whom one has long broken, heard suddenly after years, speaking to new associates.

Scotty carefully arranged my things in my cabin. I then gave him a character I had written out for him, and added something to such wages as were his due. He looked at me with eyes full of disproportionate thanks, seized my

hand, kissed it, and hurried out of the door.   I
followed him, and found him motionless half-way
up the stairs, with his head bent, crying into the
sleeve of his coat.   I turned back : I did not
wish to disturb him.

> Alas, the gratitude of man
> Has oftener left me mourning !

I leant over the bulwarks when he was once
again in his boat ; his red cap was mounting and
falling in the stern ; he looked back to the ship,
and I waved him adieu for ever.

Besides myself there were only two passengers
on board.   The saloon and cabins were full of a
kind of ghostly quiet.   We dined at half-past five
whilst we still lay off Larnaca.   When I left
the saloon we were just beginning to move.
Darkness was falling, and alone and undisturbed
I watched Cyprus melt away like a dream on a
windless sea that was coloured like a faded violet.

CHAPTER XXI

THE CHARM BROKEN

MY restoration to civilisation was, however, only gradual. By sunrise we were at Tripoli, where we lay for a few hours. By eleven we were at Beyrout. Here I went ashore with a young rogue of an Arab for an interpreter, and drove into the country amongst blue and scarlet anemones, to an old castle on one of the spurs of Lebanon. Below it was a valley full of vineyards and fountains, and under a fig-tree at the door of a small tavern I took a draught of the delicious wine of the country, which shone in the glass with the tint of a blood-orange. The whole of the following day we lay off Jaffa. My two fellow-passengers had disappeared at Beyrout, so I was left completely to myself to kill time as I might by alternately reading some numbers of *Le Monde Illustré* and looking over the bulwarks in the direction of Jerusalem. To me the prospect seemed full of an indescribable desolation and desertion. I knew that in a certain sense this impression is not just, but still the whole coast of Palestine, and its beautiful inland mountains, seemed to be saying to the world of steam and of steam-boats, " Am I nothing to you, all ye that pass by ? " Not even the presence of Cook's boatman, and the arrival that evening of two dismal English tourists, could dissipate the impression I speak of; and I closed the day with a reading that seemed made for the place and hour. It was the litany which the Jews recite at the Place of Wailing. " For the palace that is destroyed, We sit in solitude and mourn. For the walls that are overthrown, We sit in solitude and mourn. For our priests who have stumbled, For our kings who have despised Him, For the majesty that is departed, We sit and we mourn in solitude."

Twenty hours, however, had not elapsed before wailing of my own quite eclipsed that of the Jews.

By eleven o'clock next day I was in the New
Hotel at Port Said digesting the intelligence that
the P. and O. boat for Brindisi had gone yesterday, and that there would not be another for a
week. Could any prospect be more hopeless or
miserable than a week at Port Said without
friends or resources? The town is a large collection of flimsy sheds and houses built on an
island between some salt lakes and the sea, and
bounded on one side by the turbid breadth of the
canal. Twenty years ago its site was a patch of
the sandy desert; and level sands and water form
all its horizon. It is a mongrel product—a
puppy—of the modern East and West, unique
without being curious, new without being novel,
dull without being old. Such at least was the
view I took of it, as I ate my luncheon discon-
solately at the only table available, with a French
commis voyageur for a neighbour on my left and
the bloated manager of a travelling circus on my
right. In the afternoon, however, I presented a
letter of introduction to an English gentleman,
whom I need not mention by name, but whom

many will recognise if I merely say of him this—
that he is the most influential European in the
place, and as hospitable as he is influential. He
asked me to dine with him in the evening. His
house was a pleasure and a surprise. There were
broad stairs, soft luxurious carpets, a superb
mummy that eyed me on each landing, a dinner
and a dining-room that both might have come from
Paris, and a library filled with as much comfort
and literature as one would commonly find in
a country house in England. He fully sympathised with my annoyance at being delayed on
my journey. "If I were you," he said, "I should
be off to-morrow to Cairo. A small steamer—a
post-boat—starts in the morning for Ismailia, and
from thence by rail you will reach Cairo at six."
The suggestion came like a gleam of the sun
through clouds. I resolved to act on it; my
whole future brightened; and I leaned that night
over the wooden balcony of the hotel in a temper
very different from that in which I had made
acquaintance with it a few hours ago.

And now in this happier condition, and with the

kind assistance of the night, I felt as I looked down
on the Canal, that scales fell from my eyes ; and
though in some ways Port Said was the most uninteresting place in the world, it struck me in some
as being one of the most interesting. The Canal
before me was as broad as the Thames below
London Bridge ; its farther bank was black with
a mass of shipping ; lights glittered, and sometimes an unseen steam-tug whistled. As one
after another the bows of the giant steamers met
my eye in a line that seemed interminable, the
illusion seized me that I was looking at the
waters of London. The sense came over me
of the huge overwhelming city, the heart of the
world's life ; and when I lifted my eyes to look
for the roofs of Southwark there was nothing but
the hollow night and the solitudes of the endless
desert.

But there was more in the scene than this.
Presently my eye was attracted by a sight
which every night-watcher in Port Said knows
—a dazzling star, with daggers of pale blue rays,
shining low in the south, where the desert and

the night were indistinguishable. It was not
shining only, but, watching it, one became conscious that it moved. It was an ocean steamer
advancing through the Canal by electric light.
Nearly every night, and the whole night through,
one or another of such lights is to be seen from Port
Said dawning or dying on the horizon, and filling
the darkness with complicated vague suggestion.
In literal truth they are taken on board the vessels
at one end of the Canal—at Port Said or Suez—
and are put down at the other ; but these lights
for the time seem to be part of the vessels' life,
wandering portents, born in remote regions ; and
they move and move, and pass each other, like
the spirits of two hemispheres. As I stood and
looked, I seemed to myself that night to be still
in the ancient world, standing at the portals of
the modern, and to see its frontiers marked by a
river of unnatural water, and patrolled and guarded
by unnatural gliding fires.

It is true that as I went down the Canal next
morning to Ismailia in a post-boat full of
passengers who had just arrived from London,

matters assumed a more common-place aspect;
but even in daylight there is much to impress the
imagination in this broad street of water, which
for half a day's journey runs as straight as an
arrow; in the ocean steamers, now no longer
stars, but immense moving masses, succeeding
each other at constant intervals, and in the fact
that four out of every five of them gave to our
ears as we passed the sound of English voices,
and bore at their sterns some name like London,
Liverpool, or Glasgow. There is something
which mounts to the eyes and makes the breath
come quicker, in the thought that on half the
decks of Britain the sunlight is always shining.
A foreigner never knows the greatness of our
country till he has visited it: we never know its
greatness till we have left it.

The realities of modern life, as I was reluctantly coming back to them, were certainly good
enough to put their most poetical side foremost,
and it was not till I found myself in Shepheard's
Hotel at Cairo, till I saw the white shirt-fronts
and black coats of the waiters, and heard some

brilliantly dressed English ladies talking at the *table d'hôte* about "the officers," that I felt I had actually collided with fact in all its nakedness. After dinner I discovered a few acquaintances, who seemed to me like dead people come to life again ; and I went with one of them to a glittering *café chantant*, where the gilded walls and the quick crash of the music produced in the mind a dream-like feeling of Monte Carlo.

In a day or two I discovered people who were more than acquaintances—who were friends —and I went with some of them the day before I left to the Shoubra Palace, which is a few miles from the town. It is a fantastic quadrangle, filled with a marble lake ; on each of its sides is a shadowy wide colonnade with horse-shoe arches, and a ceiling daubed with pictures of pashas ; and at each corner is a saloon—in its own way magnificent—with gold furniture and heavy brocaded curtains. All four of them struck me as curiously interesting. They are triumphs of the finest workmanship enslaved to the vilest taste. They are perfect embodiments of a bar-

barism which has gone to school with civilisation, and has only learnt from it just enough to
be meretricious.

The palace, or rather the palaces, stand in a
large garden, the bedrooms and the ordinary living
rooms being in two detached buildings. The
place for a time was occupied by a son of the
ex-Khedive, who has left no traces of his presence
but a collection of French novels. It is now completely deserted except for a few gardeners ; and
though these structures are younger than men who
are still young, the ruinous stucco already is
fallen off from them, the garden steps are cracked,
and the white balustrades are crumbling. We
went out through a small door in a wall, and
there before us were the silent breadths of the
Nile, just turning golden in the light of the liquid
evening. The tall reeds stood rustling, which had
hidden the cradle of Moses, and far off were the
Pyramids standing like mounds of violet.

In the hush of the hour it seemed that all
the ages were meeting. Here, at my elbow, was
the pride of the modern world, made yesterday,

and broken like a child's toy to-day.   There in the distance was the pride of the first of tyrannies, which has seen every existing civilisation rise, and will probably live to see every existing civilisation fall.

Reflections like these were still filling my mind during all the tedious journey back to Ismailia and Port Said—thoughts of this meeting and intertangling of civilisations and ages.   Once they took a form that was curiously bizarre and ludicrous.   The post-boat, owing to a violent storm of wind, was unable to venture into the lake on which Ismailia is situated, and the passengers had to meet it at a landing stage on the Canal itself, which was some miles distant from the usual place of embarkation.   The way lay across the driving sand of the desert, and I and my fellow-travellers—only two or three in number—were at once beset by a crowd of Arab donkey-boys offering us donkeys distinguished by English names.   On one of them I was myself soon mounted—a charming little animal with the most delightful of paces.   The boy ran at its side, shouting its name at intervals ; and I could not help smiling, in spite of the drift that blinded me, to find myself cantering in the foot-prints of Joseph and Joseph's brethren on a donkey whose name I discovered to be " Mrs. Langtry."

But the Canal restored me to reflections of a more serious kind, as it mixed in my mind with certain memories of yesterday. I was watching the Canal now ; yesterday I had been watching the Nile ; and Egypt seemed to express to me all its past and present, when I thought of it as the land where the oldest of historical waters is at this moment flowing side by side with the youngest.

Some twelve hours later I was in a totally different world. I was pacing the deck of the English steamer for Brindisi ; I was in the middle of Anglo - India hurrying home to England. Around me were deck-chairs, shawls, and yellow-backed novels, plates of half-eaten sandwiches, and tumblers of brandy and soda-water. Men were moving about, distinguished by their taste in moustaches ; and there were ladies, tinkling with laughter, to whom this taste seemed to commend

itself. There was a sound in the air of such
words as "pegs" and "tiffin," and of giggles
which marked the flirtations born of a fortnight's
voyage. There was a funny man present, a well-
informed man, a man who organised various
kinds of amusement, and an extraordinary
creature in brown velvet knickerbockers. I discovered this after a few hours' watching ; and I
discovered in the evening that there was also a
musical man, who obliged the company with a
song from a London music-hall.

Here was the modern world, or a part of it,
pure and unadulterated — a world which is the
special creation of the past fifty years, and which
before the epoch of steam either was not or was
undistinguishable. It is not an idle world ; it is
the world of the professions and the businesses ; it
is the world, in fact, which gives life to capital and
capitalistic progress. For its pleasure Switzer-
land is spotted with white hotels ; and for its
profit the Alps are coloured and crowned with
advertisements. For it trains run, steamers
traverse the sea, and to Rome, to Calcutta, or

even to the heart of Jerusalem, are transferred in
all their integrity the thoughts of Clapham and
Bayswater. And yet, when I turned from this
world to look at the ship's engines, at the rhyth-
mical gray flash of the huge swaying cylinders,
and the weight of the cranks revolving, and the
light of the shining piston-rods, I thought, as has
been thought before in many a modern household,
Is not the servant a finer thing than the master?
And then there came back to me my vision of
the great Canal, with its gliding fires at night and
its moving masses by day, and I asked myself,
After all, what do these marvels mean? They
mean that bitter beer is crossing the globe to
India, and that curry and chutnee are crossing
the globe to England. This kind of interchange
is the physical reality of commerce, and the
company round me were samples of the moral
results of it. Such are the glories to which
modern progress is tending.

At Brindisi, however, I escaped in a great
measure from surroundings whose meaning to me
was so little cheering. The bulk of the pas-

sengers were going all the way by sea, and of those
who disembarked there were only a few who took
their places in the same train as I did.   My own
route was to Bologna, and from Bologna to
Florence ; and the sight of Italy, as I looked to
right and left of me, soothed my mind with a
return of the old world.   Bologna, as I wandered
through its dim red streets next morning, in-
tensified this effect.   The air of its arcades was
electric with a sense of the past, and the bells
jangled from its towers with the voice of other
centuries.   Again in the train to Florence, crossing by night the Apennines, the past also came
to me in the breath of the wild gorges, in the
voices of the torrents foaming after recent rains,
and from the outlines of the ridges over which a
young moon was shining.   But now I felt more
than ever that my last end was approaching, and
that the days, even the hours, of my respite from
reality were numbered.   As I looked out of the
window, two lines of Horace came back to me,
which turned themselves, as I thought of them
into sad homely English :—

Day is thrust out of its place by day,
And new moon after new moon hastes to wane.

My last moon of retreat had indeed waned
already. I realised this for good and all, as I
knew I should, during my first day in Florence.
Florence may be old; Florence may be full of
memories; but the life of the town to-day is as
modern as the life of London : the only difference
is that it is shabbier and less interesting, and it
appears doubly shabby by comparison with the
buildings that look reproach on it. These old
historical buildings, all of them seemed to me like
stained-glass windows with no light behind them.
The worldly pride and the spiritual life that had
once given them meaning, both alike were faded.
To many people Florence is eloquent in every
corner, and, if we may believe them, it speaks
straight to their hearts. As for me, with the exception of a few palaces, it gave me two memories
only which I cared to take away with me—only
two with any serious meaning.

One of these was a half-hour I spent in the
cathedral on a rainy afternoon one Sunday. The

26

glow of magnificence outside added to the bare-
ness of the wan and dim interior. When I
entered I heard no sound but that of my own
footsteps ; and though here and there was some
solitary human figure, the place, filled with
twilight, had an air of complete desertion.
Presently, however, far off I saw a dim twinkle of
tapers ; and as I moved down the nave towards
the opening of the great dome, a low, hoarse murmur gradually became distinguishable. Following the sound, I was led to one of the transepts ;
and there before an altar, half-lost in the surrounding space, was a small kneeling congregation,
making a black parallelogram in the obscurity.
The low voice of the priest came tremulously over
their bowed heads, only interrupted by the response of a rare Amen. The worshippers were
so few, and the sound of their worship was so
low, that the illimitable building, otherwise wholly
silent, seemed cold and indifferent to this small
act of devotion ; and I vainly tried to catch some
of the priest's words, in order to see what the
service in progress was. In time, however, my

doubts were answered. The tremulous voice all of a sudden became clearer. I heard a cadence, and I heard words which I recognised. It was the beginning of the Litany of Loretto. Then a change came over the whole proceedings. Again and again, at quickly recurring intervals, in a single volume of sound, from the lips of the entire congregation, came the cry, "Ora pro nobis." The cathedral at last was touched; and a flock of innumerable echoes every time took up the words and repeated them, with faint aërial voices, as if they were the souls in Purgatory.

The other memory which lives with me side by side with this one is a memory of a tomb in a crypt of the Certosa di Val d'Ema. It is the tomb of an abbot, whose figure in pale marble lies on the pavement, surrounded by a plain iron railing. As to its technical merits I neither know nor care anything; but on the old man's face, on his lips, and his closed eyes, more distinctly than I have anywhere else seen it, that peculiar expression rests which one thing alone can give—that ex-

pression of hope and peace escaping from a calyx
of pain, which the Catholic Church has the secret
of leaving on its children—that visible sign and
seal of the peace that passes understanding, of the
crown of life, of the aim of life, of the meaning of
life—of everything in life that the modern world
is disowning. Nothing in the Uffizi, nothing in
the Pitti Galleries lives in my mind like that
image of a lost beatitude. By escaping from this
modern world a certain peace may be found.
There is peace for the wanderer in the strange
seclusions of the East ; in secret lands where life
has preserved the past by leaving it, or where the
present itself is like the past in its remoteness.
Peace may be found there—for a time at any
rate—a peace that is not stagnant, but vivid with
a tumult of stingless pleasures, with the pulses of
a magical youth given back again to the heart of
experience. This is the peace which is known by
the true traveller, which none can imagine except
those who have tasted it, and which those who
have tasted it once ever afterwards crave for. It is
more than the peace of the hashisch-smoker ; it

is more than the peace of the opium-eater ; but if indulged in too often or too long, it would be hard to deny that its effects may be even more fatal. Compared with the other peace, it is hell as compared with heaven. If we leave too often the world in which birth has planted us, each time we return to it, it wears for us a darker aspect, and finds us more and more unfit either to choose or refuse a part in it, until at last we arrive at only this miserable conclusion — that its duties, if done, make life a meaning-less burden, and if undone, an inexplicable tor-ment.

But yet, after all, this much may be said. The true traveller, if he takes his drug in moderation —or until he has taken it, for too long, immo-derately — returns to reality with at least one faculty which makes him superior to many who have never left it. He sees with a new keenness the magnitude of modern civilisation, the infinite complexity of its wants and of its means of min-istering to them, and its enormous movement ; and he sees how little all this astonishing apparatus has really increased the sources of human happiness. He has been outside the sphere of its operations, and he has not for a moment missed it ; and he has seen more content, more hope, and not more sorrow, amongst those for whom it has done nothing, than amongst those whose lives depend on it. Steam and progress may have given much to the world, but there is nothing that they have given like what they have taken away. For this Western civilisation there may be a better future in store. Some new revelation may some day give it a meaning, like that which it once had during the ages of faith, which it ridicules ; but at present it seems to have destroyed even the materials out of which such a meaning might be made. Its highest science and wisdom result in two things only—the multiplication of superficial wants, and the disintegration of all our deepest hopes—and when we return to it, and greet it again after absence, it is hard to avoid asking in cold and sober seriousness, What does it profit a civilisation if it gains the whole world, and loses its own soul?

Could any voice of redemption from the body of this death once more say to us, "Lo, I come quickly," who of us is there—not a beast or a fool—who would not devoutly answer, "Even so, come!"

Printed by R. & R. CLARK, *Edinburgh*